W9-BGQ-341

NO LONGER PROPERTY OF
THE SEATTLE PUBLIC LIBRARY

Received on:

AUG 1 6 2013

Green Lake Library

ODD MAN OUT

ODD MAN OUT

BRANDON HEBERT

FIVE STAR
A part of Gale, Cengage Learning

GALE
CENGAGE Learning®

Detroit • New York • San Francisco • New Haven, Conn • Waterville, Maine • London

GALE
CENGAGE Learning

Copyright © 2013 by Brandon Hebert
Five Star™ Publishing, a part of Gale, Cengage Learning.

ALL RIGHTS RESERVED.
This novel is a work of fiction. Names, characters, places, and incidents are either the product of the author's imagination, or, if real, used fictitiously.

No part of this work covered by the copyright herein may be reproduced, transmitted, stored, or used in any form or by any means graphic, electronic, or mechanical, including but not limited to photocopying, recording, scanning, digitizing, taping, Web distribution, information networks, or information storage and retrieval systems, except as permitted under Section 107 or 108 of the 1976 United States Copyright Act, without the prior written permission of the publisher.

The publisher bears no responsibility for the quality of information provided through author or third-party Web sites and does not have any control over, nor assume any responsibility for, information contained in these sites. Providing these sites should not be construed as an endorsement or approval by the publisher of these organizations or of the positions they may take on various issues.

LIBRARY OF CONGRESS CATALOGING-IN-PUBLICATION DATA

Hebert, Brandon.
    Odd man out / Brandon Hebert. — First edition.
        pages cm
    ISBN 978-1-4328-2699-4 (hardcover) — ISBN 1-4328-2699-9 (hardcover)
        1. United States. Bureau of Alcohol, Tobacco, and Firearms—Officials and employees—Fiction. 2. Street life—Fiction. 3. Miami (Fla.)—Fiction. 4. Suspense fiction. I. Title.
    PS3608.E284O33 2013
    813'.6—dc23   2012051192

Find us on Facebook– https://www.facebook.com/FiveStarCengage
Visit our website– http://www.gale.cengage.com/fivestar/
Contact Five Star™ Publishing at FiveStar@cengage.com

Printed in the United States of America
2 3 4 5 6 7 17 16 15 14 13

For Carmen

CHAPTER ONE

One o'clock in the morning, Pembroke Pines patrol sergeants put Darnell Sims in the back of a cruiser. Picked him up for making terroristic threats. Calling out some white redneck motherfucker for cutting him off at the light at Southwest 148th and Pines Boulevard was the way he saw it, right as he was coming out of the Shell station parking lot. Cops saw it the other way. Racial profiling was what he said they were doing.

Make matters worse, he blew a point-one-six, twice the legal limit in the state of Florida. Got his name run in a national database and up popped a three-year-old Maryland warrant for smuggling cigarettes.

Darnell spent his next two days in a holding cell at the Hollywood Work Release Center, a lady's jail, until one of two things happened: they had a bed for him at the Broward Correctional Institute or somebody came in here and got him. Sitting up in here with his back against the wall, hardly sleeping. No way for a civilized human being to live. Shit, this wasn't his kind of thing, a couple scary brothers in here. Saw one of them eyeballing him right away, a look on his face that Darnell thought to be desirous. During the day it wasn't so bad, the lights on and all. He used that time to play devil with the hacks, always asking when someone was coming to pick him up. At dinner, telling them how he liked his chicken done.

One of the correctional officers, a young guy, said, "You made your call, right?"

"Hell-fucking-yes I made my call." Starting to get agitated with all this waiting. "Look, man," softer now, trying to show he was a reasonable guy, "I pay you to let me make another one. I'm not sure my buddy realize the predicament I'm in here."

The C.O. told Darnell to sit down and shut up, that his predicament would get a lot worse if he kept talking like that. Darnell turned away from the cell bars to find a big dude, one named Leroy, coming up behind him. Cursing himself for standing up too long, his back facing away from the wall. Leroy said that he noticed Darnell hadn't been in the shower since he got here, that he should practice better hygiene.

Darnell didn't know what to say to that.

Leroy asked if he could wash Darnell's body.

Darnell drew a breath in, having to say something; obviously something to the effect that it was okay, he could wash himself. Try to put it in a way that wouldn't offend Leroy, kind enough to offer his help.

The young C.O. on watch was looking at the two of them, anxious to see how the little guy was going to get out of it. Then turned to see a figure walking his way, flashing an ID badge at the receiving desk and being pointed this way, the hall leading to the holding area. Big head of blond hair, kind of wavy, leather jacket, older but still with some muscle on him.

The watch commander appeared and called the name of Darnell Sims.

And Darnell let out a breath he'd been holding since Leroy came up to him. Goddamn. Timing just like one of those scenes in the movies. He turned to the columns of iron bars in front of him, to hell with the rule he had made up about not turning his back. Looking out there for a familiar face, looking past a white guy in a leather jacket walking in front of him.

The young C.O. asked his watch commander who the guy was, if the police in Maryland sent a guy all the way down here just for this.

The watch commander said, no, it was the contact name at the bottom of the computer screen on the offender database when he put Darnell Sims's name in there: Max Bradford, Bureau of Alcohol, Tobacco, Firearms and Explosives.

The first thing Max said to Darnell was, "You got a warrant on you for smuggling cigarettes up to Maryland from here three years ago. You come to work for us. That's it."

This cop—or whatever they called them in the ATF—sticking it to him. *You come to work for us. That's it.* Just like that, final.

"How you know that's even me? I—"

Max cut him off. "Your name's Darnell Rae Sims. Your date of birth is October sixth, nineteen-eighty-three. I don't have your social in front of me, but you get the picture. You were identified by ATF special agents and Prince George's County sheriffs as being part of a December 2009 investigation involving the transport and distribution of unstamped cigarettes. Suspects attempted to flee, including one with an eighteen-wheeler full of cigarette cartons. By the end of it, two suspects were arrested. One suspect escaped. That's you."

"December, you say? That's Christmastime, man. You know what I was doing then? I was the Santa Claus at the Iverson Mall, up in Hillcrest Heights. Sounds strange, but they use a black Santa where they ain't no white people. Otherwise, it don't look right."

"We found your fingerprints all over the truck and cargo."

"I dunno what to tell you."

"You think someone took your fingerprints and put them on there?"

Trying to be smart now. Maybe he wasn't the usual hard-ass law enforcement officer. Somebody you could talk to. Darnell was glad at that. He said, "Could've been I loaded that truck some time before," then paused. "Come to think of it, I

9

remember helping one of my boys load a truck. Just like the one you talking about, an eighteen-wheeler. Right around Thanksgiving."

"What's your friend's name?"

See how long this convict could keep this up.

"Actually," Darnell said, "was a friend of a friend. I don't recall the name right off."

Max leaned forward, waiting. Maybe there was something more? When there wasn't, he said, "Your friend's name is Marlon Sturdivant?"

Shit.

That was it until Max loaded Darnell into the backseat of a navy blue late-model Yukon. Darnell sat back, unsure of what to say, spending the next few minutes looking out at the road, the stretch of Interstate 75 they were on, making their way to the Florida Turnpike.

Max said, "Yeah, you and Marlon go back to your days at Indian River. Sounds like a nice place, huh? Indian River. Just another name for a jail for a convict like you, though. Yeah, state time for burglary. Your buddy graduated. Federal prison up in Tallahassee. You should think about who you associate with."

Darnell shook his head from side to side, made a face, an expression like he was fed up, then a blowing sound out of his mouth and said, "Who I associate with none of your business." Darnell realizing he was wrong, didn't seem like there was any sense in trying to talk to this one. Stared out the window again and said, "I can't be for certain it was him anyway."

He saw the ATF man, special agent is what he called them earlier, looking at him in the rearview mirror.

"You better get certain," Max said. Look at this convict. Still trying to play it off. Innocent, swears he didn't do it . . . wasn't even there. "How do you think we got *your* name?"

That got a rise out of Darnell, getting him up on the edge of the Yukon's backseat, hands cuffed behind his back. Max telling him to sit down, his voice raising the more Darnell didn't do what he said. "You don't sit the fuck down, I'm gonna put your ass all the way in the back, shackles around your ankles and goddamn duct tape over your mouth."

After Darnell told Max that yeah, he was a tough guy with somebody handcuffed, neither of them said another word until they were south on the turnpike, heading towards Miami, about thirty minutes from where they were. Depending on traffic. Max liked it like this, quiet. Not too much conversation with a felon, time for that in an interview room back at the office. He spent the time with eyes straight ahead, glancing back at Darnell every so often. He could feel Darnell staring but when he looked back in the rearview, the convict's eyes were usually looking out at the cars, following the cool ones until they were out of sight. The drive got him to thinking about how to use Darnell, what he might be able to do for them. Moving lane to lane, negotiating traffic, boring. Checking his sideview mirrors, then his rearview. That's when he saw it.

Headlights on what looked like a big SUV, coming up on him fast.

Max lurched forward when they got rammed from behind, the seatbelt tightening against his chest, his head snapping back then forward again. He heard Darnell say, "Goddamn!" and turned to see him gripping the back of the passenger seat headrest, then looking past that out the Yukon's back window. Max got himself together, regaining control of the wheel, arms straight, hands at ten and two on the wheel after riding the shoulder for a bit. He was looking in the rearview mirror, in between deciding to pull over and wondering what was coming next.

"What the fuck is this shit?" Darnell said.

Max didn't have an answer and wasn't going to bother with one now. He wondered too because he could see the SUV coming at them again. That answered his question about whether to pull over or not. He saw the front bumper of the Ford Explorer run right into his rear doors, the Explorer's bumper higher than his Yukon's because of what must've been an eight-inch lift kit and metal push bar.

Max glanced at his side mirror, catching a Camaro coming up on his rear quarter panel. Not one of the new ones; the kind he would see Burt Reynolds driving in some movie from the seventies. Max had a second to gather himself while he saw the Explorer getting ready for another run.

Max got sight of the sawed-off that the guy had in the Camaro's passenger seat. That was that. This was a carjacking. Or, some kind of organized plan to run him off the road. His first thought was about Darnell. Something he didn't know about his convict? Got it out of his mind and punched it before the Camaro could get parallel with him and took the exit for the turnpike.

The Explorer came at Max's rear bumper again. This time tearing into the sheet metal, crumpling the rear cargo doors. Smashed the taillights too, Max seeing red and white pieces bouncing all over the road. He saw the Explorer back off again, giving way for the Camaro.

Max felt the Camaro make a sideswipe at him, brushing the side of his Yukon—not enough force to knock him far. Then saw it back off, Max certain the driver was making sure the bumpers weren't locked. The Camaro started veering back into Max's lane, Max with one eye on him and the other on standstill traffic up ahead.

Approaching it at sixty miles an hour.

If someone was going to get hurt, Max decided it might as well be the guys in the Camaro. The Camaro started to swerve again. Max swerved back, but the guy must've been expecting it because he moved away from the Yukon as it got in his lane.

Hell, it was time to get off the highway, the next exit a half-mile from here. Max was busy getting Darnell to calm down, Darnell's screams getting to be a distraction. Max had only turned back for a second when he heard two shots and felt the Yukon start to stutter as he tried to maintain control. A second later, shredded rubber from his blown tire all over the highway.

After that, Max's Yukon sliding off the turnpike, careening into the median.

CHAPTER TWO

They took Max to Memorial Hospital in Miramar. Told him he was okay, just a mild concussion, grade two, and possibly a cracked rib but they wanted to keep him another day, run some more tests.

His partner, Tom Mako, called. Heard about it while he was bowfishing in Louisiana, Port Sulphur, some guys from Russia in the boat with him. Told Max about the redfish that gave him a fight, took a while to bring it in, considering they were out at night. Max said it sounded like the bonefishing they'd do in Islamorada every year, the first full week in October. Tom called bullshit, said it was Max who had trouble with those, not him. Max was able to get a laugh out but cut it short when he started coughing.

Tom asked what Max was thinking, going to pick up a prisoner by himself.

"I thought I could manage."

Tom said, "I'm gonna be back next week. You could've waited."

Max grunted and reached for the glass of water on the nearby nightstand. "We don't hear anything on this guy in three years, then, bam, get a phone call out of the blue? This is a skinny punk kid. I wanted to get it out of the way, have us hit the ground running when you got back. I was gonna slap an ankle bracelet on him, have it gift-wrapped for us."

"Max . . ."

"Shit, partner, we could've had the whole damn gang."

"Well, now you're laid up." There was silence on the line before Tom said, "How long you in there for?"

"Supposed to be overnight." Max was screwing around with the IV in his arm. "I'm going crazy in here already, though."

"They going to let you go back to work?"

"No," Max said and sat up in his bed, trying to look around the corner of the doorframe from his bed. See if anyone was there. "Supposed to take a couple days off. They don't want me to drive myself for a week to ten days, either. What am I going to do? Call my mother and ask her for a ride?"

"Look, partner, you take care of yourself in there. Do what the doctor says. I'll be back soon, okay? Give me a call if something else comes up."

Max nodded and hung up. Tried to get some rest in between other people calling. His sister . . . a couple other buddies from the office. His ex-wife. *Somebody* called her. Max couldn't figure out who that was but, man, he'd like to find out. She spent ten minutes on how he liked to take risks when they were married. Calling him a lone wolf, liked to do his own thing. Leave her at home worrying about what might be happening to him. Max, thinking, *Yeah, talking about your worries with three of the neighbors. You just happened to end up in bed with them, worrying the whole time.* Then, she started in about how she was always second to the job.

It was like being concussed all over again.

He hung up with her just in time to see Don Sommers, his supervisor, outside the door to his room. Max could read Don's lips. "Is he well enough to talk?" Max yelled for Don to come in, that, yeah, he could talk. Save his boss the trouble.

Sommers asked him, "How you feeling?"

Max nodded. "Okay. I wish they had better food."

"Doing all right otherwise? See the bureau fixed you up with a private room. Can't be all that bad."

"Yeah, I'm stuck in here for another day with a headache and my ribcage is sore. It's great."

Sommers sat back in the bedside chair, a legal pad resting in his lap. "Rather be out catching bad guys, huh?"

"At least the assholes that did this."

That got Don sitting back up. "We'll get to that in a minute," he said. "First thing . . ."

Max said, "You here to take my statement?"

Sommers stopped and looked at Max, in the eye, treating it like it was a situation that warranted concern. He said, "I'd like to hear from you what happened."

"I picked the guy up. Next thing I know, I'm being accosted on the road."

Wondering if his boss would leave it at that.

"And your prisoner's nowhere to be found?"

Max didn't like the tone of voice. What the hell was that supposed to mean? He stopped, remembering to calm himself before his blood pressure and heart rate monitors started making noises, alerting the nurses.

He decided to say, "You have something to ask me, ask it."

His boss brought the legal pad up and put pen to paper. "Way I understand it, you get a call from Pembroke Pines Police saying there's a fugitive in custody, one of yours."

Max nodded.

Sommers said, "How was he one of yours?"

"It was three years ago." Max wanted to tell Sommers it was before he got to the bureau but didn't. "I was on a joint task force investigating cigarette smuggling up and down the East Coast. At that time, there was talk that al-Qaeda was profiting from the sale of unstamped cigarettes. Turns out, this lead had nothing to do with that. We busted them, but one got away until he got picked up on a traffic charge."

"How'd they get your name?"

Max was watching Sommers's eyes, closed to slits, listening, waiting. "C.O. at Hollywood WRC called, said my name was the contact on the database for this guy." Max shrugged. "Could've been anybody on the task force, really."

"But it was you," Sommers said, making sure to write down what Max just said.

"I just told you, it could've been anybody. I don't even remember giving my name, but I guess I did. Who knows?" Max laid his head back. "It'll be in my report."

Sommers reviewed his notes, looking for the next question. He said, "Why'd you go alone? You know it's against bureau policy to transfer a prisoner without two-person integrity."

"I thought I could manage." He gave his partner a better answer on the phone, but decided that was enough for his boss.

"What made you think that?"

Unless his boss forced the issue. Still, all Max said was, "This was a punk kid, a nobody. I didn't foresee him as being trouble."

Sommers scratched his nose and waited. Looking down at his notepad, he said, "Let's go over what happened after that."

Ah, getting to it. Max could feel Sommers studying him. Like some body language expert, looking for a tell. Looking at the IV drip, then back at Max.

"I got on the interstate, followed it to the turnpike. That's when I got rammed from behind."

"By the Explorer?"

Max nodded.

"Then what happened?"

"An older Camaro pulled alongside me."

Making his boss work for it.

"You sure they were working in tandem?"

Max thought, *Yeah, unless they met up at the gas station and decided to do this for fun.* "They got me boxed in, in the right-hand lane. At that point, I see the Camaro passenger with a sawed-off and get hit from behind again. I swerve for the Camaro, but he swerved too."

"Hold on," Sommers said. "You're swerving in a car chase on the highway?"

For chrissakes, man. Max said, "There weren't any civilians around at that time." He stopped to let Sommers write that down. "I turn around to calm Darnell down, he's screaming and it's distracting me. Next thing I know, my tires are blown and I'm in the median."

"You blacked out after that?"

Max said, "Hit my head on the wheel," and saw Sommers looking up at the knot on his forehead.

"You woke up, there's an ambulance there . . . onlookers around but no prisoner?"

"Yeah, Darnell's gone." Max tried to sound as contrite as possible.

Sommers looked up from what he was writing. "Before, he was your 'prisoner.' Last two times you mentioned him, he was 'Darnell.' You two get chummy?"

Max had caught that and was waiting. "Outside of why I was there, we didn't say a word to each other."

Sommers crossed his arms over the legal pad in his lap and looked up at an angle, thinking. "Why take that route? Why not just stay on the turnpike?"

Max thought there'd be less traffic this way. Or, at least, what traffic there was might move faster. He shrugged and told his boss the same thing.

"I keep thinking about what's so special about this guy that somebody would take that kind of risk. Ambush a federal agent in broad daylight on a busy interstate."

Max said, "When I find them, I'll let you know."

Sommers got up and started to turn away. "I'll see you, Max.

We'll talk more later." He paused and turned back. "Even more curious, how'd they know where to find you?"

That was a good question.

Darnell would say, "Hello?" and wait.

No answer.

"Who's out there?" In a whisper.

Nothing.

So he'd sit. A folding metal chair in the middle of the room, but Darnell didn't bother with that. He was more comfortable on the floor. A far corner, away from the door.

Where the hell was he? The last thing he remembered was running off the road with that ATF guy. Max, that was his name. Last name started with a B. What was it? Aw, hell, never mind. What happened to him? Didn't matter, they'd never see each other again.

He had to worry more about what was going to happen to him. This shit was getting scary. He *did* remember being hauled off after the accident. Remembered a little, at least, coming to for a few moments before passing out again. Remembered two white guys—one with a denim shirt cut off at the sleeves—sliding him into the back of a car. It happened fast. He didn't recall them saying a word to each other. Fact, the last voice he remembered was Max. Yelling at him to shut up.

Asshole.

Woke up here, a house. He was sure of it. Took Darnell a few minutes to realize that, not that it was some shack in the middle of the swamp somewhere. He hadn't known how long he was in the car or how long he was out, so that was possible. Even with black shades over the windows—so he couldn't see out and people couldn't see in—he could feel that it was a residence in a neighborhood somewhere.

He hadn't seen anyone since he opened his eyes, about forty-five minutes. He could hear shoes shuffling around outside in the hall. Two guys, maybe three. Darnell put his ear up to the door. See if he could hear anything, find out who they worked for, hear a name. Nothing. He pressed harder, asking himself if these sons-of-bitches ever said a word. Kidnapped by a bunch of monks.

Darnell wasn't sure who they worked for . . . but was dying to know. He decided to give it a shot and said, "Look, you tell Johnny I wasn't going to say a thing," leaning into the door. He heard them moving around out there; rubber soles, tennis shoes scurrying across wood floors. "Johnny, that you?" Still trying. "Look, you know I'm good, man."

No answer.

Darnell had to get himself calmed down. Thought about a minute and said, "You tell Johnny we can make a deal. I'll split my half with him." Then decided that wasn't smart and said, "Fuck it, tell him he can have it all," and waited.

No answer.

He started to get agitated. What the hell was going on? Ain't nothing like this ever happened to him before. Yeah, he been in trouble with the law . . . But this? Kidnapped? Shit, kinda wish that ATF man would've left him in that cell. It would've been better than this. He would've figured out a way to deal with Leroy. In the slam, he could have his posse; there was always a crew he could hook up with. A lot of guys with time on their hands, nothing to do *except* come up with groups of people who would watch each other's backs. On the outside, forget it, he'd smoke whoever it was running around on the other side of that door.

Or, at least, find somebody who could.

But, right now, he was alone. By himself in a place he didn't know. People on the other side of that door, he wasn't sure who they were. Then something obvious hit him. It was a kidnapping, right? He said, "You wanna play some kind of a game? You know I work with Johnny Stanz, right? He gonna have your ass if he finds this out." Darnell paused. "Let's help each other. You let me out, I'll walk away. Pretend this never happened. No one will be the wiser."

He waited.

Darnell said, "I told you I wouldn't mention it," and wondered if they believed him. Probably not, since no one had come to the door or acknowledged him yet. He shut up, figuring it didn't work, and sat back, on the floor against the far wall. He thought he heard them moving around again. Minutes passed. Darnell had started to put his head down against his arms, folded across his knees, when he heard the door open.

He looked up to see a white guy standing in the doorway. Black leather jacket, black leather pants, just about black leather everything. Scruffy beard, sunglasses on inside. A biker, not anyone he would have recognized. The guy took his glasses off and smiled, like he was waiting on Darnell.

They stared at each other, the guy standing over Darnell now, until Darnell said, "Who are you?" with no tone in his voice.

"Ain't important who I am." The guy had a baritone in his voice. Darnell guessed he dressed like that, all black, to match. Figured the guy thought it fit. Darnell could feel the guy staring at him, waiting for Darnell to say something or lose his cool, give the guy an excuse to stick a shank in his mid-section. Fuck him, man, for trying to play a game. Darnell was *about* to get to his feet, fuck it, and square off when the guy said, "You a friend of Johnny Stanz, huh?"

Hey, maybe they weren't so bad. Darnell had a sense of relief. A small sense, but hey . . . He tried talking to the guy, in a way that he could understand. Telling stories about him and Johnny. Old buddies, all the way back to when they stole cars in Riviera

Beach together. Their early teens, Darnell couldn't recall the exact age. They lost touch when Johnny went to Starke on a felony firearms charge in the sale of MAC-10s. The judge had it in for him was the way Johnny put it. He tell you that? It was Marlon Sturdivant was his cell mate, how him and Johnny got back together.

See if that did anything.

The big guy let him finish and said, "See, only problem, Johnny ain't in charge no more." He was halfway to the door before he turned back, Darnell seeing this macho asshole was doing it for effect. Trying to put a scare in him.

"You never met Raoul, have you?"

The biker, Billy Poe, found Johnny Stanz in the living room, behind the wet bar, pouring himself a shot of vodka, straight up, and asked him, "You hear all that talk about you?"

Johnny downed it and nodded. "I been knowing Darnell a long time."

"That's what he says." Billy took a seat on one of the bar stools across from Johnny. "Says y'all go way back, all the way till when y'all were teenagers."

Johnny started to pour another then paused. Felt like something stronger and started sifting through the cabinets, see what was there.

Billy said, "If you two are buddies or if you think you're gonna have a hard time," he saw Johnny's head come up from behind the bar counter, "maybe you should stay here."

Darnell knew they were moving him.

The last person he saw was the biker, the guy who had come in the room earlier. The one who had mentioned somebody named Raoul. Somebody else had come in with him. Then, darkness and realizing they were blindfolding him. Tied tight around the back of his head. There were two sets of hands that wrestled him to the floor, Darnell able to yell, "Get the fuck off me!" before they got the duct tape over his mouth. He was kicking, bucking hard, trying not to make it easy for them. Swinging his arms before they got him face down on the floor. He wasn't sure what was next but hoped it wasn't *that*. No, bound his wrists with plastic tie-wraps and flipped him back over, thank God.

The edge of the tape over his mouth was touching his nose, tiny strips of it waving back and forth with each breath. Darnell shook his head side to side, hard jerks to let them know he was having a hard time breathing. Shit, he didn't see the need for all this. He heard one of them say, "Where we taking him to?" but didn't hear an answer. Darnell tried to calm himself down, concentrating on breathing through his nose, never mind the tape was bothering him. He would be okay if he just did that; not thinking he was going to suffocate to death.

They got Darnell up, each of them hooking an arm under his, and started to march him outside. Didn't know where they were going but Darnell was ready to be brought to the woods or the Everglades or someplace remote and be shot. Maybe ask him some questions before, but he wasn't sure. About what? He didn't know that, either. If that was it, he hoped they decided on Alligator Alley; there was a toll booth going out there and maybe the police could track them like that, they could get their just desserts for doing this to him, dammit.

Under the blindfold, he heard another voice. A third guy, someone he did recognize. Couldn't place it, though, because of his disorientation. It said, "I'm gonna take him." Take him *where?* That's all Darnell thought about while they dragged him down a hallway and shoved him back in a room.

A minute later, after hearing voices arguing outside, the door opened again. They got him up, one guy taking each arm again, and outside. Threw him into the back of a car and closed the door after him. Darnell started for the other door, thinking he could turn his body and be quick about it, before he heard the door locks click. Not the same car, this one had the new car smell.

They were moving, thoughts in Darnell's head of where they might be going, trying to guess at anything. Losing track of what direction they might be going in after a few turns. He believed they were driving for less than ten minutes before they stopped. A voice said to him, "I'm going to let you out. From here, you're on your own."

Darnell felt the blindfold pulled from his face. Left it hanging around his neck and looked to the front seat. Then tensed up, wondering if this was a joke . . . but saw the driver and sat back.

Johnny Stanz said, "You take off. We never see each other again. I'm gone."

Johnny cut the tie-wraps around Darnell's wrists with a pocket knife and left him there. Darnell walked along the street in a residential area, looking in the driveways of little red brick houses for the car no one would expect to be stolen. Found what looked like a ten-year-old Toyota Camry and decided on it.

He slipped in, the door unlocked, and sat in the driveway. Trying to do this without calling too much attention to himself, thinking about Johnny just letting him go like that. *I'm gone.* Where to? He got the engine turning over and gunned it back out. He could think about all that later. Right now, if he could just figure out where he was . . .

CHAPTER THREE

Darnell could only think of one place to go.

LaKelle Evans lived in Oakland Park. Grew up near Wimberly Fields Park, Northeast 41st Street. Moved to a rent house with pink stucco and bars on the windows not five minutes from her mother. Had dropped out of Northeast High her senior year—a year after she first met Darnell. Worked on her GED and found odd jobs to make ends meet, but told herself that she would never stoop to pleasing a man for money. Didn't have to after the first time Darnell asked could he stash some guns at her house that a friend was trying to sell. Sure, just give me some money. When Darnell objected to that, she said, "Well, you can take 'em somewhere else then," knowing he didn't have somewhere else. Darnell gave her two hundred dollars on the spot. She told him that was good for two days' worth of storage.

Even with that, Darnell kept coming back with the occasional guns, or a pound or two of drugs. Sometimes he'd throw some her way. But she reminded him that was a gift, on top of the payment he still owed her. She liked the grass, never touched the hard stuff. Got to a point where she had squirreled away a few thousand dollars and Darnell would send friends over to hide their own stuff, let them pay their own damn way.

All that stopped when LaKelle got pregnant with Darnell's little girl.

She let Darnell in, loud knocks on the door, and made him take his shoes off before coming inside. Darnell said he didn't have time for that, he needed to come in *now*. LaKelle told him how she just passed some Fabuloso on her floors and she didn't want him tracking anything in.

Or he could just go somewhere else . . .

Darnell was pacing across the kitchen floor in socks, talking to himself a mile a minute, LaKelle letting him work off the steam. Shit, now baby LaKeisha was up and crying, time for her afternoon feeding. That boy, didn't even think about that when he came over, banging on the door like the police, creating a ruckus.

LaKelle looked up from the baby. "What's going on?"

Darnell kept pacing. It was like talking to a wall. She said his name, a little force behind it, and that got him looking at her.

"I asked you what's going on."

"You ain't gonna believe this." Darnell came over and gave his little girl a peck on the forehead. He gave LaKelle his story about his kidnapping—he stressed that word—and how he was held hostage. That was the first time he thought about it like that. Yeah, he was a hostage, dammit. Then told her about Johnny Stanz just up and letting him go.

"You serious?" LaKelle had a half-grin, her head cocked to one side, like she didn't believe it.

"Hell yes, I'm serious, woman. You think I'm making this shit up?"

"You watch your mouth around her." LaKelle turned back to LaKeisha, stroking her baby's head in case she heard her daddy's foul language. "I think you been smoking too much of that junk, that's what I think."

Darnell waved her off, she didn't know nothing. Grass don't even do that to you, give you delusions like that. He stood over by a window, pouting.

LaKelle had LaKeisha in her arms when she walked up to him and said, "What you gonna do?" Then thought for a minute.

"They don't know you're here, do they?"

"You think I'd do that to my little girl, put her in harm's way?"

LaKelle did feel a little bad about saying that, what it implied. He was a good daddy.

Darnell said, "I left the car I stole a couple streets over, off Prospect. I wiped it. Nobody knows I'm here."

LaKelle had a look on her face, pacing back and forth from the kitchen to the living room. Darnell watched her. "I know you about to say something. Just go on and say it."

LaKelle, baby LaKeisha in her arms, said, "How about Johnny? He knows you ain't got nowhere else to go."

By the time Max got to his office, Don Sommers was already there. Sitting in the chair across from Max's desk, legs crossed and waiting.

When Max walked in, Don said, "How you feeling?"

After the hospital, Max wasn't sure if Don was really interested or not. He said, "I'm feeling great." There was a pause while Max sat down. "Wouldn't you be?"

Don didn't answer. Instead, he decided to say, "You're on restricted duty. Doc's giving you five days to recuperate, get that bump on your head to go away."

Don's comment made Max feel his head, a knot at his hairline on the right side of his skull. It wasn't *that* big. The way Don said it, he made it sound like Max looked like some freak show monster, a Frankenstein. Rubbing Max's nose in it.

Don didn't let up, saying, "Give you some time to work on that report of the incident."

Jesus, this guy. Max said, "I'll get to it," and looked out through east-facing windows at the morning sun over a horizon of ocean, palm trees, and the low skyline of Miami Beach in the distance.

"I should've brought in a court reporter, have you read your recollections off while you were laid up. That's my fault."

"What's wrong with doing it now? Christ, Don, I just got here."

"Yeah, but it's been two days now. Get it on the record while it's fresh in your mind, that way there's no inconsistency."

Max sat back, feeling at his head again, listening to his boss sounding like a lawyer. When Don said, "Because the OPR'll have some questions about it," Max knew why. OPR. Short for Office of Professional Responsibility and Security Operations, the bureau's internal affairs. Yeah, Max agreed they'd be interested.

Still, Max was curious about why Don was so quick to think so, something he didn't like in his boss's tone. He asked that and Don explained it to him: "Number one," Don held a finger up, "you're picking up a prisoner alone." They had gone over that but Max didn't remind him, Don was on a roll. "Number two, somebody knew about it. Number three, your prisoner's vanished." Don had his three fingers up, on the edge of his seat, but put them down as he sat back, a move that signaled to Max he had calmed down. After a few seconds, Don said, "This whole thing stinks, Max."

"You sound like I planned it that way."

"I don't think that, no," Don said. "But those OPR guys are real disagreeable people. They might not see it the same way I do."

There it was.

Max said, "You saying I'm under suspicion here?"

"Not by me." Don ran a hand down his tie. "But you need to get your story straight. I'll make you a copy of my notes from the hospital to help you out with the first part . . ."

Max cut him off. "When's the internal affairs interview? You know if they scheduled it already?"

Don shook his head. "Not yet." He started to get up, saying, "I can postpone for a few days with you on restricted duty. Those interviews can be long, no way for an injured person to spend their time."

That gave Max five days.

Don was on his way out when Max called his name. "Before, you said your notes would help me out with the first part . . ." Don nodded and Max said, "What's the second part?" He was curious where Don was going with that.

"Max," Don said, stopping in Max's office doorway. "You're a good agent, never been in trouble. But I've seen this before, guys misstepping or *being perceived* as misstepping. These OPR guys don't play around."

Max was listening close.

Don said, "You got a fugitive that disappeared under your supervision . . . A high-profile accident on a very visible road that could be a simmering public relations issue unless we can keep it under wraps . . . your fugitive is running around out there for God knows what reason." Max watched him turn away, Don smoothing his tie again. "There's a lot of loose ends."

Max was already thinking about how to tie them up.

Max figured he'd try the Hollywood WRC, where he picked Darnell up. Talked to the warden. Tried to be as delicate about it as he could without coming out and asking if one of his guys was dirty.

It was a dead end.

Went by Pembroke Pines Police after that, but they didn't know shit.

On his way back to the office, thinking about it the whole time in the car. What Max did, after lunch from a vending machine, was look up Darnell's old arrests. Put his name in and had to go back twelve years to find a relative listed. Darnell's first arrest. Burglary from a dwelling. Sentenced to a year and a day plus probation, did a little over three months.

Delores Mae Brown. Identified in the database as Darnell's mother, an address on Northwest 10th Street, Overtown. Max wondered if she was still living, if her son hadn't given her high blood pressure over the years to cause health problems; if she was still kicking, would she be willing to talk to him about her little boy? Families were tough to get to turn over on family members. Moms were the worst of the bunch. Minority families were really tight-knit. What was he gonna do, haul in a seventy-year-old lady for questioning?

Half an hour later, Max was parked on the curb in front of Delores's little yellow house, the smell of liver and onions coming from inside.

Max knocked on the door, not hard, and waited. Hands in his pockets while he looked up and down the street, rows of little square Florida bungalows, with yards that needed to be fixed up.

Watching young black kids come out to the street to see him, nothing better to do. One after another, standing in groups next to cars parked on the street. Some propping a leg up on a car's bumper, leaning to look cool or mean, put on a show. Showing him they weren't scared, in their little crowds whispering to each other about him.

Max's mind wandering while he was waiting, he half-wondered if something would be spray-painted on his vehicle when he came out. Or maybe find it up on cinder blocks.

The door opened.

"Miss Brown?"

By her face, Max could tell he'd guessed right about her age. Around seventy. She nodded, a puzzled look on her face.

Showed his ID and said, "Ma'am, I'd like to talk to you about

Darnell, your son," and spent the next two minutes, solid, explaining through the crack in the door that he was ATF. Not Dade County Sheriff or Miami Metro. Having to convince her of it. Had to tell her what ATF meant before she said, "Firearms? What he doin' with firearms? That don't sound like my Darnell."

Poor woman, she sounded experienced.

Max took a second to listen for movement from inside or a male voice, either Darnell's or maybe the father. If he was still in the picture. When he didn't hear anything, Max asked to come inside.

Delores said, "I guess so," and looked down the block. "People starting to stare."

Max stepped inside, closed the door behind him, and moved into the living room. Delores was already on the sofa and offered him a seat.

"What's this about Darnell?"

It was the voice of a woman that stayed up late many nights, a mother worrying about her boy. Max couldn't help but feel sorry for her, Delores already clutching her dish towel waiting for more bad news.

"Ma'am, Darnell could be in some real trouble. I picked him up two days ago in Pembroke Pines and was transporting him to my office for an interview." Delores didn't ask what "picked up" meant. "We were run off the road. I blacked out. When I came to, Darnell was gone."

"You mean to tell me he run away from you?"

Max shrugged. "We were deliberately run off the road. Whoever did it left me." He could tell by the look on Delores's face that she got the idea, then Max catching sight of the dish towel being clutched a little tighter.

"You think they hurt my boy?"

Max's tone lightened, or he tried the best he could, to put

31

Delores at ease a little. "Ma'am, I'm just trying to find out what happened. If you know where he is, it would be better for all of us. I can help him if I can find him."

Delores was rubbing her hands, anxious, the dish towel folded over her lap now. "He got a child, you know? LaKeisha, my little grandbaby. Darnell always bring her over, though. I don't go to the baby's momma's house 'cause she a no-count bitch. I don't like the way she treats Darnell. First, took her about a month before she even invite me over to see little LaKeisha. A month? I'm that baby's grandmother, can you imagine? When I do go, she starts in on why I didn't bring a nicer onesie for LaKeisha to wear. I bought the best I could. I wish I could give that little child the best of everything."

Delores shook her head. "Shit," looking away, "I'm on a fixed income."

Max started to say something but Delores cut him off. "So, I told Darnell to please bring LaKeisha so I could see her. He want me to babysit? Fine. But, he need to bring her over here 'cause I ain't going to that little bitch's house."

"Do you have Darnell's number? Or the address of the baby's mother? Either of those would be extremely helpful."

"The girl live somewhere in Oakland Park. I couldn't tell you where. Time I went, I made Darnell come get me. I don't like to drive."

Delores got up and waddled off, her voice trailing off as she walked away from Max before it blended into the sound of voices coming from the TV a few feet from him.

She came back and said, "You never know if his phone cut off or not, depends on if he pays the bill every few months, I guess." She stopped, looking at Max like she was making a decision.

Delores said, "You gonna help my boy if he's in trouble, right?"

32

Max nodded. "Miss Brown, he's a lot better off with me than without me right now."

"I'd like to see him straighten up and fly right. I thought having a child would do that. I guess it didn't." She said, "You can't get ahold of Darnell, he got a friend, Johnny Stanz. He's white but a good boy. Grew up around here, him and Darnell used to play in the street, they's old buddies. He might know where Darnell's at, case Darnell's phone out again."

Max waited.

"I get his number for you too." Delores turned for the kitchen. "You have to excuse me first, though. I need to get my dinner off the stove before it burns."

By the time Darnell got to Johnny Stanz's house, Johnny was almost finished packing. He'd mentioned that he tried to call two or three times. Got tired of hearing the phone ring with no answer and decided to come over. Johnny said, "Bad idea," and told Darnell that he wasn't answering, no matter who it was. Darnell asked what if it was his mother? Johnny said, "Fuck it," shrugged, and said he was throwing the phone away.

"How people gonna get ahold of you?"

"They won't. That's the point."

Darnell stopped, not sure what to say to that. He watched Johnny throwing things into large duffel bags, big ones; the kind that a person could fit in if they curled up in a ball. Not really packing them, folding them like you would if you were going on vacation. Grabbing things from dresser drawers and throwing them in there, clothes from the closet still on the hanger when they went in.

Darnell said, "What the hell's going on here?"

Johnny didn't stop long enough to look at Darnell when he said, "When they find out I let you go, they're gonna come looking for me. They're gonna want to know what happened. I want to be somewhere else."

Darnell waited, pausing to let Johnny do his packing. *They.* Johnny kept saying it. When *they* find out . . . *They're* going to come looking for me.

Darnell couldn't wait anymore. He said, "Who the hell are *they?*"

That got Johnny sitting on the edge of the bed, strung out, letting out a sigh. "They some ruthless motherfuckers, man. Fuckin' bikers, you know how they are."

No, Darnell didn't specifically know that but didn't say anything.

"They don't give a shit about anything, ain't got no kind of respect for their fellow human being, no respect for the dignity of human life. Not like you and me, we're good guys. They'll kill you just as soon as look at you."

Darnell waited for Johnny to say more because that didn't tell him much. He let Johnny catch his breath, the poor guy looking like he was about to explode. Darnell looked around the room, touching little things here and there on dressers and nightstands and whatnot. Something to pass a few seconds before the guy calmed down, got in a state of mind where he made sense.

"You remember that job you did in Homestead?"

Darnell nodded. "I done plenty jobs down there. I could tell you yeah, but I'd have to think about it."

"The one after you got back from that thing in Maryland?"

Darnell nodded again, remembering the one Johnny was talking about. He said, "You mean the one where we robbed that dude?"

Johnny put his hands up to his face. "That dude is the guy looking for you."

Darnell made a face and looked away. "Man, that guy don't remember me." He thought about it for a second. "That was three years ago, how he gonna know me?"

34

Johnny raised his face from his hands and said, "A guy's not going to forget somebody who ripped off a half million dollars from him."

That got Darnell's attention. His head bobbed back, surprised by what Johnny said. "I know I ain't got no half million dollars sitting around somewhere. You seen where I live, man?"

Johnny got up from the bed and walked over to Darnell. "Somebody does. You had two other guys with you, right? Somebody got away with something."

Darnell was busy thinking back. Yeah, there was LaRon, his cousin, and one of his buddies. A guy LaRon called Tweety. This was the first he heard of this.

Motherfuckers.

Johnny said, "The guy you stole from is named Raoul Garcia."

Darnell remembered hearing that name.

"He's a P.R. Got a real mean streak."

Darnell said, "Look, I'm just going to sit him down, man to man, and tell him I ain't got his money. I don't know nothing about it. He can go see LaRon if he want to."

Would serve his cousin right, leaving Darnell out like that.

"Your cousin got shanked at Starke. He was doing a bid for possession of Schedule 3. Took it right in the mid-section. Took several, actually. Died right there, walking the single file line back from the yard on the way to chow."

Shit.

"That was Raoul's doing. He hired some skinheads on the inside to do it. Only, he said to hurt him enough to get him in the sick bay. That way, they could get to him better there. When the nurses weren't looking, one of the trustees could cut off his morphine drip until he talked, some shit like that. They went too far, though."

Darnell didn't know how to react. Pissed a minute ago.

He said, "What about Tweety?"

Johnny shrugged. "Never heard from him again."

Darnell watched Johnny starting to pack again, going through a nightstand, throwing underwear and socks on top of the pile already in the bag. Johnny said, "Look, you can talk to him but you'd be good just to let well enough alone. He might not be able to find you again."

Might not?

"But if he does, it wouldn't matter. He wants to know where his money's at. And, he wants to restore his reputation. You know how that shit goes. That'll be all he wants to talk about."

"Well, I ain't got his money."

"He thinks you do, that's all that matters."

Johnny finished packing and zipped his bag up. "We better get out of here. I'm going far away. You'll probably never hear from me again."

Darnell could see Johnny getting a little emotional. It made Darnell a little choked up, too, considering. Johnny standing there, it looked kind of pitiful. Shit, man. Darnell took his friend and gave him a hug, a gesture; a look on Darnell's face that told Johnny thanks for what he did.

Darnell followed Johnny out of the room, stopping for a second to grab Johnny's cell phone sitting on the top of the dresser.

Hey, Johnny said he was just gonna throw it away.

Was a perfectly good phone.

CHAPTER FOUR

Max had called Johnny Stanz's number three different times before he was out of sight of Delores's house.

He had an idea the number might be bullshit. Even if Delores wasn't just giving him a line. She seemed sincere enough, even asked Max if he was going to help her boy. Gave him a look before she asked, making a judgment on Max before she said it.

Decided to call the office and have Johnny Stanz's name run. The voice on the other end came back with three different addresses on multiple arrests dating back a dozen years. Max asked for the most recent one, a house on Burlington Street in Opa-locka.

For a possession bust two years ago. Two years, it would probably end up a runaround. Just like the phone number.

What the hell, he'd try it anyway.

When Darnell got home, LaKelle was busy cleaning her house. The woman was always cleaning, she should do it for a living. He didn't know what else she did for money . . . but he knew it wasn't *that,* selling herself. She would never, not with a baby under her care. He could call the woman what he wanted, curse her to himself—never out loud, though—or think of her what he wanted, but he'd give her one thing: she loved her baby and wouldn't be so irresponsible to invite strange men into her life. Plus, she knew that would hurt his feelings.

LaKelle hadn't asked him about Johnny and Darnell knew

she wasn't serious. *How about Johnny's?* She *had* to be joking, realizing what a life-threatening ordeal he had just been through.

The only thing she told Darnell was to watch where he was walking, not to step in her dirt piles while she was sweeping.

He made it to the bedroom, a separate room from LaKelle's. He wasn't allowed to cohabitate with her seeing as he only came around on occasion. He wasn't sure if that was the right word, cohabitate, but that's the word she told him once and he remembered it. She had an extra room with two mattresses on top of each other, no frame or box spring, and a small closet. Darnell had fit what he could in the closet and the rest was packed in big, black lawn and leaf bags on the floor. Once a week, LaKelle asked him when he was going to get rid of his extra clothes. He could see, one day, he'd come in and they would be gone, off to Goodwill.

What was he going to do now? How long was this going to go on? How long would he have to look over his shoulder? He had a baby girl, responsibilities. What he needed was protection. A way out. Not one of those hood rats. Somebody with more scruples than that. Darnell wasn't sure he could trust one of them any more than this Raoul character. Or Max, the ATF man; both of 'em probably crooked as all get out. One would send him back to jail, one would send him to his grave.

Darnell leaned back on his mattress and ruminated on it, trying to decide which would be better. Some of the guys he knew, they saw jail time as a badge of honor, some screwed-up rite of passage that they were actually proud of. Not him, fuck that.

Of course, Max had talked about working for him. They didn't get a chance to talk about it beyond that before the incident. That's what it would be for the rest of his life. The incident. He could see himself talking to LaKelle in ten years: "You remember the incident?" He could see her telling him not to walk in the kitchen yet, she just mopped. Not even answering his question.

Truth is, the ATF man got him *out of jail* for whatever he had in mind. Maybe there was something there. He was a cop and they had their ways. He could do what the man asked and still end up incarcerated. Darnell wondered if it would come down to that, a choice between prison or death.

Max saw them as soon as he pulled up to Johnny Stanz's house: two white guys in jeans and t-shirts around the side of the house past the driveway. One with a leather vest over his white t-shirt, both of them with small chains running from their wallets to a belt loop. He knew the type but never understood the chain thing, what the purpose was. To stop from getting your wallet stolen? Or show how tough you are, a chain hanging from your clothes and all? He'd seen some get ripped off guys walking on the street, some kid running by and just yanking the hell out of it. Just a little clasp left hanging on the belt loop.

Whatever the reason, Max asked them about it walking past a Jeep CJ5 parked in the driveway. No look of surprise on their faces, both of them chatting away as Max approached them.

No answer to his question, though.

Maybe they didn't hear him, too busy talking to each other like he wasn't even there. He said, "Hey fellas, why you wear those chains on your wallets?"

A friendly tone of voice. Max thought it was jovial, even.

They still didn't answer. The two of them stood there staring at him.

Max said, "One of you guys Johnny Stanz?" getting annoyed with this. He could feel the tension starting to build, nobody wanting to back down, look like they were giving in. Jesus, he was just trying to talk to them.

Max said, "Guys, just relax," reached into his back pocket

and took out a leather case. Held it open to show them his ID badge.

One of them leaned in to read it and said, "Why's the ATF looking for Johnny?"

Max figured the guy wasn't Johnny but had to ask anyway. The guy shook his head and Max said to the other one, "What about you, partner?"

The other guy shook his head. Either of them could be Johnny, Max wouldn't know. "Maybe you guys can help me out. I understand Johnny lives here. Is that right?" Max waited, watching these guys decide whether to answer him or not.

One of them shrugged.

Max said, "That mean you don't know?" trying to lead up to asking them what they were doing here if they didn't know, until one of them spoke up.

"Yeah, that's my understanding, too."

"Your understanding, huh?" Max smiled, meaning it to give them a little attitude. "You a friend of Johnny's?"

The guy shrugged.

Max said, "What's your name, partner?"

The guy stood there, trying to make up his mind, and the other guy spoke up.

"Why don't you tell us your name, *partner?*"

Max turned to him. "You want to start talking now?" Max pulled out his ID again, holding it up to the guy's face, making sure he had enough time to look at it good.

"So," Max said, "you know my name. Know what I do for a living. Know more about me than I do about you." Max turned to face the first guy. "You want to tell me what you're doing here? What I see, looks like a couple guys snooping around, looking to break into somebody's house. That's just a wild guess."

"Sir, we weren't snooping around. We were looking for our

friend is all." The guy sounding pleasant now.

"So, you are friends of Johnny's?" Max said. "What's your name?"

"Bobby."

Max waited.

"Davis. Bobby Davis is my name."

Max turned to the other one.

"Lester Long."

Max said, "You putting me on?"

Lester shook his head, not sure of what the ATF man meant.

"Name like that, you should be in adult movies."

Lester smiled, not giving it much.

"So you two haven't seen Johnny for a bit? You over here checking on your buddy, worried he might be hurt?"

Bobby said, "Yes, sir."

Max waited, let them think he was going to say something. He didn't, hoping to make it awkward for them. He knew the whole thing was a line of shit. Checking on their friend? C'mon. He let them get nervous, think that the ATF man standing in front of them was getting suspicious. He could ask for IDs, but that would get them thinking. He'd run the tag on that Jeep in the driveway when he got back to the office, find something out that way.

Lester said, "We hadn't seen Johnny for about a week. We were getting worried."

Max said, "You guys hang out a lot? You close to Johnny?"

Bobby looked at Lester and shrugged.

Max said, "You don't know?"

Bobby said, "I guess we ain't really that tight. Just buddies, you know?"

"You have any idea where he is?"

Lester said, "Didn't say."

"He didn't say? When's the last time you talked to him?"

41

"I guess it was a couple nights ago. I can't remember. We talked on the phone for a couple minutes."

Then Bobby said, "But we ain't seen him for about a week."

Like they were getting their stories straight.

Max said, "You have Johnny's number by any chance? I don't have it and I'd like to get in touch with him."

Lester said, "It's in my phone. Only thing, sir, I don't have my phone with me."

Max passed business cards to both of them, then turned to Bobby, who said, "I don't know his number." Bobby pointed to Lester. "He always calls Johnny if we gonna get together."

Now Lester said, "What we can do, sir, is tell Johnny to give you a call when we see him, tell him you'd really like to talk to him."

Max shook his head—overwhelmed by the generosity—before looking up at Bobby and Lester with a sort of grin, appreciative.

"Really? You'd do that for me?"

Lester said, "You shouldn't have given him a fake name. That's gonna piss him off."

"You were the dumb one to give him a real name," Billy Poe said. "But it's weird enough to where he thought it might've been fake."

Lester remembered the ATF man's face when he said his name. Asking him if it was real. Whatever. He said, "Well, you could've thought of one better'n Bobby Davis. That's lame."

"I was on the spot," Billy said. "What you want? I hesitate, he's gonna know. They trained to sniff out that type of stuff."

Lester nodded and let it go, knowing Billy was bullshitting him. How would he know what federal agents were trained to do? He said, "What's he doing now?"

"Standing there. The man looks frozen."

"Why's he not leaving?"

"He's checking things out."

There it was again. Billy giving him pages out of the federal agent handbook. Billy and Lester were in Billy's Jeep; had made the block and parked in front of somebody's house, watching Max Bradford looking up, down, and around Johnny Stanz's house. Writing something on a little notepad. Lester wanted to ask what Max was writing down, see if Billy could tell him that too.

Lester said, "What you think he's doin' here?"

"You heard the man," Billy said. "He wanted to know if we knew Johnny. Obviously, he's looking for him."

Billy was full of smartass comments today. In a bad mood. What Lester meant was, "How do you think he knew to come here? I mean, to Johnny's house?"

"I'd guess he looked it up in the computer." Billy was scratching his beard, starting to get edgy. "Either way, that don't matter. All that matters, he's here."

Lester stretched his neck out, like he could see better that way, and said, "What the fuck is he doing?"

Billy shrugged, not really sure. The man didn't appear to be doing anything different. Walking the grounds—if you could use that word with Johnny's little piece-of-shit overgrown yard—taking notes every so often.

Lester thought him and Billy might be thinking the same thing, so he asked it. "Suppose Johnny's in there? Suppose he's waiting it out, hiding in a closet, waiting for everybody to leave but gets tired of it and comes out before the fucker leaves? What if he gets seen?"

"Or if he's out and comes back, pulls right in the driveway without thinking, wondering what the hell's going on?"

See, they were thinking of the same thing.

They could see Max walking away now. Back to his car and

pulling away and going in the opposite direction from them on Burlington.

Billy said, "He's gone."

Lester let out a sigh, sounding like he was brought back from the dead. "That was close."

"Don't loosen your ass cheeks yet. He might double back."

"You think?"

"You said it yourself. Suppose Johnny's in there, waiting to see if the coast is clear before coming out?" Billy was nodding. Meaning Max, he said, "He's slippery enough to try that trick, come back and surprise him."

Lester was up in his seat, squinting at the gold car in the distance, getting smaller and smaller going away from them. He said, "You think so?"

"It's what I would do."

Max believed looking up members of the task force from three years ago was a waste of time but felt he had to do something. It was nagging at him, that sense of not knowing if there was something going on in the office. He thought of the internal affairs interview, coming up in four days' time or so. He'd have to check with Don to see if that was set up yet.

Yeah, he would tell his story in his quiet tone. Look up and see stern OPR faces, one of them sure to act bored, showing his confidence that they already had the story and were there as a formality.

Max decided to look through some files.

They were all on computer now in an automated database, but he needed things you couldn't see on a screen. Looking through handwritten notes was best, you could learn a lot more that way. So he went down to a records room and told the guard on duty he'd look through them himself if that was okay, he didn't want to sign anything out. Max saw names of guys on the task force. It wasn't big, him and two other guys. Russ Bennie, an old-school agent; a cowboy built like Wilford Brimley who wore a Stetson and boots to work every day. If he had to wear a tie, it was one of those skinny bolo ties. Somebody said once Russ reminded them of Jack Ruby the way he always had that hat on. Max could see it.

Russ was transferred to the Phoenix office not long after their task force wrapped up. His wife, Phyllis, needed the dry air to deal with her emphysema. Max could call out there—it would give him an excuse to catch up—but the last he heard, Russ was fifty-nine, close to retiring, taking care of Phyllis on a two-acre ranch and busy with congressional inquiries into the Phoenix office because guns were ending up at murder scenes across the border.

Carl McDermott was a different story. To your face, he was a good guy but had a bad attitude he couldn't hide. He could be one of those OPR people. The kind of guy that would bad-mouth you to other guys behind your back. What Carl didn't know was that nobody liked him so they'd end up telling the guy what Carl said. When they were on the task force, Carl had told Russ that he didn't like the way Max would interrogate some of their suspects, that he was too friendly. Russ asked what that meant, did he think Max was in cahoots? Carl didn't say anything, just gave his half-ass shrug. Trying to tell Russ that he thought maybe so or get Russ to agree. Russ told him to fuck off.

That was the only time Max worked with Carl. He heard Carl was transferred to the Canine Training Center in Front Royal, Virginia. Max bet the dogs didn't even like him. After that, Carl retired to Nashville and nobody'd heard from him since, and Max wasn't sure anyone wanted to.

Max was flipping through pages of handwritten scrawl. Neither guy liked to type and only bothered to transcribe some of their notes. Max could recognize Russ's writing even if he couldn't always make it out. Carl was better about it, but not much. Hundreds of yellow sticky notes, each of them a reminder about a different question to ask one of the suspects. Russ liked to do that, jot things down on yellow sticky notes. Max came across his report on one of the suspects: a Lebanese-American named Ishaq Mukarram Sarkis. He remembered the assistant U.S. attorney asking if he was profiling Mr. Sarkis and Max told him he thought that was his job, something he had to do in anticipating potential threats to the United States. That shut him up for a minute. Then he wanted to know if that was an accepted practice, to single out an individual based on appearance. Max told him no, except when that individual has relatives with ties to known terrorist cells in Islamabad. Then it was accepted practice. Max liked that last part, when he turned the attorney's snot-nose attitude around on him.

The assistant U.S. attorney asked how could Max be entirely certain of the information, could he absolutely trust the intelligence? Not outright accusing Max of dereliction, but it wasn't far off.

Max said, "What're we supposed to do, wait for a bomb to go off?"

Max remembered liking that line. Don, Max's boss, kept him away from the assistant U.S. attorney for a while.

Max read the rest of the report then kept looking.

He came to a page on Darnell and dog-eared it. He finished the file and didn't find much else that interested him. Came back to the page on Darnell and looked at it. Darnell's personal information: height, weight . . . an address in Maryland. All the stuff that Marlon Sturdivant gave them.

There was something funny at the bottom. Carl's name was printed in the contact area. When Max got the call from Hollywood WRC, the C.O. told him *his* name was listed. Maybe somebody changed it when Carl was transferred out to Virginia? It was possible, but for a three-year-old warrant for a fugitive way down the food chain? Not likely.

It could be nothing or it could be something.

Darnell wondered how he was supposed to watch his baby girl with that phone ringing all the time. Johnny Stanz's phone. He left it on vibrate, not even thinking about turning it off since he took it from Johnny's house. Thinking about answering it; wanting to, bad. Decided against it for fear of who was on the other end. That Raoul guy Johnny was talking about. Shoot, that guy sounded scary as hell. Like Johnny said, let well enough alone.

Only, every time he'd go to clean up little LaKeisha when she spit up, that phone would ring. Damn LaKelle. He come back from Johnny's house, first thing she does is run out for groceries. He told her everything Johnny said—including that part about his cousin getting killed in prison—and what does she say? "I'm sorry, baby, but you got some money? I need some Fabuloso and some lottery cards. I wanted to get some Powerball. Ain't nobody won the Mega Money yet, either, so I was gonna get some of those." That girl and her cleaning supplies. Darnell just about wiped out walking in his own house nowadays. He didn't say that out loud, she'd be quick to ask him where his half of the house note was.

Darnell gave her what he had on him, a twenty, and she stared at him like she was expecting more. He looked back and said whatever lotto money she won, half was his.

He turned back to LaKeisha, crying but not spitting up anything disgusting this time, and waved toys in front of her. Little dolls, a stuffed turtle, anything to try to get her to stop. Man, this girl's lungs worked, that's for sure. She settled down a bit and Darnell cradled her on his shoulder, patting her back to keep her that way.

Walked around the house with her and used his free hand to figure out the voice mail on Johnny's phone. Shit was confusing. He hit a few buttons, could see there were two messages. Held the phone up to his ear and heard a gravelly voice on the other end; definitely a white fella but didn't identify himself. Sounded like somebody who'd been smoking two packs a day all his life. Saying all kinds of derogatory things about Johnny and what he was going to do to Johnny when they found him. Shit, now Darnell was using that word. *They.* Man, this stuff was mean. That guy must be some kind of psycho, talking a streak like that. Darnell stopped the message and listened to the other one, holding the phone a little ways from his baby girl's ear, not wanting her to be exposed to language like that. He was curious if the second message was Raoul. Johnny said he was Puerto Rican but voice didn't sound Spanish or have any accent like that.

It was the same cigarette-smoking guy.

He put the phone down, intent on calling his momma to let her know he was okay after LaKelle came back from the store. Damn, girl, don't take that long to buy cleaning supplies and lotto cards, does it? Either she was spending more than she took with her, shopping for other things, or bullshitting with somebody she ran into at the store. Probably telling them about her baby's daddy's recent kidnapping ordeal.

The phone started ringing again. Man, this was something else. He watched the phone, lights going on and off, the hard plastic vibrating, making a buzzing sound flush against the laminate kitchen countertop.

Darnell looked at the phone for a moment or two, thinking about picking it up. Thought hard about it. These guys weren't going to go away. Not if he understood those messages. They were serious.

They didn't know where he was. They wouldn't know how to

find him. It was a cell phone, Darnell could be answering it from anywhere. He didn't even have to say anything. Hang up on the guy if he started talking crazy again.

He reached for it.

What did he have to lose?

CHAPTER FIVE

The minute he picked it up, Darnell had second thoughts. He pressed a button to answer and waited.

A voice on the other end said, "Johnny?"

It sounded surprised.

When Darnell didn't say anything, the voice said, "Johnny?" again.

It didn't sound like the cigarette smoker's voice.

"Johnny, this is Max Bradford with the Bureau of . . ."

Darnell hung up.

Oh shit. What was *that* guy doing calling Johnny's phone? Darnell thought, *looking for me?* Had to be, unless Johnny was in some trouble with him too. Could be.

The phone rang.

Darnell let it ring, looking at his baby girl; precious little baby, her eyes starting to close. Should he answer it? Could be asking for all new trouble getting the ATF man involved. But didn't he say something about going to work for him? Not anything about putting him in jail. Actually, he's the guy got Darnell out of jail if you wanted to look at it that way.

The message light on Johnny's phone was blinking.

The phone rang.

How about going to work on this? Surely, Mister Max would be interested in this Raoul character. Wasn't no way Darnell could handle this alone. Sic the ATF on him, that's what he could do. Be a better chance of seeing his baby girl grow up if he did that.

The phone rang.

Same number as before. Four straight calls. Darnell told himself to play it cool and answered. He said, "Hello?" and heard Max ask him if he was Johnny Stanz.

"No, this is Darnell."

Silence.

"You know who this is?"

Darnell said, "This is Max Bradford, right? You with the ATF."

"You know I've been looking for you?"

Darnell said, "I'm sure," and thought about it for a second. "I been through some crazy shit the last couple days." Trying to get some sympathy. "I guess we should talk."

Almost sounding like a question. Feeling the ATF man out, seeing if he was angry.

When Max said okay, Darnell felt better. Then Max asked where Darnell was, that he could be there right away, Darnell said, "Unh-unh, not here."

"Tell me where."

"You know a place called Colors, in Pompano?"

"What's that, some kind of titty bar?"

"It's on Dixie Highway, almost to Atlantic Boulevard. You meet me there in one hour."

There was a hesitation before Max said, "That'll be two o'clock in the afternoon. It's gonna be open?"

Darnell said, "It'll be open. It's gonna be the skanks working that shift but it'll be open," and hung up.

Billy decided that he and Lester were going to drive back to Johnny Stanz's house and wait. The house on little Burlington Street that Billy always had trouble finding. Lester wanted to ask him how come Billy couldn't find it, they were here twenty minutes ago. But he didn't. They watched the little stucco house, hibiscus growing out of control, complaining about Max the ATF guy. It was the only time Billy made conversation, when there was a problem.

"You see him give us his card?" Billy was looking at it, holding it between two fingers. "He wants us to know he's out there."

Lester said, "Can you blame him?" without going further.

Billy took the time to turn to Lester and said, "Whose side are you on?" and Lester said, "Our side," then tried to make it better by saying, "We shouldn't have left him there."

Billy turned back to look straight ahead. Lester could tell Billy's mind was far off. Billy thinking that Lester was right, but they were told to take the black guy only, leave the white guy. He remembered those exact words, *Leave the white guy*. Billy shrugged it off and watched the street. Older cars moving up and down, smoke trailing from tailpipes and ball joints in need of lube jobs squeaking. Then Lester said something that Billy hadn't thought of until now.

"You think the ATF guy is still here, watching us watch for Johnny?"

It was a thought that made Billy start looking around. He didn't remember what Max was driving but spotted an Explorer come past them. No, not Max, but Billy felt himself watching close.

Lester said, "You gonna tell Raoul about this?"

Billy nodded and watched a gold Impala creeping up the street. He couldn't make out a face but tapped Lester and said, "Check it out," sitting upright now. "Is that him?"

Lester leaned across Billy to see. Not leaning too far, then it would look like they were gay and he was giving Billy a blow job. Just enough to see without looking like it. He said, "I can't be sure," shaking his head. "That looks like something somebody in the government might drive." Lester looked for government markings. He sat back as the Impala turned on a side street before it came to them, out of view now. "I couldn't be sure."

Well, Billy decided he was definitely telling Raoul now, if there was any question before. This guy was going to be a problem, Billy could tell that already. Felt it again holding the man's card in his hand, then spooked by cars on the road. Whether that Imapala was him or not, he was out there. Billy looked at the name on the card again. Max Bradford. Even his name sounded like trouble.

Darnell went over the tone of Max Bradford's voice in his head. It wasn't angry. He sounded interested. What Darnell didn't want was a SWAT team coming with Max. Bust in the strip club, his favorite place, yelling to get down—repeating it over and over like you didn't hear it the first time—then have a shotgun pressed against your head while you're figuring out what's happening. Use one of those flash grenades he'd seen in the movies, they'd clear the place out.

That happened, he'd never be able to show his face in there again.

He heard LaKelle calling him to take out the trash, that she had some other chores for him while he was at it. Darnell let it go for a minute, he was busy thinking. She'd come back here in a minute anyway, asking when he was going to do what she asked.

The more he thought about Max, the more comfortable he got. Maybe comfortable was too strong a word, but it was the first one that came to his mind. What he still couldn't understand was how the man knew about Johnny Stanz. It freaked him out, but Darnell told himself the man was with the government, he had his ways.

Darnell wondered should he take himself a gun. Look at that, comfortable one minute, thinking about personal protection the next. He didn't have one and didn't know where he could find one this fast, telling Max to meet him in an hour. *You know I've been looking for you?* No shit, get in line. It didn't sound too bad the way he said it, but you could never tell. Darnell shrugged it off, thinking back to when they first met; when Max picked him up at the Hollywood WRC. Darnell telling himself the man wanted you to go work for him, not shoot you, so chill out, okay?

That wouldn't be easy. LaKelle would be coming soon, asking him why the garbage hadn't been taken out yet. Did she understand what he had just been through? Darnell told himself *guess not* and piddled around the bedroom. Picking up clothes scattered around—his t-shirts, his jeans, his Nikes—before she added that to the list.

Darnell decided it rested on what Max meant by working for him. He could see himself walking into a room wearing a wire, sweating his ass off from nerves. Working undercover might be cool, but a wire? No, sir. You get killed on the spot if a bad guy finds that. Darnell figured it was something him and Max could discuss.

He was reaching for a Kangol he'd bought but never wore, something he missed making his first pass around the room, when he heard footsteps. That flat tap of LaKelle's bare feet against the wood floor of the hallway. He got lost looking at the hat—a charcoal gray one that would look good with a black shirt he had—staring at the cute little kangaroo on the back, when he heard LaKelle say, "What you doing, Darnell? There's chores to be done."

Yes, he knew. He told her that and she said, "You best get to work, then. That trash ain't gonna throw out itself. After that, the filter in the air conditioner needs changing, there's food in the fridge needs to be thrown out . . ."

Darnell started tuning out when LaKelle told him the yard

needed to be mowed. He could pay a young boy down the street for that. He could wear his hat to meet Max, look cool. Like he wasn't nervous. His black shirt to go with it. Yeah, there were a couple of girls he had his eye on the last time he was there, they would probably like the way it looked on him. "Oh, Darnell, you lookin' good." He glanced at the hat one more time, thinking about how he'd look and, yeah, he could imagine them saying that.

Except that right now, LaKelle was telling him, "Oh, and there's part of the fence that needs to be reattached in the backyard. Some of the chain links come loose, see if you can take care of that."

That girl, when she got on one of her kicks . . . Darnell decided he'd go to the club early, see if those girls were there. He told LaKelle he had somewhere to be, he'd take care of his chores when he got back. He promised.

"That's fine," she said, starting to dust as Darnell was walking out the bedroom door. "Just don't forget that trash on your way out."

Max raced up 95, steady traffic, going over what he knew. Hoping that he'd have an epiphany, something that he hadn't thought of before would come to him.

Darnell gets arrested. He picks up Darnell. They get sideswiped, run off the road. He wakes up, Darnell's gone. Does some looking, comes up with the name Johnny Stanz. Old buddy of Darnell's. Goes by Johnny's last known address and finds two douchebags hanging around. One guy lied to his face. The Jeep in the driveway was registered to one Billy Poe, not Bobby Davis or Lester Long. Yeah, they could have borrowed it—or stole it. Something that Max would find out soon enough. Still, Max was willing to bet it was Billy who was the liar. Shame on him.

He'd deal with that later.

So, far as Max knows, Darnell's a fugitive at this point. Max calls the number he was given for Johnny Stanz. Christ, must've tried it twenty times. Then, just like that, somebody picks up. But it's not Johnny, it's Darnell.

Did this tell him anything?

That Darnell arranged his own escape?

It was something Max had thought of from the start. The most obvious explanation.

But if Darnell was the mastermind, planning a highly visible escape on a crowded highway in broad daylight, why even pick up the phone? Why meet with the guy you escaped from?

He was setting Max up.

The idea: get Max alone, strike up some conversation to initiate trust; get Max to let his guard down. Then some dude jumps out of the shadows to put a bullet in the back of Max's head.

But Darnell said the place, Colors, would be open. Even at two o'clock in the afternoon. Max could believe that. The hunt for tail never sleeps. Plus, was Darnell going to have somebody shoot a federal agent in a public establishment in the middle of the day? Talk about bringing fire and brimstone down on yourself. Double that with the escape scenario and this guy, Darnell, either had more balls or less brains than Max gave him credit for.

Those were the feelings Max had, even if they didn't make any sense. Being a mastermind didn't seem like Darnell's speed. He might be a crafty guy, though. Street smart. Not an organizer or leader of men. You need a certain something for that.

Max didn't think Darnell had that something.

Continuing north on 95, Max remembered something else Darnell said when they were on the phone. Something about what he'd been through in the last couple days. Max figured it to mean since they had been split up.

What was up with that?

Since they got home, Lester had asked Billy twice if he was going to tell Raoul about Max. They hadn't been in the door fifteen minutes. Shit, yes, he was gonna get around to it. He told Lester to get off his back.

Lester said, "I was just trying to be helpful."

Billy was busy looking through kitchen cabinets, searching for something to eat, saying, "Well, you're not." Nothing there. He closed the cabinet, making a show by slamming it, and said, "It's getting on my nerves."

Lester couldn't stop Billy before he was gone—while Lester was busy figuring out what was in the house that he could cook.

Billy called from the road. Lester picked it up but didn't get a chance to say anything because Billy said, "I had to get outta there. You were aggravating me with your questions."

"I was just trying to make sure we don't miss nothing."

Billy said, "We won't."

There was a pause where Lester thought Billy might be watching the road. He said to Billy, "I found some pancake mix. I can make some if you want."

Billy said, "It's probably expired." Another pause and Lester heard Billy honking over the phone. Billy came back on the line and said, "I'm thinking, do we know somebody who knows somebody who might know where Johnny is? Or can help us get to Darnell?"

"You don't think Johnny's home now?"

Billy shook his head even though Lester couldn't see it. "He ain't there. We hung around. I might swing by while I'm out, but I ain't expecting nothin'."

"I don't know about finding Darnell outside of Johnny," Lester said. "You thinking of cutting Raoul out?"

"We can't cut him out. He wants the man, he has the resources."

"You see a way to make some money here?"

"I'm just thinking out loud," Billy said. There was a silence while Billy was driving. "I'm going see a lady friend. I'll be back later."

Lester said, "You think you have time for that?"

Billy said he wasn't going to be long. "Besides, she ain't the kind of gal wants you to hang around after and cuddle."

"Okay," Lester said. "Just don't forget to call Raoul when you're finished, all right?"

CHAPTER SIX

Raoul was never home in the mornings.

That's why it surprised Billy Poe when he called, sure he was going to get Raoul's answering machine. Leave him a message and then spend the next couple hours screening his phone calls. Instead, Raoul's voice, a deep one, came on the line and told them to come over, the accent sometimes making it hard for Billy to understand him.

Billy and Lester were inside the house off Tamiami Trail when Raoul came out of the bedroom, closing the door behind him; Raoul lounging in his robe, hanging open, boxer shorts and house slippers. A sliver of white residue left under his nostril. Doing lines. Billy started to talk until Raoul held a finger up to his lips and motioned for them to go outside. It meant he had a woman in there.

Raoul pulled a chair out from a frosted glass-top patio table and settled into the deep cushion on top of the chair. Looking like the man had a rough night.

Billy decided not to make mention of that. He got straight to it and said, "We didn't find Johnny," watching Raoul's head slump. He tried to figure if the man was disappointed or sleepy.

"That's very unfortunate."

Raoul said it with his head resting on the table, making it hard for Billy and Lester to hear. They let it go, thinking they heard it well enough to know the answer was that he was disappointed. They squirmed in their seats a little waiting for Raoul's next move. The guy could be unpredictable, prone to flying off the handle when he didn't get his way.

They watched Raoul get up and walk around. Rub his belly for a minute, not a big one but there was something there. Massaging it through the opening in his robe while he stared off at the rest of Florida beyond his backyard fence, moving his hand on occasion to run it through the hair on his chest. Running fingers along his mustache now, a thick one that Billy once heard a woman say looked like Magnum P.I. Billy didn't see the resemblance. Running it through there over and over now. Thinking.

Billy leaned close into Lester and said, "He starts rubbing his pecker, we're leaving."

They waited while Raoul contemplated. Wondered if his woman might come outside, see what was going on. Maybe catch a glimpse of her bush, that would be something.

Raoul straightened out, putting his hands at the small of his back and arching. He said, "Tell me what happened."

"We kept calling," Billy said, "but didn't get no answer. Finally, we just went over there."

Billy and Lester knew what was coming.

"Why not just go over there to begin with?"

It sounded like a question but really wasn't. Not something they had an answer for and Raoul could see it. He paused to rub his mustache again, Billy noticing the black onyx pinky ring Raoul liked to wear. He thought Raoul wore it for show—like a James Bond bad guy sort of thing—but was told it absorbs negative energy.

Raoul got up and stretched his back out again. Man, that chick must really be wearing him out. Billy heard him mutter some words in his native tongue, then heard him say in English, "This is very disturbing."

Billy waited, exchanging glances with Lester when Raoul

wasn't looking. Wanting to say *some*thing.

Raoul said, "What the fuck are you in my employ for?"

That change in tone told Billy and Lester the pinky ring wasn't working. Wondered again if they should say something, defend themselves. But that's not what this was.

"I pay you so shit like this doesn't happen." Raoul was burning off steam, the inflection in his accent stressing the cuss words.

Billy looked close but didn't see the bulge of a gun in the pockets of Raoul's robe.

"You fucking up, my man." Raoul started again in his P.R. Spanish, then continued in English, saying, "Now what the fuck you expect to do? You can call this Johnny piece-of-shit all you want but he won't pick up. How do you fix this?" That was it before he said, "I want this fucking Johnny dead, too."

Billy thought about saying something right then. Put his hand on Lester's arm when he saw Lester about to open his mouth. There was no pleasing Raoul at this moment.

"I want his fucking balls on my kitchen table. I want to eat them for breakfast." Raoul paused to look at Billy and Lester. "Mix them right in with my Apple Jacks, just like they were chopped up little strawberries, this sack of shit."

That kind of talk made Billy want to get up. Got him nervous, wondering if his boss was about to lose it.

"And how will you find this nigger that ripped me off?"

Lester couldn't take it anymore. Billy tried to grab his arm again, stop him from making it worse. Lester brushed him off, reaching in his pocket to take out that ATF agent's card.

Raoul stretched his arm out and grabbed it. Stared at it for a moment. Max Bradford, Special Agent, Bureau of Alcohol, Tobacco, Firearms and Explosives. He stared at Lester. Maybe waiting for an explanation. When he didn't get one, Raoul said, "What am I supposed to do with this? You like me to wipe my

61

ass with it, this piece of scrap paper?"

What's going on here? Lester couldn't figure out why Raoul would react like that. He said, "We ran into that guy at Johnny's house."

Raoul paused to think about what Lester was saying. Tried to understand why Lester was excited about telling him this. He said, "Did either of you give him your names?"

Billy shook his head and looked at Lester for him to do the same thing.

That was something.

Raoul said, "But now we know his."

Man, the guy was on his game, huh? Billy thought Raoul might be coming around, seeing things their way. He said, "We can let that guy find Johnny for us. Or his nigger friend. He has more ways to find people than we do."

Raoul sat back in his wrought-iron chair, getting low and relaxing on the seat cushion. "You plan to follow him?"

That was the plan and Billy told him so. After that, Raoul said, "You could use my car. It's fast. Four-hundred-twenty horsepower."

Billy knew Raoul was talking about the Camaro, the new one. He nodded when Raoul said, "You can drive a stick?"

Raoul watched Billy and Lester smiling. "You like that, huh?" That got Raoul up out of his chair. He stared at the card again, looking at it closer this time. Giving himself time to examine it, noticing things he hadn't noticed before when he took the card from Lester. In a blind rage at that time.

Bureau of Alcohol, Tobacco, Firearms and Explosives.

"I want you to listen to me," he said. "I let you use my car. I'll find something to use in the meantime. But don't do anything until you hear from me. Do something with your Jeep. Please don't leave it here. I couldn't stand to have that backwoods vehicle seen in my garage."

"Any way to prove that?"

Darnell shrugged.

Max said, "You want to end up like that? You have a little girl to think about."

That stopped Darnell.

"How you know about that?"

"I spoke with your mother."

And that reminded Darnell he forgot to call her.

"She practically gave me your whole life history. She's a good woman, you should do right by her."

Darnell wanted to tell Max to leave his momma and little girl out of it but said, "Shit, I'm trying."

"She even gave me your phone number."

Max was pleased with himself.

Until Darnell said, "That been cut off a long time ago."

Max hunched over the bar and started playing with a stack of cocktail napkins, getting the feeling he was hitting close to home. He said, "What about this other guy, Tweety?"

"Ain't heard much from him of late. About three years, to be exact. Johnny told me he hadn't heard nothing about him, either. I ain't really thought to look until now, be honest with you."

Max waited.

After a moment, Darnell said, "He got a girl, though. She keeps a room at one of them hotels down in South Beach."

Max turned to the stage, looking away while he couldn't help but smile a little.

Darnell took a sip and said, "Least she did when I was banging her."

"never heard Raoul that angry," Lester said. "All that talk about putting Johnny's balls in his cereal. That was creeping me out. You think he meant that?"

Billy and Lester watched Raoul smiling now—look at him. Not a bit upset.

Man, that onyx ring must be magic.

Max thought Darnell looked different now. Worn out. Nervous. Couldn't put his finger on it, but different from when Max first met him a day and a half ago, making faces when Max told him about working for the ATF. Darnell looked happier in jail. Max watched him take a sip from a glass in front of him before looking toward the stage.

"I told you they have some skanks in here at this time."

"Yeah," Max said, "you sure can pick 'em."

Darnell turned back to Max. "Hey, you come in here at seven, eight at night, prime time. You see some fine bitches up in here."

Maybe so. But all Max saw right now were teeth and eyes. It was fucking dark in this place. He took a look around, glancing over his shoulder; midday light coming in from the front door opening on occasion.

"In case you didn't notice, there's no bouncers at the door."

Darnell said, "Never any before nighttime at this place," not sounding surprised.

"What I'm telling you is, I brought my piece in, if you were thinking about doing something stupid."

Darnell jumped. "Shit, man, it ain't like that. What you think I am?"

Max really wasn't sure yet.

"Everything's cool, man." Darnell motioned towards the bar. "You want something?"

Max shook his head. "I'm working."

"Really?"

"Yeah, interviewing an escaped convict."

Sounding serious.

Max said, "I should haul your ass in right now."

But Darnell knew he was curious. "Look, this ain't my fault, Mister Max." Darnell brought a hand up to this chest. "I was *kid*napped, you understand? They meant to kill me."

"C'mon, Darnell, you expect me to believe that crap?"

Darnell nodded, his eyebrows arching to show how serious he was.

Okay, let him prove it.

Max said, "Who?"

"All I know is somebody named Raoul. Last name of Garcia."

Max asked how he found all this out and Darnell told him about being taken to a house after the wreck—he didn't know where it was—and being told that name by one of his captors. That's the word he used. Captors.

Who was the guy that told you that name? Darnell said it was a white guy, biker dude, bald on top but had hair on the sides long enough for a ponytail. A goatee, too.

"Billy Poe?"

The description matched.

"I don't know that name. Like I was saying, I didn't know any of these guys before two days ago."

Max smiled. "So what, they just pick your name out of a hat? You think they go around doing this for fun?"

"Me and some guys robbed a guy three years ago, down in Homestead. We got, like, twenty grams of coke." Darnell tried to make it sound as innocent as he could. "Supposedly, the guy we robbed was this Raoul."

"That's what you got, twenty grams?"

"That's all I knew of."

It wasn't a complete lie.

Darnell said, "I didn't even know what to do with it. I'm not into moving a lot of drugs. That's not my thing."

Max shifted in his chair. Trying not to get comfortable, hav-

ing drinks and conversation with a felon. "What next?"

"Fortunately, one of my buddies was at the house were gonna drive me somewhere. Shoot me dead l broodmare, I 'magine. He offered to take me out the way, he stopped the car and let me go."

"What's your buddy's name?"

"Johnny . . ."

". . . Stanz." Max nodded. It caught Darnell off gu

Max started replaying the events in his mind, fi now where Johnny fit in.

Darnell was still wondering how Max knew remembered he answered Johnny's phone when Max

Speaking of which, Max said, "You still got that ph reached to take it from Darnell. He scrolled th numbers and said, "Anybody call you on this besides

Darnell nodded. "There's a couple messages bu rang in a while."

Max said, "Stay here," and disappeared outside.

Darnell ordered another drink, straight Hennessy, a Passed the time watching a young woman named Sp bling onstage to music he didn't recognize, in six-inc pasties covering her private parts.

Max came back a few minutes later. Didn't expla was doing outside. Darnell stared at him while the picked up an empty glass and asked Max if he needed

Max told him no thanks and waited until the walked off before saying, "That robbery you were talk who else was with you?"

"Was my cousin and a guy named Tweety. They d cousin. A shank in the ribcage while he was at something unrelated. Least that's what Johnny says. was this Raoul guy responsible for that, too."

Billy gave him a look. "Are you serious?"

Lester shrugged, he was just asking. "Looked like he calmed down after I gave him that ATF business card."

"That was kinda weird," Billy said. "He was probably just thinking how ridiculous it was that you had that."

Lester said, "You had one, too," knowing Billy was just arguing, looking for something because he didn't think to do it.

Billy didn't say one word. He was too busy looking at the Camaro; buttons on the dashboard that did different things if you hit a certain one, like a spaceship with wheels. Billy wondered what one of those NASA control panels looked like, if it was like this.

Lester was looking at Billy when he said, "How you think he's gonna have us do it?"

Billy was lost in the control panel. "Do what?"

Lester raised his voice. "Find Darnell." Then had to ask, "What else you think I'm talking about?"

Billy shrugged. Driving off, he saw Raoul in the rearview mirror standing at the end of his driveway. Out in his robe like a parent watching their kid borrowing the car.

Lester said, "That's your answer?" mimicking Billy's shrug but exaggerating it.

Billy was driving, pressing buttons, finding the first main drag he could and making a right turn. He wasn't sure what street he was on. It didn't matter. He said, "Don't make no difference. We're the ones gonna find Johnny. After that, Darnell'll be easy."

Billy sounding like he'd made up his mind.

"So you been thinking about that, what we were talking about?" Lester said. "Sounds like you been."

"I hadn't given it much thought."

"You thinking out loud again?"

Billy grunted. Lester looked over. Billy was still playing with buttons. I wonder what this does? Showing some of them to Lester now. Like a kid with a new toy.

Lester said, "When you decide, I guess you'll tell me."

Billy's mind was somewhere else. "Man, this is a nice car."

CHAPTER SEVEN

It took Raoul some time to make phone calls, line up backup plans in case Billy and Lester didn't work out. When he came back inside, Gloria was waking up. Wiping her eyes and asking Raoul where he'd been. She was a good-looking woman for her age, forty-eight by Raoul's estimation, but had a knack for asking questions. Raoul wondered how much of his conversation with Billy and Lester she heard but wasn't letting on.

Still, he had to be careful with her. Raoul sometimes stored drugs at this house—his house, but she was here often. Coke purchased from straw buyers that Gloria recruited, people she knew working strip clubs and illegal betting parlors before Raoul found her. He felt the woman could have a mean streak if she made up her mind to; do something with the information she might have overheard. If he could find another woman to replace Gloria, quick, then he might gently ask her if she heard any of what they were talking about. Bring it up in conversation.

She said, "Are you coming back to bed?" and it made Raoul look up from the vanity. At the time deciding what jewelry he was going to wear that day. Or maybe counting it, seeing if Gloria tried to sneak a piece while he was outside. He let her think that if she wanted.

He watched her, spreading her arms across the pillows as an invitation; parting the crook of her thigh to show she wasn't wearing panties, running her fingers along down there. Putting on a performance for him.

Raoul smiled, continuing to watch her. It reminded him of last night: Gloria letting him watch her pleasuring herself, flying high on cocaine, a new shipment that she had just brought to him. He could control the urge to use drugs, especially before lovemaking, but he had to watch the woman's intake. He remembered having to stop her on more than one occasion, that she had a habit of not stopping herself. He wanted to enjoy her, not fuck her as she lay unconscious. He wondered if she thought of that—his selflessness—when she was partaking in illegal narcotics.

Now Raoul was on the edge of the bed, asking if she would do it again. Gloria asked what and he said pleasure herself. Gloria said she would prefer him to do it and asked if he wanted to, parting her legs some more. He said, "Yes, my dear," because she liked talk like that. Being called "dear." But if you bone a woman over a billiard table within twenty minutes of meeting her two years ago, Raoul's feeling was that the mystery would evaporate soon. So why rush things? Asking for the occasional indulgence would help keep that mystery. Maybe she didn't think of it that way.

Gloria said, "You don't want to touch me, my sweet?" There was another one, "my sweet." To which Raoul said, "Nothing would give me greater pleasure, my love, but I would like you to ready yourself." He said, "Afterwards, I will make love to you as I never have," thinking that would do it.

It did and Gloria started, what sounded like genuine moans coming from her as Raoul let his silk robe fall to the ground. It was weird, but in that moment, the ATF business card that Billy gave him came to mind. He told himself to forget it, there was a beautiful naked woman in front of him.

Too late. Gloria took one look at him and the moans stopped. "If this doesn't excite you," she said, Raoul standing limp in front of her, "why do you ask me to do it?"

★　★　★　★　★

Max and Darnell walked into the lobby of the Clark Hotel, South Beach, Ocean Drive across from Lummus Park, what a hotel guide might call a blend of classic sophistication and contemporary chic; Latin music coming from the bar, tourists waking up from the previous night heading out the door. They crossed to the stairwell, a glance coming from the desk clerk, a good-looking young blonde.

Max followed Darnell up to the second floor. Darnell stopped, moving aside to let Max knock on the door.

A Hispanic girl in a gray tank top and tight jersey shorts answered the door, barefoot. Could be cute if she cleaned herself up and brushed her hair a little.

Darnell popped in the doorway and said, "Alondra? Girl, how you doing?"

Alondra leaned against the doorframe, resting one bare foot on top of the other, and looked at Darnell. No reaction, not looking especially happy to see him. Then looked towards Max and said, "Who are you?"

"My name is Max. May we come in?"

Alondra glanced back into the room, then turned back and said, "I don't think so."

While Max was looking past her, noticing what he guessed was the bathroom door, closed; a few beer cans on the floor; a mess of clothes thrown on the bed, bath towels; he heard Darnell say, "Max here is with the ATF. He just want to talk for a minute."

"About what?"

"Look," Max said, "I'm not real anxious to drag you out of here and do this at my office. You let us in, we'll be gone before you notice."

Alondra took a moment, thinking about it, and moved away from the door. She turned her head again and Max and Darnell looked at each other.

"Alondra, huh?" Max said. "I don't think I've ever heard that one. It's a beautiful name."

"It's supposed to mean 'defender of mankind.' "

She reminded Max of girls he'd arrested before: seen-it-all, playing it cool like it was no big deal. Even sounded like those girls, her voice flat since she answered the door.

Darnell said, "We wanna know if you seen Tweety?" and Max wondered how him and Alondra hooked up.

Max wanted to step in, make it clear that he was asking the questions, but let Darnell have that one. He felt Alondra staring at him and heard her asking for his ID.

"Here you go," Max said, getting his badge out, "Bureau of Alcohol, Tobacco, Firearms and Explosives. I'm not looking to give you a hard time, okay?"

Alondra said, "This is bullshit," looking at Darnell, and Max felt himself losing control of the situation again. Darnell said something back, Max wasn't sure what it was, some kind of street jive maybe. She started in on Darnell, something in Spanish, and it started to sound like a lovers' quarrel.

"Everybody be quiet." Max held out his hands. "Let's not make this harder than it has to be."

The girl, Alondra, rolled her neck at Max and Darnell. Gave them some kind of brush-off with her hand. Max ignored it. He said, "Look, all I need to do is talk to Tweety. You tell us where he is, or if he's staying here, and we'll be out of your hair."

Alondra said, "I ain't got to tell you a damn thing," and gave Max her neck roll again—this time smacking her lips to go along with it—and Max could feel Darnell opening his mouth again.

"This here some *buuull*shit," Darnell said. "Look at this, god-damn trash everywhere. This about some dissolute livin', girl. He either here or you fucking dudes around the clock."

Max shook his head in Darnell's direction, thinking they were going to have a serious talk after this. Alondra started in on Darnell again. Going crazy with her Spanish cuss words, Max not able to make out all of them but got the idea. She stopped and did it again.

Looked away from them, in the direction of the closed bathroom door.

Feeling like she might be trying to tell them something, Max moved towards the bathroom. One hand on the holster on his hip, Max put the other hand on the doorknob. Okay, he'd fling the door open, pull his nine-millimeter, fly in there . . . Christ, feeling a chill as he readied himself.

CHAPTER EIGHT

The knob turned in Max's hand. Shit, somebody right there on the other side of the door. It flew open, knocking Max back, and he caught a glimpse of a black kid; heavy, but from muscle tone. Max could tell that much. He yelled for the kid to stop, got to his feet, and decided quick not to get a shot off. In a moment, it was over, the kid throwing Darnell into a glass brick wall near the bed before he was in the hallway.

Max glanced at Darnell on his way out the door.

He moved into the hall, careful but not hesitant. Nothing in either direction until he heard a door slamming to his right and followed it.

Down a flight of stairs, Max pushed open an exit door, paused to look around, and saw the kid running back towards Ocean Drive and the front of the hotel. Max started after him, tough to do in heavy cowboy boots, and heard footsteps coming up from behind him.

And saw Darnell blow by him in sneakers, following the kid who was going north on Ocean Drive by now. Past all the art deco hotels, cafes fronting their lobbies, filled with tourists; college kids or young professionals strolling up and down the sidewalk; through the slow crawl of traffic separating the hotels from the beach.

Darnell saw Tweety—yeah, that was him—hang a left into a load-in alley at the back of the strip of hotels. Darnell skidded across the hood of a car, angling himself to slide across on one butt cheek, gave a look back to see Max following in the distance, and took off.

He saw Tweety in front of him, hopping over small stacks of wooden loading pallets, twisting around garbage cans. Throwing some of that in Darnell's way. Just to make it hard on him.

Kitchen workers, Spanish folk talking to each other in their native language, came out in cooking aprons and hairnets to throw the trash or haul out boxes. Getting in Tweety's way enough to slow him down a little.

Darnell was going at full speed, the alley coming to a T at the end of Ocean Drive, where it intersected with Fifteenth. Running past streaks of sunlight between the buildings, he wasn't sure how long he could keep this up. By the grace of God, Darnell saw Tweety trip over a crate in the alley, some Spanish kid forgetting to pick it up, and stumble enough to give Darnell a chance to catch up.

He jumped on Tweety, the two of them coming down on smooth pavement. Smooth or not, that hurt. Darnell hanging on for dear life while Tweety tried to wrestle away from him. Jesus, this was a big boy. Bigger than Darnell remembered three years ago. Fucking steroids or something. Bet it made his wee-wee small, why Alondra practically ratted him out.

Darnell had his legs wrapped around Tweety, locking his ankles around Tweety's mid-section. Trying to hold it until he heard footsteps coming up behind, big cowboy boot footsteps, getting heavier.

Then felt the barrel of a gun against the back of his head.

"Get the fuck up."

Darnell looked up and saw Max standing over him.

Supposed to be partners.

Right?

Darnell said, "What the hell you doing, man?"

"Darnell," Max said, "get off him. Do it slowly and go stand over there," pointing across the alley.

Max heard Darnell say, "I ain't the one you need to be worrying about," the words trailing off as Max tuned him out to concentrate on the guy in front of him.

"That's him."

Tweety looked at Darnell, in the eye, and said, "You done it now, boy. You in a world of shit now," before Max swung him around and put handcuffs on him.

"The fuck you think you doin'? You fuckin' dead too, my man."

Max leaned in close and asked Tweety, "You always talk that way to an ATF agent?" and saw Tweety roll his eyes and blow out of his mouth all in one motion.

"I dunno what this is, but I ain't got nothing to do with no ATF. I'm clean, I tell you."

"Just shut up," Max said and backed off, taking a break. All that running. Before Tweety could even ask, Max brought out his ID and put it in Tweety's face. "Three years ago," Max looked back at Darnell, who nodded, "you were involved in a robbery in Homestead. You, Darnell, and a buddy of yours, LaRon Jefferson. You remember that?"

Tweety was silent.

Max took time to pat Tweety down, ask him if he had anything in his pockets Max should be aware of. Tweety was silent. Didn't have a wallet or ID on him. Max said, "What's your name?"

In the silence, it came to Darnell. "His name Alvin."

"Alvin? No wonder you like Tweety."

Tweety was silent.

Max said, "Okay, I'll talk some more." He tugged at the waist of his pants, settling in. "I can talk all day about this. You want me to do that?" He waited. "Nothing? Okay, so you rob this guy, his name's Raoul Garcia. Sound familiar?" Max waited again. "No? Well, he's been looking for all of you. Your boy, LaRon? He's gone."

Tweety, turning his head, gave Max a look.

"That's right," Max said. "Took one in the ribs from some nasty friends of Raoul's. Darnell here was kidnapped, goddamn near killed me in the process. He managed to get away, but they'll try again."

That got Darnell wondering.

Was he serious?

Tweety said, "That's a bunch of bullshit," facing the wall.

"Partner, it couldn't be less bullshit. Now, there's a reason this guy's got a hard-on to get after the three of you. Darnell says he doesn't know. He's in the dark. He says *you* know what's going on."

Darnell's head snapped around. What the fuck was this? He never said that or, at least, didn't remember putting it that way.

Tweety turned his head to look at Darnell.

Max said, "Yeah, he says you were the brains behind the whole thing, know everything that's going on."

Tweety shook his head, looking down, and said, "He giving you some bum information, my man. I don't know shit."

"What'd you come away with?"

Darnell tensed up.

Tweety hung his head again and said, "A few grams of coke."

Max asked him to repeat it, louder so he could hear. Tweety raised his head and said it again.

And there it was. The same thing Darnell told him.

Max said, "You're lying to me, I know it," and felt like he was fishing for information now.

Tweety said, "That's all we got, I'm tellin' you. I mean, yeah, we moved it, but that was it."

Max looked at Darnell, who said, "I told you I didn't have nothing to do with that. It ain't my thing."

Max paused a moment, thinking about it. He put his hand on Tweety's shoulder. "When I let you go, don't do something dumb. Don't start trouble here . . . Don't even *think* about going back to that room. Just walk away and keep walking. Understand?"

Tweety nodded and Max uncuffed him.

They started in opposite directions, Max and Darnell walking the alley looking for a spot to cross back to Ocean Drive; salsa, mambo, different kinds of Latin music muffled in the background.

"Where we going?"

"Back to the room. I wanted to get the information off Tweety's license."

Darnell glanced over his shoulder before saying, "What's up with that back there about me saying Tweety's the brains behind the whole thing, that I said he knows everything?"

Max detected the attitude.

He didn't stop to spell it out for Darnell. Kept walking as he said, "You let me question my suspect. It's a tactic to get him talking."

They found a place to pass, a narrow opening between buildings leading back to louder music, traffic, women walking by in bikinis, and the clippity-clap of flip-flops. Civilization. The opening was too narrow to walk side by side, so Darnell followed Max through to the Ocean Drive sidewalk, salt air coming in from the Atlantic breeze.

Darnell stopped and put his hand on Max's arm. "A tactic? What the hell is that? You're gonna get me killed, man."

Max put his finger in Darnell's chest. "Look, I know you got a family. But truth is, you're a goddamn felon and I don't trust you. Your big lead turned out to be a steaming pile of shit. So I'm going to do what I have to do."

Well, Darnell was glad they finally understood each other.

★ ★ ★ ★ ★

Alondra was smoking a cigarette when they got back to the room at the Clark. There was a pause when Max knocked and he noticed a shadow over the peephole before the door opened.

Max walked in, Darnell following when Alondra said, "You're not gonna, like, arrest me for smoking, are you? Being with the ATF and all."

Max smiled it away and said, "No, I'm not concerned. The hotel might not like it too much. But I'll let it slide." Wondering if she was getting his jokes.

"Good." Max saw Alondra smile for the first time. Really white teeth showing up against dark skin. " 'Cause I need a fucking cigarette right now. I wasn't about to walk my ass all the way outside." She blew a whiff of smoke away from her. "What happened?"

"We caught up to him." Max glanced beyond Alondra, watching Darnell looking out a window at Ocean Drive forty, fifty feet down, palm trees in the distance. "He won't be coming back . . . for awhile, at least."

Max looked around for a pair of jeans, dress trousers, anywhere he thought to look for Tweety's wallet. "You don't happen to know where your boyfriend's wallet is at, do you?"

Alondra pointed to a nightstand on the far side of the bed. "In the drawer," she said. "And he's not my boyfriend."

Max nodded at that and said, "I'm going to take down the information from Alvin's driver's license. You want me to get a warrant?"

Alondra shrugged. "Go ahead. I don't give a shit."

Max wrote it down, an address he recognized as Liberty City. Huh, expired six months ago. He could still be at that address. Who knows? He'd check on it.

Max said, "You got somewhere you can go?"

Alondra said, "I got an apartment. You saying I should go to my mother's?" and Max felt like asking what she used the room for.

"No, I guess your apartment's okay. Far as Tweety knows, I opened that door because I was suspicious." Max looked towards Darnell. "Ain't that right, partner?"

"Yessuh, Mister Max, it sure is." Giving Max a Negro slave accent to poke fun.

Max nodded, took out one of his cards, and handed it to the girl, reminding himself to check in on her later, give it time and drop by to see how she was doing. "He gives you any trouble, give me a call." Feeling friendly for some reason he couldn't pinpoint.

Max saw Darnell look at him and smile.

They were in the hallway—Darnell telling Max she was good in the sack if that's what he was thinking—when they heard Alondra say from the doorway, "By the way, I really like those boots. Are you a real cowboy?"

Before Darnell had a chance to say something else about Alondra, Max got a call.

After a minute, Max hung it up and said, "I had a trace run on those last few phone numbers that called your buddy's phone. Prepaid cell phones, no way to trace."

Darnell nodded, understanding that was cop business. He hesitated but said, "Mister Max, I been wanting to ask you something."

"What?"

"In the jail, in Pembroke, you said I was to come work for you," Darnell was talking with his hands now, "in some, uh, capacity for the ATF."

Max nodded.

"Does this count?"

CHAPTER NINE

Billy decided he wanted to cruise South Beach before heading back to the house. He'd never had his hands on an automobile like this and, fuck it, he wanted to make the most of it. Lester told him not to, that it wasn't business. Billy told him this wasn't a company car, calm down for chrissakes. A friend loaned them his car, what was the big deal? Lester asked Billy if that's really what he saw this as and Billy told him it would be fifteen minutes out of the way at this time of day.

The only problem, and Lester knew it, was that Billy would want to cruise around for a couple hours. Drive up Collins and down again. Drive up far enough to pass the Fontainebleau and Eden Roc and then turn around. Slow along Ocean Drive windows down, the radio blaring. Multiple times. He might even try Star Island, Billy was just crazy enough for that. This would take hours.

Lester did admit, though, that "This is a nice car."

"A lot of power." Billy revved the engine at a stop light at Collins and Eighth, in front of the Victoria's Secret, thinking some chick working the sales floor would step outside to check him out. People would turn to look. "You don't see this kind of engine in foreign luxury cars like Ferraris and Lamborghinis."

Billy didn't know if that was true, but he put that out there expecting Lester to ask how Billy knew what engines were in Ferraris and Lamborghinis, but he didn't. Billy's experience in foreign luxury cars was at car shows, but Lester didn't know

that and Billy would have said he'd driven a few back in the day if it came up.

Billy tore away from the intersection and that had people looking at him again. He was aware of this and slowed down, looking at passersby on the sidewalk, then looking away. Putting a serious look on his face, leaning back on the driver's seat, being cool.

He said, "You get some serious trim in a vehicle like this."

Lester could see that. He could also see getting seriously pulled over by the cops if Billy did that at every stop light. He let it go as useless, Billy was going to do what he wanted. They got pulled over, there wouldn't be any outstanding record. Billy had served his six months on a concealed weapons charge. Lester's marijuana arrest was nolle prossed. No probation, they would be clean. But Lester didn't see why they needed to push it.

Billy found a girl that was willing to look back at him. She smiled and Billy said, "How you doing, sweetheart?" They were at Collins and Seventh. Lester couldn't hear what she said. Maybe she didn't say anything, but she was still smiling.

That gave Billy a bigger opening. "You wanna come ride?" Lester thought it was a bad idea and shook his head. Looking straight ahead, he saw the light turn green and was waiting for Billy to pull away. He hung around instead, making conversation with this girl that wasn't half-bad looking. Now, Billy had people looking at him for other reasons.

Billy got the hint and eased away from the intersection. Lester heard him telling the girl, "Next time," with his head hanging out the window. Like there would be another time.

Lester said, "What are we doing here?" Then added, "When are we gonna get back?"

"I'm just having a little fun." Billy slowed to power brake in

the middle of the street. "You heard him talking about my Jeep. 'That backwoods vehicle.' "

"Yeah, so?"

"Maybe he was right. Maybe it's time to step up to something like this."

Lester said, "Unless you have a job I don't know about, I don't think you'd be able to afford it." Lester wasn't sure a Camaro was right for Billy anyway.

"That's what I'm talking about," Billy said. "You need to make your own luck."

"You been thinking again?"

Lester said it not expecting a reply, but Billy said, "I'm working on it," and he felt the engine come to life, Billy revving it up again. Lester looked over to see Billy making faces, a grunting look, sneering with the rise of the RPM gauge.

Then it got quiet, Billy cutting out the hot-dogging as quick as he started it. Lester looked around, expecting to see police nearby, but didn't. Billy's eyes were looking straight ahead, focused on the sidewalk ahead of them.

Lester looked that way and saw them. Two people that looked like Max the ATF agent and Darnell, their escapee, on the sidewalk coming this way. He said, "Is that who I think it is?"

Billy said, "Uh-huh," and slid down in the seat.

"What are they doing here?"

Billy didn't say anything, shrugged, and kept looking. He watched them walk past, looking intent, like they were going someplace. He watched them in the rearview mirror now, taking a right turn at one of the streets back there and heading out of sight.

The light turned green and Billy sped away, watching his speed before he told Lester, "We should go. There ain't nothin' to see down here anyway."

★ ★ ★ ★ ★

Alondra heard the door open behind her and turned to see who was there.

Tweety said, "Didn't think I had my key, did you?"

She was still, tense, so Tweety went up to her. Standing so close, Alondra was looking up at him.

"It doesn't matter to me if you did or not."

No emotion behind it, the little woman looking straight at him, saying it as if she wasn't scared. Tweety grinned at her. "I bet you care if I walk in and you jerking off some dude, telling yourself it's your work, huh?"

"I don't do that." Alondra backed away from him. "Get out."

Tweety said, "That's a bunch of bullshit," moving a couple of paces forward to cover the distance between them now. "I know you up here skeezin', making your money. Don't be ashamed, you got to get along like the rest of us."

"If you worked at a job half as hard as you work at being an asshole, you might be something."

Tweety moved away, staring at her while he did it, showing how cool he was. "That's how it's gonna be, huh?" Tweety dropped his head in what she thought might be shame. "I guess when you got busted with blow, you needed this nobody to bond you out."

"It was my mistake," Alondra said. "I should've just stayed in the fucking jail instead of putting up with this." Whatever he was trying to do, she was getting tired of it. "What do you want?"

"I wanna know how come that cop knew to look for me in the bathroom."

"It's a hotel room, a small one. Maybe he saw a closed door and got suspicious. I don't know. You'll have to ask him."

"When I come out the door, he had his gun in his hand . . . like he was ready." Tweety had to stop and think. "How'd he know to be ready?"

"I told you, you'll have to ask him." Alondra put some shoes on, wanting to get out of there. She started towards the door, not looking up, and brushed past Tweety, knowing he would try to stop her.

And he did, putting his hand on Alondra's right arm, saying, "I already talked to him. Now, I'm talking to you."

Chapter Ten

Max almost passed the driveway looking for Billy Poe's house, an address on Jann Avenue where the Jeep he saw at Johnny Stanz's place was registered to. He'd passed up and down the road twice looking for six-thirteen, the house number, then realized the six on Billy's house was loose. Turned upside down to look like a nine.

No sign of Billy's Jeep in the driveway. An orange Camaro sitting there, parked, shining bright in the early afternoon sun.

After sitting in the road for a minute, Max backed up the Impala, the car he was using while the Yukon was in the shop, and found a spot along the curb across from the house.

Darnell woke up after a slap on the arm, snoozing on the drive over, and saw Max staring at him. A look on Max's face like he was glad to wake him up. Darnell took a breath and looked around.

"Where we at?"

Max pointed across the street and said, "That's supposed to be Billy Poe's house."

Like that was supposed to mean something.

"What we doing?"

"Waiting."

"How long?"

This guy. Listen to him. Max said, "You have somewhere better to be?"

"I could think about a million things better'n this. Bet you could too, huh, after meeting Alondra?"

Max got Darnell's meaning and said, "Don't you have a baby at home? And that baby has a mother?"

That got Darnell silent. Not for long, though, before he said, "Well, my baby's momma does her own thing."

"What's that mean?"

"That mean she don't bother me about where I go."

"You don't think she'd like to have you around, babysit on occasion, so she can get out and enjoy herself?"

"Hey," Darnell sat up. "I'm in my baby's life. What you think I am? My baby gonna know her daddy. I ain't going nowhere."

For her sake, Max found himself hoping so.

"Besides," Darnell said, "if you saying I need to watch my girl every once in a while so LaKelle can go out and get a piece of ass, I ain't worried about that. She don't do that."

Max glanced across the street and sat back in the driver's seat. "What is she, a nun?"

Darnell closed his eyes and slumped in his seat. "She know better. We got an understanding."

A few minutes passed. Max letting it go, back to watching the little brick frame house across the street with overgrowth and a yard that needed to be mowed.

In the silence, Darnell said, "What about you? You got a woman?"

Max wasn't about to get into a discussion about his ex-wife with Darnell. Joyce. Didn't want to get into how she acted like an invalid, in her invalid voice, and ask him to get her glass of water and pills for whatever was ailing her that week; didn't want to get into the nagging because of his long hours. Hell, it was the job. She couldn't work, could she? Not in bed with a different life-threatening disease every couple of weeks; didn't want to get into the guilt trips over those long hours, going so far as to follow him sometimes, make sure it was work he was doing and not fooling around. When she was well enough to get out of bed. He'd spot her on occasion, but never said anything about it at home. The way she drove, it wasn't hard to pick out their yellow Toyota FJ Cruiser. A color that reminded her of a canary.

Then there was the thing with their neighbors.

Max tapped the wheel for a second before saying, "I'm seeing somebody. She's a flight attendant . . ."

Before Max could go on, Darnell said, "She gone a lot. I bet you tap that when she in town, though. I know how that feel, I just got out of jail."

Max looked at Darnell. "You were in there overnight."

"And it was very traumatic for me. Don't forget, I was *kid*napped after that."

Max nodded, like there was no way he could have forgotten.

Darnell shifted in his seat. "Could we put the air on, at least?"

Max turned the ignition over and rolled the windows down. "And I'm thinking about putting an ankle bracelet on you."

Darnell frowning at him now, shaking his head.

"Are you serious, man? How am I supposed to live like this? What if I need to run out and get something for my baby?"

Max didn't say it but figured they could work something out.

Darnell kept going, Max trying hard not to pay too much attention. He heard Darnell say something about wanting to go see his momma. Was that allowed? Max didn't answer, looking across the street past Darnell.

That's when he saw it, tucked in the carport, hidden behind the orange Camaro out front; every part of it covered by a tarp except the right rear quarter panel.

Another Camaro. No doubt about it.

Just like Burt Reynolds used to drive in the movies.

Lester said, "What's he doing?"

"Nothing," Billy said. "He's sitting there. Across the street in a car, with our black friend."

"Why doesn't he leave?"

"I suspect he's waiting for us."

Billy kept the house dark, no lights on, even at this time of day. No curtains moving except for a sliver of one drawn back so Billy could look outside. Just a sliver, though, not enough to draw suspicion. Like his foster mother would do when she was spying on the neighbors. Until one day, Billy was a kid then, he asked what she was doing and pulled the curtain back all the way. Enough for the neighbors to see her staring back. They gave her looks from across the street. Disapproving looks. Billy got put on his knees on a burlap sack filled with grains of rice on top of having his mouth washed out with soap. He couldn't figure out the soap part. It didn't make sense to him, that part. He hadn't said anything bad. Now, when he'd call her a cunt bitch to her face, he could understand.

Just not for the curtain thing.

Billy turned to see Lester, kicked back in a recliner, slurping his oatmeal and watching afternoon TV. And not cool stuff like a monster truck show on cable. Dr. Phil, Dr. Oz, or one of those other doctors that liked to tell you that everything you were doing was killing you, stuff like that.

Billy said, "Knock that shit off," meaning the oatmeal slurping. "Who eats oatmeal in the middle of the afternoon?" He turned back to the window. "I can't even concentrate on what I'm doing."

Lester couldn't see where staring out a window needed much concentration, but okay.

"What's he doing now?"

Billy turned back again, like he was trying to make a point when he said, "Nothin'."

"Why don't we just go out there?" Lester put his bowl down, looking for a table to rest it on but settled on the floor. "We could probably run out there and surprise him."

"What you want, a shootout in the middle of broad daylight? I live here." Billy felt the curtain move a bit in his hand and it made him jump. He got it back into position, thinking the movement wasn't visible from outside. Couldn't be.

Lester was walking over to Billy when Billy said, "Will you stop moving? He's gonna see your shadow or something," and Lester looked like he'd froze, eyes glued to Billy like he was about to get hit head-on by a car.

"Should we call Raoul?"

"He's gonna tell us the same thing. That we should lay low, be smart about it."

Lester didn't see how that could be. Hell, they'd tried running the man off the road on a busy highway in the middle of the day, what's the difference? Maybe he meant, be smart about it *now*, considering. He shrugged and said, "Can I move?"

Billy turned back and nodded. This guy, you had to tell him everything.

He looked back, the black fella, Darnell, was in the car by himself. Looked to be handcuffed to the steering wheel, his mouth moving a mile a minute. Billy could tell they were curse words. What the hell was that about?

Then the blond ATF man, Max, walking up the driveway alone.

There was a two-way radio in the car, but it was never on. Darnell found himself wishing Max would've turned it on and ran through how to use it in case something happened. Go through the codes with him. Darnell was sure there were codes. I got a two-eight-five, agent in distress. Or whatever the number was. He knew ten-four, everybody knew that one.

Max left his cell phone in the car. Darnell could see it tucked between the seat and console. He could use that. Probably no time to look for numbers, he'd just dial 911. Darnell picked it up, maybe there were some interesting numbers on there, that flight attendant Max was talking about. See if that was for real or if he was making it up.

Nope, the screen was locked.

Darnell didn't fool with it, but saw that it told you to press a couple of buttons to unlock it. Okay, he'd have to remember that. See, it was a good thing he checked.

He didn't see it as being nosy. A good government agent is always prepared.

Billy hid behind the sofa and called Raoul.

He said, almost in a whisper, "He's here. Looking all over the place. He's in my backyard now."

Billy had watched Max come up to the house, taking a look in the windows, looking around. Thank God Lester had the sense to hit the remote and get that doctor off the TV on his way to the bedroom; heard the federal agent walking through the carport. Shit, his other car, the Camaro, was out there. Maybe he wouldn't recognize it. There was a lot going on at the time they tried to get him off the road, he might not remember it.

Raoul said, "What's he doing now?"

It pissed Billy off that Raoul sounded calm. Over there probably getting a blow job while he was on the phone.

Must be nice.

"I can't tell. I saw a shadow out the back window of my living room."

"Well, if he sees that mess of a yard, maybe he'll think nobody lives there."

Fucker.

Billy held the phone away from him, peeking around the corner of the sofa for the ATF man; covering up the mouthpiece on instinct. Not that Max could hear Raoul's voice on the other end from outside.

Shit, there he was. Right there. The shadow of a guy, going over six feet tall, had to be, through the curtains on Billy's back porch sliding door. Curtains the landlady left from her previous tenant.

Man, if he had his nine-millimeter, the one with the extended beavertail that looked cool when he held it sideways, he could end this right now. Put a few in mister federal agent, run out, snatch the nigger, and go. Fuck the rent. He was already three months behind anyway.

Goddamn Raoul. Billy could hear him in the background, demanding to know what was going on.

Billy waited it out, watching the federal agent get bored and turn away from the sliding door. Followed him through windows around the side of the house and back out to his car.

Billy, still in a whisper, said, "He's leaving."

And heard Raoul say, "Billy, don't tell me my car is in front of your house . . ." as he hung up the phone.

Max was driving Darnell home when his phone rang. Back on 95, going north again. Second time today. All this driving around, he wondered when he would find the time to get some work done.

He let the call go to voice mail while Darnell said, "What if they leave while we gone?"

He had a point and Max knew it. They couldn't sit there all night, like he tried to make Darnell think they were going to do. He said, "They're not going anywhere. For all they know, we're still there, parked down the street."

Max hoped Darnell would accept that, his head was starting to hurt after he forgot to take the medication for his concussion.

"You serious? You think that, that they not going to leave?"

So much for hoping.

Max nodded and thought about it. Yeah, he was serious. He had Billy Poe's address; sure of it when he saw that older Camaro in the driveway (but who had the Explorer that rammed him?)—and the tag number on a newer Camaro that was in the driveway. That was the job, following leads.

It was silent for a stretch while Max's Impala rolled along, passing high rises and beachfront property to their east. Max was thinking about tomorrow: back to Billy Poe's, find out who owned that Camaro, knock on the door this time . . .

"So you gonna put an ankle bracelet on me?"

Max knew Darnell didn't want to ask by the sound of his voice. He looked over to see Darnell staring out the passenger window, his chin resting in an open hand.

Max let it hang there for a second, figuring the pros and cons. Shit, the little guy was trying to be helpful. Busted his ass chasing down Tweety. Something Max wasn't sure he would've been able to do in his boots. Besides, it wasn't like getting an ankle bracelet happened with the snap of his fingers. There was time and paperwork and he had a headache.

Max was looking straight out the front window. He said, "No, you go home, play with your little girl." Trying to make it sound like he was a good guy, cutting Darnell some slack. Sounding different when he said, "Don't think about going far, though."

It was silent again. Max catching a glimpse of Darnell smiling to himself out of the corner of his eye. Max took the same time to check the voice mail on his cell phone, that call from earlier. The voice sounded like it was crying.

After a minute, Max could tell it was Alondra.

He hung it up. Didn't say a word about it to Darnell.

CHAPTER ELEVEN

The sun going down, Billy kept the house dark, the TV off. When Lester came in from the outside, Billy said to him, "He out there?"

"I didn't see the car." Lester shook his head, getting tired of the questions. "What else would I be looking for?" It pissed Lester off. Taking the trouble to skulk up and down the street, hiding behind neighbors' bushes, banana trees; worrying that somebody was going to end up calling the cops on him . . . While he was looking for a cop. All that to come back to this?

"You call Raoul back?" Deciding to turn the questions around on Billy, see how he liked it for a change.

It straightened Billy, hunched over looking out the front window, the phone in his hand. "I'm waiting."

Lester wanted to ask for what, why he didn't just call Raoul, tell him the ATF agent was gone, but decided he was heading to the bedroom instead and take a nap. They weren't doing anything here anyway, why stay up?

Before Lester could make it to the hallway leading to the back of the house, he heard Billy say, "I got an idea," and came back. Decided he would make it look like he was listening to whatever Billy was saying, *then* head back to the bedroom.

"Way I see it, Raoul'll do just about anything to get his hands on the colored fella, right?"

Lester nodded.

Billy had a gleam in his eye. "He tried to snatch him in broad daylight . . . Says we can do anything we have to, to get our hands on him, right? You heard him, he's committed to seeing that guy hurt."

"Yeah, so?" Lester was thinking about the bed.

"What about paying to get him?"

Lester didn't follow. Maybe if he was more awake . . .

"What're you talking about?"

Billy stepped away from the curtain, first time in half an hour. "What if we took him and asked for a ransom?"

Lester was awake now. "From Raoul?"

Billy nodded, smiling.

Lester looked at the man like he was crazy.

Billy started to move around the room, excited instead of nervous now. "We did it Raoul's way. We don't do it like that this time. And, we don't have Johnny Stanz to stab us in the back. Just me and you."

The way Lester saw the difference: "Me and you would have every guy that Raoul has after us. This ain't a hostage situation, it's a suicide mission."

"Not if we smart about it," Billy said. "Look, we know Raoul wants this guy bad. It's his fucking ego. As for his guys, we're the smartest he's got. That's why he picked us for this. We got to use that to our advantage. We talked about this a little bit."

Lester remembered it. They mentioned it, didn't really talk about it. He said, "How we gonna do that?"

"I haven't figured that part out yet."

"Momma, there some white guy come to see you, asking questions about me?"

It was the first time Darnell had a chance to call his mom. By now, it didn't matter how Max found him, he was just curious.

Delores said, "There was somebody come around here. Yes, he was white. Tall with blond hair."

That was Max.

"I remember I was cooking smothered liver with rice and gravy and green beans that day."

Darnell's mouth started to water but he said, "What'd you tell him?"

She said, "I gave him your number," and stopped. "Oh, wait . . ." Darnell knew his mom had her hand against her face, like she always did when she said that. "I gave him Johnny's number too on account of yours is disconnected a lot."

"What'd he say?"

"He said you were in trouble, that he picked you up and that you had gone missing." Darnell didn't want to tell her what happened. Delores said, "He showed me his ID. He looked respectable and I seen my share of law enforcement."

Darnell felt a little sting from that but let it go.

"Why, baby, did I do wrong?"

"No," Darnell said, "you didn't do wrong, momma."

"I was worried about you, my boy. You got a little girl now, you got to stop all this monkeyshines."

Darnell changed the subject and asked his mom how she was doing, if she was feeling okay; asked her if her ankles still hurt and she started telling him about her left knee giving her trouble. Something new. Darnell asked her did she make an appointment to see a doctor and Delores said she was calling tomorrow. Darnell said to tell him when it was and he would drive her.

They hung up and LaKelle came in, asking Darnell how his momma was doing. He told her she was okay, with an off-guard expression because the question surprised him. He didn't go into his mom's various ailments too much.

LaKelle's tone changed when she said, "How about you, you have fun with your friends today?"

It wasn't what he would call fun but Darnell said, "I[
okay."

"Good. I'm glad to hear somebody had some fun." La
was standing there, watching him. "Because that fence i
backyard ain't gonna fix itself."

Soon as Max knocked on the door, Alondra's voice on the
side, "Who is it?"

Max said it was him through the door and it opened; Al
on the other side, different from what she was befor
watched her raise a hand to brush hair away from her fa
bright red mark on her cheek. Eyes swelling, some of it
crying, some of it, Max guessed, from Tweety.

Max didn't move any closer, didn't touch her face, wh
said, "What happened?"

She looked up, glancing away from Max. "After you
chasing him out of here . . ."

"He came back?"

She nodded and said, "I guess he didn't see things the
way you did."

Max was feeling guilty, having the chance to lock the g
but not doing it. Feeling guilty, not something he was pro
do. He said, "You call anybody?"

She shrugged. "Like who?"

"Your mother, maybe? Didn't you say you could go
there?"

Alondra nodded. "I guess so."

She didn't sound too thrilled by that and Max wonde
something else was going on here.

Still, he said, "You want to go over there?" Max had his
across Alondra's shoulders now. "I can drop you off if you v

"Would you?" She looked at him for the first time, smi
little. A tired one, but some of the attitude from when the
met showing through.

"You get cleaned up a little before I take you over there."

Max watched her disappear into the bathroom, catching a glimpse of Alondra putting makeup on over the marks on her face. Rubbing it in, wincing when she pressed too hard. She caught him looking and smiled again, right at him, not the least self-conscious now.

Alondra packed a small bag and slipped into some flip-flops, not saying a word. In a hurry to get out of there. Fact, neither of them spoke until they were outside walking to Max's car double-parked on Collins with hazards flashing. He asked if she was okay and Alondra said, "I'll be fine."

"You get to your mom's, you explain to her what happened," Max said as he opened the car door for her. "Then you tell her you've got a cop friend looking into it."

Billy was back in the living room, keeping watch just in case Raoul was coming around. Raoul had been here once and made ugly comments about it. Snickering at the way him and Lester lived. Refusing when Billy offered him a bowl of cereal. Cocoa Puffs. Raoul asked if that was all they had to eat. Billy told him no, normally they had a better selection—usually two or three brands, but he caught them off guard, they hadn't been to the grocery store lately. Usually, they had Frosted Flakes, Lucky Charms, *and* Cocoa Puffs. The Cocoa Puffs were for variety, with the chocolate flavoring and all. Rice Krispies if they were on a health kick. Raoul had just made that cereal comment that Lester was hung up on, so Billy didn't see where that was coming from, thinking back on it. Rice Krispies would be good, all the fast food lately was giving Billy an upset stomach. It was the crisped rice taste. Jesus, Rice Krispies, he could taste it.

Billy remembered Raoul waving off marijuana smoke the minute he walked in the door. Making a big show about doing it. Waving his arms real dramatic through the air, like it was

soooo bad. The man was known to use his own product, something Billy saw recently—little specks of white powder below Raoul's nose. Hell with him, the man was such a hypocrite.

What made Billy jump were thoughts of backstabbing Raoul. They were just thoughts, some of it thinking out loud to Lester. Well, it was becoming more than that. They were making plans, becoming more concrete. The man, Raoul, had an almost mythical way of finding out information, what you were talking about, thinking . . .

Billy was looking out the front window at cars passing up and down Jann Avenue. Wondering what car Raoul might be in if he drove up since Billy had his Camaro. He did see a Mercedes earlier, tint too dark to see inside. It would be something like that, but that one kept going, it didn't stop. There were a couple others, but they were just cars, old jalopies.

The phone rang and Billy answered it.

"You said the cop was at your house."

It was Raoul's voice. Billy caught his mistake the second the phone was in his hand. What he should've done was hang it up, it wasn't too late. Say they had a shitty phone with a bad connection if Raoul called back later. He heard Raoul's voice say, "Billy?" and thought the idea might be more trouble than it was worth.

"Yeah?"

"I asked if you said the federal cop was at your house."

Billy said, "He was . . . earlier. He's gone now."

"Did you speak to him again?"

"No," Billy said. "What you think I am, some kind of dummy?"

Raoul didn't answer quickly, but did say, "William," using Billy's real name. He had a habit of doing that. "I just want to ensure that you didn't inadvertently divulge some information."

Billy wasn't totally sure what that meant, but it didn't sound great. Was it about their plan? They just started talking about it. Did he know about it already? See, there was the man's powers at work again. Billy felt his neck get rigid and decided he needed to be more careful from here on out.

CHAPTER TWELVE

Max drove home seeing Alondra with that mark on her face, something that Max had a hard time with. Violence against women. It reminded Max of his old man, coming home from work at a Dothan, Alabama, car dealership. Long days in the sun pushing the 1976 Chevette. A fifty-one horsepower engine and four-speed stick shift. He remembered his dad complaining that if anyone came looking at the *Corvette,* that's all they did, look. He would say, "If you can't afford it, why even look?" and then say it was the insurance that was the killer. Too expensive. There was one time in particular that Max remembered where his dad came home drunk, salesman trading stories after work at a bar across the street from the dealership. Yelling at his mom about people looking at the Corvette.

He remembered his mom having problems with her wrist and it was hurting that day. It was like his old man knew and when she said, "Mike, don't worry so much about that," he grabbed her, his dad's hand wrapping all the way around his mom's right wrist. Max had come out of his room and remembered his mother's eyes, how she looked at him like she wanted Max to be somewhere else. His mom asked his dad not to do that in a voice Max hadn't heard before, like the optimism had gone out. He was five years old and that's when the abuse started.

He hadn't thought of that in a long time.

On the way to her mom's, in the car, Alondra had asked,

"You ever just wanna get away?" As they were coming to the airport, like seeing that made her think about it.

Max said, "Sometimes, sure," and looked over to Alondra, seeing her stare out the window at airplanes, hordes of people heading off to different points around the world.

Alondra said, "I do. I want to get on one of those planes and go far away."

Max let her talk. She said, "Just get on one and never come back."

"You'd have a lot of people that would miss you."

Alondra didn't look away from the window. "Outside of my mother, I can't think of anybody."

Max hadn't heard her mention a father yet, but didn't ask. He did say, "That's more than some people have."

To change the subject, she said, "You mind if I smoke?" Max shook his head and hit the window button for her side. Alondra lit up, blew a stream of smoke out the window, and said, "I'm sorry if I'm having a pity party."

Max said, "It's not a problem," and meant it. It was understandable. He didn't mind listening to her. His mother had never talked about it and it made him wonder if that's how she felt; if she wanted to leave their two-bedroom house on Morris Street . . . and go to the Greyhound station. Then he wondered if she didn't because of him.

He did say, "You don't have to be scared, though. I'm going to have this guy locked up tonight if I can. He's not going to bother you." Trying to explain the situation if that's what she was worried about.

"You're going over there now, right after you drop me off?"

Max couldn't figure out why she sounded surprised. He said, "I'll probably wait until it's dark," and wondered if there was a misunderstanding.

Alondra didn't say anything to that and Max assumed it was

okay. She said, "Just be careful, please," and that confirmed it for him.

Max got on the Palmetto Expressway, going south, and said, "You need anything before we get to your mom's house?"

"I could use some female items."

He tried to picture a store out this way.

She said, "I don't suppose you'd want to get down and get them for me?" and it reminded him of doing that for his ex-wife. "Don't worry, I'm just kidding."

It was the first time she'd smiled since they got in the car.

"So you need to stop?"

"It's not an emergency or anything. I can wait, really."

"You sure?"

Alondra shrugged. "Yeah, I don't feel like getting down anywhere."

Max glanced at her to be sure.

She was staring out at the road, saying, "I look like I just got beat up."

Darnell had his white woman, Kelly, in an apartment in Pompano Beach. Really, it was her apartment but he liked the idea that he was keeping women all over town. On his way over, he stopped at a liquor store on Dixie Highway looking for something special for the occasion. Kelly liked vodka. Darnell looked at rows behind the counter, a burnout behind the register with an I'M DURNK, WANNA FUCK? t-shirt on; the word *drunk* misspelled on purpose, one of those hip t-shirts that was supposed to be cute.

There were vodkas imported from Russia, Finland, Sweden. From everywhere but the USA. Darnell looked for the cheap stuff but didn't see any.

The boozer looked up and said, "What can I get you?" A tone in his voice that said he didn't want to wait while Darnell looked around, undecided.

Darnell stood there. He could tell the guy was getting impatient. Fuck him.

Darnell was taking his time, not prepared to pay thirty bucks for a fifth. Jesus, he liked Kelly but, damn, not *that* much. He'd have to explain to LaKelle where that money went. He could feel the boozer staring at him, not surprised by a black guy taking his time. Had that feeling like the guy was ready for another black guy to do something stupid, and Darnell saw a hand go under the counter and stay there for a second.

The guy said, "Look, nigger, either shit or get off the pot. I got other customers. You like, there's a store down the street has all the malt liquor you want."

Another swamp-rat-country-fuck mouthing off. Was the same thing that got him busted in Pembroke. Darnell knew better now, realized he had to keep his cool, that's all. Screw up again and it was his ass.

Wasn't that how Max put it?

Alondra's mom asked her, "It was one of those men, wasn't it?"

More of a statement than a question, her mom, Sylvia, reminding Alondra of her dislike for her daughter's chosen profession. Sylvia said it while she was putting an ice pack on Alondra's face to keep the swelling down. She heard her daughter say, "Please don't give me a hard time, okay? I have enough problems."

And Sylvia said to that, "I'm just worried about you. I hate the thought of you with strange men," fussing with ice cubes in a Ziploc bag wrapped in a dish towel.

Alondra moved away, holding the ice pack to her face. "It wasn't a strange man. It was someone I knew, if you have to know."

"A friend? That makes it even worse."

Alondra shuffled down the little hall to her room, sure her mom was locating her rosary by now and would deep into Hail Marys by the time Alondra's head hit the pillow.

Alondra found her room—full of boxes that Alondra couldn't guess what was in them. They never had this much stuff when she was growing up. Reusing the kid's room for storage after they leave, it must've been something parents did. She found a blanket in a drawer and threw it on top of her single bed, sheets already on there.

A shadow moved in front of the light behind her and Alondra knew it was her mother.

Alondra said, "I'm supposed to tell you I have a friend looking into it, a cop."

"A cop?" Sylvia said. "One's a cop, the other a thug who hits you. You sure got some different kinds of friends, my child."

Max found Tweety's place, the one Alondra told him was a little cream-colored house in Para Villa Heights. Exactly what she said, cream-colored duplex. For some reason, Max found it odd: Alondra being that exact even in her time of distress.

She wasn't totally sure of the house number, but Max knew he had the right place. He heard the hip-hop music from the street, music Tweety could've been getting high by, and followed the beat to a house on the corner, cream in color. The music was on full volume, something Max knew guys liked to do while maintaining their high, usually in groups.

Only tonight, peeking inside, Tweety was moving to the music, dancing and mouthing the lyrics. Or, what passed for lyrics in that kind of music. Maybe his buddies were relieving themselves or getting another hit in another room. There was a smell of reefer wafting around. Might get stoned just walking in there, who knows? Point being, Tweety probably wasn't doing that dancing all by himself.

Max moved around the side of the house, past wild fern and a tangle of shrubs, taking a second to look around; see if anyone was watching nearby. Decided to try around back and found an unlocked door. He heard voices from the front of the house. The living room he saw through the blinds from the road. Just a small hallway connecting that to where he was, the kitchen. Heard footsteps coming his way until a figure appeared in the hallway.

Tweety said, "What the fuck?"

Max drew his gun and Tweety didn't move, so Max went over to him and drug him back into the kitchen. Spun Tweety around and kicked his legs out from under him. Sure nobody heard it over the music.

Max put handcuffs on Tweety and left him face down. On his way out of the kitchen, Max asked if there was anybody else in the house. Tweety shook his head, visibly pissed. Max knew better than to trust that and had his gun up making his way through different rooms.

It didn't take long to cover, the house had to be around eight hundred square feet. Left the music blaring while he did it, but it didn't help his headache.

It was in the bedroom where he found two Beretta M9s and, shit, a Ruger Mini-14. That Ruger was a fucking sniper rifle, for chrissakes. The M9 was military issue, the equivalent of a civilian 92FS. Max shook his head, not the kind of stuff you walk into a store looking for. He thought about Alondra. Man, she was lucky all she ended up with was a scrape on her cheek and a bruised eye. Considering.

Max checked the rest of the house, finishing up in a bathroom that looked like it belonged in a bus stop somewhere. Pulled back the shower curtain—surprised it was drawn closed in the first place—and found nothing.

He was wrong.

Tweety was dancing by himself.

★ ★ ★ ★ ★

Darnell felt good, good about himself for controlling his temper in front of that asshole cracker at the liquor store. Shelled out thirty for a fifth of Absolut to show the man his ugly racist words didn't make any bother. Decided to treat himself to some out of the bottle on his way to his white girl.

Hung on to that feeling until he got to the door. Kelly took one look at him, said, "Oh," and left the door open for Darnell to come in.

What, she wasn't excited to see him? He asked her that, but didn't get an answer. Wait till he told her about his being kidnapped, that would change her tune.

Darnell closed the door behind him and said, "What you doing?"

Kelly shrugged. She was never one for much conversation but, shit, this was ridiculous.

He had been through a very traumatic situation.

Kelly was in the middle of the living room, shag carpet under her bare feet, aluminum foil on the windows behind her. She had fixed the place up since the last time he had been here, but it still looked like she could move out in about half an hour. Not like a place you lived in and called home, personal shit lying about. A TV tray for a kitchen table, things like that.

Okay, she wasn't moving so Darnell went over to her, the fifth of vodka still in his hand. He looked at her face, no color in it in all this tinfoil darkness. He put a hand on her shoulder, running it down to her elbow. "You ain't happy to see me, baby? I got your favorite." Darnell held up the bottle.

Kelly bothered herself to look up at the fifth in Darnell's free hand. "I see you done drank damn near half." She said, "Thanks," and took it into the kitchen.

"Shoot, girl, I done been in jail, kidnapped . . . Now I'm working for the federal government. I needed that."

Now Kelly was warming up. She walked over and put her arms around Darnell's neck. Uh-huh, see what the tale of his plight would do? She said, "Oh, I'm sorry to hear that, baby."

All right, she didn't sound too surprised, no big deal.

Darnell let it happen and moved in closer when Kelly said, "But I got some company right now."

Darnell heard a voice say, "What you mean, working for the federal government?" and jumped away from Kelly.

He saw Johnny Stanz come out of the bedroom in his underwear with a kind of a smile, saying, "And you weren't held for that long."

Not sounding the least bit sorry, looking straight in Darnell's eyes, like he was making a joke. But he did move to Johnny and said, "How you been? What you doin' here?" Tried to hug his friend, happy to see him.

Johnny didn't move. He said, "Whaddya mean, working for the government?"

Darnell had to stop and think. What was going on here?

Johnny could see the hesitation on Darnell's face. The Darnell that he knew, that always liked to run his mouth, sometimes at the wrong time.

Johnny got the feeling this was one of those times.

"Why don't we have a seat?" Johnny said. "You got a fifth, why let it go to waste?"

Chapter Thirteen

Lester Long had a Budweiser tall boy while Billy was busy on a joint it took him five solid minutes to roll, the size of a cigar. Look at Billy: a little while ago a hostage-taker, now lost in a cloud of white smoke. He could come and go like that.

How he thought about going into the drug business about twenty years ago. No, had to be longer than that because *Miami Vice* was big on TV. Lester remembered that much. Billy had his white suit and pink t-shirt picked out. Bought the electric razor that left stubble like Don Johnson had, on purpose. Lester remembered asking at the time if that meant he had to be the black guy. Billy told Lester he could if he wanted to, but that he couldn't use his razor.

"Then you got sent to prison for that drug thing," Lester said, raising his beer.

"Dumb luck," Billy said, a hint of disbelief in his voice. "Thousands of guys bring drugs all over the place, from Point A to Point B. Do it without anybody ever noticing. I do it, I get picked up."

That was before they met Raoul.

"We done pretty good since then." Billy took a drag, a big one, and waited. Let the smoke get way down there and coughed. "Shit, I'm getting old." He looked up at Lester and said, "Would be nice to be back on our own."

Lester wasn't altogether sure about that, but didn't say anything. Billy said, "That's why we're gonna do that thing we talked about earlier."

Lester wasn't really sure that they talked about it, like it was some conversation they were having. There was a silence. What Billy said made Lester picture Darnell, the colored guy, in some room full of bugs, rats crossing the floor, cracked pipes dripping overhead, the hostage huddled in a corner chained to a radiator.

He had never seen a house in Florida with a radiator.

Darnell said, "I thought you were gone," seeing Johnny's face, his grin telling Darnell exactly what Johnny was thinking.

"I made a stop on the way."

"I see that," Darnell said and thought about it. "How long you intend to stay?"

"Depends." Johnny shrugged. "What are you doing here?"

Two old friends feeling each other out, surprised to see each other.

"I needed to get out of the house."

And now Johnny was giving Darnell that little grin again, saying, "No, I meant what are you doing *here?*"

Darnell said, "What, in town?"

Johnny walked closer, Darnell watching that confident look on his face; Darnell wondering what was going on when Johnny took the bottle of vodka from his hand.

"In town . . . In Florida . . ." The words trailed off as Johnny looked for glasses. Then, like he had just thought of it, Johnny said, "In the United States, for that matter."

It was Darnell's turn to grin, a way of letting Johnny know he was serious. If that's what this was, a serious conversation. "What you expect me to do, up and leave my baby?"

After a moment, Johnny said, "Why not take her with you?"

Wait a minute, what the fuck was going on?

Now Kelly was starting in. "What's going on?" Hands on her hips, a tank top and stringy hair that needed a wash. "Are the two of you in some sort of trouble? I don't need that shit right now. I'm on probation."

They turned to look at her at the same time. Darnell told Kelly that of all the people in this room, she was in the most trouble and that got him some attitude, some sort of gesture from her that she wasn't interested.

Johnny calmed her down; telling her it was okay, just two buddies talking. He used the word "baby" a lot. He asked Kelly could she go outside and she said, "This is my fucking place, motherfucker." Darnell shook his head to himself. The mouth on that girl.

She said, "Y'all can take your bullshit outside and not come back."

That brought more "baby's" from Johnny and she agreed to go into the bedroom as long as there was something good on regular cable. If not, she was coming back out to the living room where she had the expanded cable package, two-hundred-fifty channels. They could talk around her if they didn't like it.

With Kelly in the bedroom, out of the way, Johnny said, "I stuck my neck out for you, man. Way out . . . and this is how you repay me? By hanging around so you can be caught again?"

"Look," Darnell said, "I can't go nowhere. I'm working for the government to try and catch Raoul. I leave, I'm in more shit than before. They gonna take my kid away from me."

"They told you that?"

Johnny, he just didn't understand how government agents worked.

"They don't have to," Darnell said. "It's understood."

"What they have you doing?"

Johnny stared like he couldn't believe they would ask Darnell, almost as if he were jealous they didn't ask him.

Darnell shrugged and pulled out a chair from the table. "Right now, just looking at mugshots, pictures . . ."

"Does he have one?"

"Who?"

"Raoul."

"I haven't seen it if he does."

"What you gonna do?" Johnny said. "Pick him out of a lineup?"

"I don't know."

Johnny let it hang and took out two glasses, dusty ones with some kind of fast-food logo on them. "These'll have to do."

He poured straight vodka, nothing in the apartment to chase it with, and sat down across the table from Darnell. "They must have something good on TV in there, she hasn't come out bitching. That gives us a chance to catch up."

Darnell seemed to consider it, still trying to gauge Johnny. "How much catching up we got to do?"

"Your government work, man," Johnny had that smile again, "it's interesting. Tell me everything."

Lester asked where they were going to keep Darnell and Billy said, "Sure can't be here. I was thinking maybe Johnny's, but I ain't sure about that either." Billy stopped to think about it between hits on his cigar-sized joint. "Maybe we just get one of those places in the swamp."

Lester said, "How we going to do that? There's not people living in those places? What're we going to do, move in with a family?"

Billy didn't always think things through when he was high.

"Not all of them. There's bound to be one that's unoccupied. Hunters coming and going from their camp between seasons, something like that. Be even better if it's full of palmetto bugs and stuff. The worse the conditions for him"—meaning Darnell—"the better."

The guy still wasn't thinking clearly.

Lester said, "Where we going to be? Out there with all those bugs? You know what kind of fucking swamp creatures are out there where you're talking about? Shit, we got rattlers in the backyard, we don't go out."

Billy took another drag and looked at the joint, half of it gone already. He'd be feeling better if Lester wasn't being such a downer.

"Why you putting up such a fight on this? All we have to do is get him out there and chain him up until we call Raoul."

"With what, bicycle chains?"

Billy seemed to be thinking about it and shook his head. "I was thinking something bigger. I used to see on the news where guys in the Middle East used to use, like, chains with links a couple inches thick, with clasps for the wrists. At least it looked like that to me."

What Lester meant was the kind of bicycle chain that you wrap around a bike rack or something so that nobody steals it. Those were pretty strong. What Billy was talking about . . . Two-inch links? How you wrap that around a man's ankle? He guessed you could wrap it over and over, but still. If Billy started talking about cutting people's heads off on the Internet, Lester was out of there.

But as long as Billy was on a Middle East kick, what about food? They couldn't starve the guy, he'd die. What good would he be then? Lester didn't know what kind of food they served hostages.

Maybe Billy saw something about it on the news.

Billy made a face, half of it looked like he was in pain, half like he was annoyed. "Les, you're worrying about the wrong things. The most important thing we need to do," an anxious tone in Billy's voice, "is ask for enough money."

"How much you think that is?"

Billy shrugged. "Depends on how much Raoul thinks the man's life is worth."

★ ★ ★ ★ ★

Max brought Tweety, handcuffed in a tank top and baggy shorts, to the Miami-Dade County Jail, the main jail. Checked his gun at the sally port and the door opened to the intake area.

Lieutenant Daniel Remedios was there waiting.

"Goddamn, he's a big one."

"Dan, this here's Alvin Wright. Likes to be called Tweety."

"Like the bird?"

Max nodded. "I guess it beats chipmunk jokes." He looked past Remedios to people shuffling around the intake area. Corrections officers directing traffic, murderers to strung out junkies to college kids with fake IDs moving from street clothes to orange jumpsuits. "Busy tonight."

"This here's standard." Remedios turned back to look. "Nothing out of the norm. Just another Tuesday evening." He looked up at Tweety and said to Max, "What's his deal?"

Max sat Tweety down and took Lieutenant Remedios away from him, to a corner where they could get away from the controlled chaos. "He's a small part of an ongoing investigation." Max rocked his head from side to side. "I'm running kind of under the radar on this one."

"But he's done something worthy of being jailed, right?"

"Over the years," Max said, "I'm sure he's got a litany of offenses against his fellow man that would be the envy of anyone in here. For now, how about beating up his girlfriend? I get over to his place, I find a damned arsenal. Two military issue M9s and a Ruger . . . a Mini-14."

"You serious? That's heavy duty firepower." Remedios glanced back, then turned to Max. "Nice one, man."

"I got 'em in the trunk of my car if you can hang on to them for a bit."

Remedios said, "I'd love to get a look at that sniper rifle," and stopped to think. "How's the girlfriend fit in here?"

"She doesn't really, just gave me a reason to get him in here. I'd really appreciate it if you can hold him until I can figure out something else or this blows over."

"I won't ask what 'this' is, for now." Remedios looked around the main jail intake. "We got two hundred people in here a night. Stack that on top of people waiting from two or three night ago," thinking in mid-sentence, "it could be twelve, fourteen hours before he gets processed."

Max nodded.

"We'll stick him in the holding tank. After that, it's finger-printing, medical testing, you know the drill. We can't keep him forever, but we can drag our feet on it a little. I'll arrange for a bunk in one of the dorms at Metro West after that."

"I really appreciate you doing this, Dan."

"Like I said, I won't ask what's going on right now. At the same time, I am curious why your people aren't in the loop on this, you understand?"

"I know the line about not knowing who to trust is a cliché," Max said. "But in this case, it happens to be true."

"You can't trust those two," Gloria said to Raoul Garcia in Spanish. "They're idiots."

Raoul knew she meant Billy and Lester, but had to think first. She was here all day—and mentioning this now? At this time of the evening? She was beginning to grow tiresome, even before trying to discuss his business. He said, "Don't worry about them."

"You gave them your car . . . You don't worry about that?"

No, but she did. Well, maybe he did a little. She might have had a point, they were *idiotas*. It was not his best decision, but he was high on coke and not thinking correctly. He could see that now. But he knew this was Gloria wanting to be paraded around in a fancy automobile.

Gloria said, "I don't how you can be so calm about it."

Raoul listened to her thinking and tried to figure a way to shut her up. He hated to throw Gloria out in the night; looking forward to enjoying her delicate nether regions one more time before doing that.

"Legally, I don't own that car," Raoul said. "It belongs to a fictitious character named Fernando who lives at a different address. True, they could get picked up, but would not tell on me for fear of retaliation." He shrugged. "Who knows, they may get lucky and do what has been asked of them."

Raoul decided right there he should have a backup plan . . . in case they didn't.

"What if they aren't fortunate?" Trying hard to speak her best English.

Raoul slid his hand under Gloria's camisole, the feel of satin giving way to bare skin around the crook of her hips. "Let me worry about that."

"I'm just worried you're taking risks . . ."

And costing you fancy cars and nice things?

Gloria put her hand on top of Raoul's, who was starting to rub the line of fabric on her panties that ran over her hip, and said, "If they do this, are you going to reward them?"

Raoul ignored Gloria's hand and moved his down further.

"You obviously don't know me well enough."

Darnell got home, ten o'clock, he could hear LaKelle's snores coming from the bedroom. Not girlish little snores but big ones, some moaning on top of that. Moans so loud, he felt like he had to go in there, make sure there wasn't a man in there with her. Certain that wasn't the case, she wouldn't possibly betray him in that manner. She didn't wake up when Darnell made noise . . . probably wouldn't wake up if he wanted some either.

You would think with a baby in the house, she would hear

the door unlock and come out, wide awake.

A baby in the house.

It was about that time that Darnell heard little LaKeisha start to move around, about to let loose with those lungs. All up in the middle of the night. He went into the bedroom, grabbed LaKeisha from her crib, and set her over his shoulder. Patted her back to keep her calm while he paced the living room.

That Johnny Stanz, his old buddy, trying to get him slap drunk so Darnell could tell him about his undercover work with the federal government. Wait, was it undercover? Darnell didn't know, but it sure sounded good that way.

What Darnell did, he came up with a story that he was being framed to help the government catch Raoul Garcia, a nefarious drug dealer and general rabble-rouser. He used those words, not sure if Johnny was convinced. Seeing as Johnny most likely had ill feelings towards Raoul, it should be a likely story. That Max, an ATF agent, found him after the kidnapping by talking to his mother. That much was true. Told Johnny that he hadn't done much but look at mugshots and paperwork since then. Johnny had a look like he wasn't believing Darnell and kept trying to ply him with alcohol hoping there would be more.

Shoot, the whole time he was at Kelly's, around an hour, he had but one drink. In a hurry to get out of there.

And what was all that business about Johnny being gone? That's what he said. "I'm gone." What did that mean, a twenty-minute car ride to the house of a known prostitute? It disappointed Darnell, being lied to like that by an old friend.

Darnell heard movement behind him but didn't want to turn around quickly for fear that LaKeisha would be disturbed from her delicate sleep. Just starting to doze off, her little eyelids getting heavy.

He felt something digging into him.

LaKelle said, "Don't fucking move," in a whisper.

"Baby, it's me," Darnell believing that LaKelle couldn't make out LaKeisha on his shoulder in the darkness. "And I do believe you have a gun pressed against my asshole."

CHAPTER FOURTEEN

Don was in Max's office by the time he got there.

Before Max could sit down, Don said, "How's your head?"

It was okay but Max had the feeling it was about to get worse. Max said he was okay and sat down. There was a silence, Max expecting Don to say something, waiting for it.

Don said, "You been resting?"

"On and off," Max said, trying to remember the last time he rested.

"Well," Don said, "what've you been doing?"

Max wondered if Don was playing a game with him. Trying to come off like a good guy without going too far with it, leaving himself an out to play the heavy if he had to.

He said, "Trying to tie up loose ends."

Don asked Max how that was going and before Max had a chance to answer, Don said, "You find your fugitive yet?"

Max didn't want to give too much away just yet. "I got a lead on him."

"So he's alive?" Don sounded surprised.

Max nodded without trying to look like he did. That made Don ask, "He's in custody?"

Max said, "He's scared."

"No shit, he's scared." Don was up in his seat now, changing roles, getting more interested. "He's on the run . . . from us, Lord knows who else." Don sat back and Max could see the wheels turning. "You think he's pulling your chain?"

Max said, "No," left it at that and hoped Don would respect his judgment. He worked to change the subject. He said, "I was looking at the case file from three years ago. You know Carl McDermott was the contact name on Darnell's warrant?"

Don didn't seem fazed, but did say, "I thought you said you were?"

"I said I thought I was. Or figured so since I was the one who got the call." See how Don liked that.

"You thinking someone on your team had something to do with it?"

Max wasn't sure how far he wanted to go with this. He said, "I'm looking into anything I can."

Don looked up, like he was thinking. "Russ's in Phoenix now," saying it as if Max wasn't aware. "I think Carl's retired." He said, "You think something's there?"

"Like I said, I'm just looking into it. There might be something in the file I can use, you know, like a lead."

"That would help you with OPR." It was like Don hadn't even heard Max's comment at the end. "You have some information, they'll put a spotlight on that."

Max could feel Don reverting back to his good guy persona. He said, "What do you think about that?" At first wanting to drop it, but curious now.

Don shook his head from side to side, considering it. "I don't like it, but it takes the heat off an active duty agent."

Max saw a third side of Don: the politician. He could see where this was going: set up Carl McDermott, a retiree, as a scapegoat. Max knew it wasn't that simple.

Don started to get up. "You let me know when you talk to your fugitive. Don't sit on it. You've got four days before your interview. You don't have this wrapped up in three, we're putting together a group to hunt this guy down. I'm not going in that room with my dick swinging in the wind."

Max looked at his watch. He was picking up Darnell at his house in forty-five minutes.

Hey, the man said not to sit on it.

Max phoned Alondra. It wasn't early, eight-thirty, but maybe too early for her. He gave it a shot anyway.

He could hear sleepiness in her voice when she said, "Hello?"

"Hey, this is Max. I'm sorry I woke you."

Alondra moved up on one elbow and put a hand to her face. "It's okay," she said. "I should be the one saying I'm sorry." Sounding like the morning after a couple has a fight.

"It's not a problem," Max said. "How're you feeling?"

"My head hurts like hell. My face has gone down."

"Your mom taking care of you?"

"Yes," Alondra said, making a sweet voice. "She made me an ice pack and put me to bed." Then back to her regular voice. "I think she's going to do a novena, praying for my safety and welfare. I think she wants me to do a Marian devotion."

"I wanted to tell you that I picked up Tweety. He's locked up so you don't have anything to worry about. He won't be bothering you."

"Where is he?"

Max said, "Jail," wondering if Alondra wanted him to be more specific. "He's in jail, we'll just leave it at that."

"Is there any chance he could get out? I mean with bail or anything like that?"

"It'll take time to process him. I doubt he has a lawyer, so it could be weeks before the public defender gets to him for his first appearance. The prosecutor will press for whatever bail amount I recommend. Based on a prior record and the weapons in his possession, it'll be substantial. After that, another one to two months before his arraignment comes up . . ."

Max was thinking about his meeting with the state's attorney, what his offer to Tweety would be—if any—while waiting for another question from Alondra about Tweety's release, wondering if she was having second thoughts.

"I just don't want him coming after me."

Max told Alondra he wouldn't, that he would see to that, without going into detail.

"Did he give you trouble?" Alondra said. "I know he can be a handful."

Tell me about it, Max thought. A handful was a nice way of putting it. Max didn't want to talk about Tweety anymore, so he said, "It went fine. It's taken care of."

She must've sensed a tone in Max's voice because there was a silence on the line while Max stared out his car window, on his way to pick up Darnell.

After a moment, Alondra's voice came back. She said, "Thank you," quieter than normal.

"It wasn't a problem," Max said. "You just worry about taking care of yourself."

"If you want," Alondra said in a different tone of voice, "you can come over sometime . . . when you have the time. My mom can make some *asopao de pollo* or *lengua rellena.*"

That sounded good. Max said, "The first one's chicken soup, right? I think the other one involves beef, but I couldn't make it out."

"Stuffed beef tongue."

There was a silence.

"Or," Alondra said, "my mom might go bingo at the community center that night. In that case, we could just hang around here, you and me."

Darnell was outside waiting for Max, motioning for him to find a parking spot down the street. No room in the tiny driveway, the fender of LaKelle's 1998 Honda, the homemade tint job bubbling up on the rear window, hanging over the curb already.

Darnell saw Max roll his window down and said, "You early."

It was nine A.M.

"C'mon, let's go."

Darnell came over and leaned into the window. Max almost told him to back off, that it looked like a drug deal was going down. A reflex, he guessed, not seeing much of a difference it would make.

"Look," Darnell said, "I been up all night with my little girl. Crying her little head off for some reason or another. Mostly 'cause she an infant and that's what they do. I need some time to adjust."

To what?

Max figured, *What the hell* and found a spot about fifty yards down the curb. Darnell waited in the drive while Max walked back to the house. He brought Max around the back door, grill-work covering windows on that side, into the kitchen (which was one big room combining the kitchen, dining room, and living room), told Max to make himself comfortable while he brushed his teeth.

Max sat, wondering if Darnell drank coffee. He'd had his already and was picky when it came to that. Wondered mostly for Darnell's sake, if that would get him moving faster or if he could make some, save Darnell the time.

Before he could ask, Max heard voices from the hallway connecting the kitchen–dining room–living room area to the bathroom where Darnell was and a bedroom. At first, the voices were loud. A female voice said, "Who the hell is in my kitchen," and Max immediately started to plan an explanation and his exit. He heard Darnell answer. Something like, "Lower your voice," but Max couldn't make out what came after that. A few moments passed, Max readying himself in case of a quick exit.

The voices lowered and there was more discussion. In a

whisper and Max didn't try to listen. A woman came out from the hallway in a t-shirt and jersey shorts. About Darnell's age, maybe a year or two older. A butt like he's seen on black girls before but nothing hanging out around the mid-section. Not bad looking.

She introduced herself as LaKelle and asked Max if he wanted some coffee.

Max thanked her and said no.

LaKelle was over the coffee machine, fitting a filter in, when she said, "You the guy my baby's daddy's been spending all his time with?" There was a smile but something behind it, curious about an answer.

Max nodded and Darnell—from the bathroom—said, "LaKelle, don't be bothering him with questions like that." Max waved Darnell's comments off and waited for Darnell to come out, but he didn't.

"Darnell's helping me on an investigation. It's in his own best interest."

LaKelle pulled a chair out from the table and sat down across from Max. "It might be in his best interest. But it's in my interest that he home to help me take care of our little girl. You know we have a baby?"

Max nodded. He thought of asking LaKelle how Darnell being in prison would be in her best interest.

She slowed down and said, "Look, I appreciate what you doing. I know Darnell could be a knucklehead and know you trying to help him. I don't know everything, but I know that much."

"Well, he's in a bit of trouble but, with a little help, I'm going to try and get him out. It's gonna take some time and effort on his part, though."

"Effort?" LaKelle looked back towards the bathroom. "It's an effort just to get him to take out the garbage." She took a sip from her coffee cup, shoulders hunched quickly as her lips got singed. "It's the time part. He got responsibilities here. Lord knows he loves that little girl, but can't be coming home late like last night."

Max shook his head. He didn't remember the exact time but said, "I dropped him off around four. Before that, I think."

"He took off again, said he had to do something for you. I was asleep when he got home, 'bout scared me half to death. I came out here with my gun."

LaKelle was staring at Max over her coffee mug. "Well, if he wasn't with you, where the hell was he?"

The minute Max turned on to Billy Poe's street, he said, "I hope they're still there."

Darnell knew Max was talking about how long it took him to get ready.

Max drove the Chevy up the street once past Billy's house. Orange Camaro still sitting in the driveway, parked behind other cars. He ran the plates on the Camaro and it belonged to somebody named Fernando Navarro. Sounded made up, but he'd have to check that out later. Nothing looked out of place, like someone had left. Max made the block and found a spot down the street that gave them a clear view.

"Don't bitch, man," Darnell said. "I ain't used to all this . . ."

"What are you used to, then? Sitting around on your ass all day?" Max looked away. "I bet your old lady don't take that long to get ready."

"I didn't know you'd be coming that early."

Max said, "That's why you went out late last night?" Deadpan, letting Darnell know he wouldn't forget about it.

"It wasn't that late, about ten. And I had to get some pussy, okay?"

"It's not okay. You need to let me know. I gave you a get-out-of-jail-free card. You want to keep it, you won't pull any more stunts like that."

Darnell was supposed to feel guilty, or at least look like it. So he did. Because Max was being a good cop, doing his job, and because he had been nice in doing what he did. Felt he had a little reason to feel guilty anyway, he got to see his little girl instead of being locked up. Okay, give him that one.

"What's wrong with LaKelle?"

"What you mean? For humping?" Darnell said. "Shoot, man, I done wore her out. That's my baby's momma and all, but I ain't about to hit that again."

"She won't put out for you, huh?"

Darnell stared out the window. "Not even after my kidnapping."

Max stared up and down the street for a minute, wondering how long it would take before they were noticed on a street lined with little pink and blue crack houses and late model cars junked in front yards. Thinking about it, he said, "So who's the other chick?"

Darnell said, "Kelly's my white girl, stays over in Pompano," eager to talk about it, almost before Max could finish the question. "She a working girl but that's all right. Her stuff so good, I can look past that."

"I hope you're taking precautions, you being a father."

"If you're asking do I wear protection," Darnell turned to Max, "I wear two rubbers when I see Kelly. The night LaKeisha was conceived I was inebriated. Don't mean she was a mistake." Darnell held a hand to his chest. "I love her more than life itself. Just that I wasn't as cautious as usual."

Darnell asked could they roll the windows down again, like last time they were here, and said, "Did you eat yet?" It was near eleven on the dashboard clock.

"Before I went to pick you up."

Well, that had to be, like, maybe three hours ago. Darnell didn't stop to eat; he saw the look LaKelle gave him when he

126

came out the bathroom and decided it was best just to leave. He didn't know what that was about.

Maybe Max didn't understand what he was getting at about eating.

Before Darnell could ask again, they could see the rear bumper of the orange Camaro start to nose out into the street. Max and Darnell watched it, Max telling Darnell to get ready to get low in his seat if it came this way.

The Camaro was on the road, backing out and going in the opposite direction, when Max sat up and turned the ignition.

Darnell said, "We gonna follow them?"

Max nodded. "I'm curious to see where they're going, aren't you? These are your abductors." Max put it in drive and started north after Billy Poe. "Any luck, they might lead us to Raoul."

Darnell made a face and wondered how long this would take.

"Maybe they'll stop by a drive-thru on their way."

On their way out to Hendry County—to look at camps on Osceola turkey hunting leases that Billy knew about—Lester asked if Billy had ever heard of Stockholm Syndrome.

Billy's head rattled from side to side. "Sounds familiar. Wasn't there something like that in that Bruce Willis movie?"

"Only the guy calls it Helsinki Syndrome, but it's the same thing . . ."

"That was a kick-ass movie, huh? When he says yippee-ki-yay, motherfucker," Billy at the top of his lungs now, fingers pointed to look like a gun. "I love that part."

Man, sometimes it was work keeping this guy on track.

"Anyway," Lester said, "the thing is that sometimes the hostage starts to, I dunno, like their kidnappers. Like there's some weird thing comes over them and they start to side with the people that's holding them."

Billy looked in his rearview mirror, open fields and pasture around them. "That's about the craziest thing I ever heard. You sure you're not making this up, pulling my chain?"

Lester shook his head. "It's real, I'm telling you. There's proof. You ever hear of Patty Hearst?" He waited. "No? Well, she was kidnapped by some terrorists a long time ago. I don't know what kind, probably some A-rabs."

"Like al-Qaeda? We're not like that."

"Some different A-rabs, I'm not sure. I don't know how long they been around exactly, but I'm pretty sure this was before them. Point is, she goes from being held for ransom to robbing banks with these guys."

Lester waited for Billy to continue their conversation, not that they really talked much. But Billy didn't say a word back or make a comment about their kidnapping plan until, a few miles of scrub brush, swamp ponds, and orange orchards behind them, he said, "Let's try this one. There ain't no cars, but if somebody comes out, we're just going to say we got lost."

Billy turned on a dirt road, dust and stones kicking up underneath Raoul's car. Shit, now he'd probably have to go get it washed when he got back to civilization. The man could be touchy. Billy maneuvered while the car moved in and out of holes in the road, then came to a stop in front of a neat-looking brown wood house. More like a lodge.

Billy and Lester got out and took a walk around the lodge. Billy pressed his face close to windows on the back side of the building. Covered his face to block out the reflection, looking in at a nice little living room. Hey, they had a TV in there. Perfect. Billy backed his face off the window and looked up. A fuckin' satellite dish. That was good. He didn't know how long they'd be out here, maybe have to bunk a couple nights. He thought about telling Lester about the TV, but he'd notice soon enough.

Billy made one more round of the place and saw Lester standing there, not doing anything. That sad-sack look on his face.

"Nice, huh? Better'n you thought, I bet."

On his last pass, Billy caught sight of a small shed out there about thirty yards from the back of the lodge. Small, but not small enough to be an outhouse. No place with satellite TV is going to have a pisser out in the woods anyway. Billy tried pulling the door open, the wood rattling a couple times before he realized there was a padlock.

He got to one knee and told Lester to go around the other side, see if he could see through the boards. Billy found a spot where he could see through the slats. This building was older than the lodge and the wood planks were separating a bit. Probably re-did the lodge when they put the satellite in.

Billy saw some shelf work on the walls, leading down to table tops where they cut the turkeys up; looked like some old farming equipment sitting on the shelves, but he couldn't be for certain. A four-wheeler . . . a generator. Those could come in handy. He could see Darnell now, chained to one of the table legs. It might give way, so they'd have to find something else, but there was bound to be something.

Whew, it would be scary out here in the dark.

Billy said, "Ya know, Les," and Lester came around the corne of the shed, "we get Darnell in here, I doubt he's gonna like u side with us, or any of that nonsense you were talking about."

Max had to drive past where Billy Poe turned off. In the mi of the country, he couldn't just pull off and wait.

He thought that maybe Billy and Lester might have scoping the place out, thinking about leasing for hunting or part of it. Anxious, trying to figure out when they make it out here in their free time between kidnappings tempted murders of federal officers.

What it could be: a place for Raoul. Someplace for h low for awhile? Max shrugged. He was a quarter-mile p

the camp was and double-backed. On their left, the little camp was getting bigger. Max slowed to look around and saw Billy staring into a shed out back. He kept going.

Now he stared straight ahead as he drove away from the camp and Darnell said, "What's out here?"

"Nothing," Max said. "We can't hang out here, in the middle of nowhere. They'll make us."

"You think we could eat?"

"I'll drop you at home. You can eat there." Max was thinking. "I got a couple of things to look into this afternoon."

Darnell had his body turned, rubbernecking in the opposite direction as Max drove away.

"What you think they doing there?"

Max swung back by the office, took care of something, and walked into Don Sommers's office. He said, "I called Carl Mc-Dermott, see what he was up to."

Don's head snapped back a bit. "You did?" He must've caught himself, that Max could tell his surprise, because the tone changed when he said, "How is old Carl?" It was a tone that sounded genuinely interested, something that Max had never heard in anyone in the office's voice about McDermott before.

"He enunciated a lot. I think he was half in the bag."

Don looked at a wall clock. "It's, what, two in the afternoon over there?"

Max shrugged. "There was music on in the background. 'Take This Job and Shove It.' "

"Who was that? Merle Haggard?"

"Johnny Paycheck," Max said. "Carl says he plays it over and over on a loop every afternoon."

"Guess Carl's glad to be retired. Sounds like he's going the way of all those outlaw country guys . . . Waylon Jennings . . ." Don stopped, trying to think of others, ". . . drinking himself

away." He said, "What else he have to say?"

"Between the long pauses where he was swigging alcohol, not much. It's like talking to a child, really. I kept at it, looking for a way to talk to this guy. When he starts going off about politics, I think, oh well, that's it. I'll be on the phone all day with nothing to show for it. But then, out of nowhere, he says, 'I talked to somebody from the office a couple months ago.' "

Don said, "Really," in that way that didn't sound like a question.

"Get this." Max lowered his voice to a whisper. "He says, 'It was about that thing we did a couple years ago.' "

Don was smiling at Max. "That could be anything."

Max told him that he and Carl only worked together once.

Don said, "Oh." Then, "He say anything else?"

Max was going to tell him no, that Carl was too far gone to remember who it was that called him, but Don's cell phone buzzed and it saved Max from discussing it further. Don checked it and said, "Keep me posted."

Which Max already decided he wasn't going to do. Not until he knew more, had more information. He had to be sure. It was the kind of thing that could end up as a headline on the evening news or some website.

Max gathered himself, ready to leave the office for the afternoon. Tie up those loose ends his boss kept coming back to. On his way out, he had a thought. What if he tried the jail where he picked up Darnell again? Call them and ask them how they knew to contact him?

Talk to somebody different. You never know how that might turn out.

CHAPTER FIFTEEN

Max wanted to talk to Dan Remedios to clear something up. Darnell mentioned his white girl, Kelly, living in Pompano. Showing Max what a slick guy he was. It was closer for Max from Darnell's house than going all the way back to the office.

In case he decided to run back by LaKelle's, make sure Darnell was home.

"I took a chance you'd be there."

"I didn't get out of here until about nine last night," Remedios said. "Back in here at nine this morning, maybe a little later. Never stops."

"How's my guy?"

Remedios knew Max was talking about Tweety. "He hasn't even been processed yet. It's been slower than even I thought, but it won't be long." Remedios looked away from the phone at some commotion in the intake area, then turned back. "What's up?"

"I got one more favor."

He could talk to Dan, the lieutenant never giving Max the feeling like he was wasting his time. Max told Lieutenant Remedios about Kelly. Asked if they had any Kellys in their database with a Pompano Beach address that were picked up for solicitation. Max remembered Darnell called her a working girl.

It might've been a long shot, but when Remedios came back after a few seconds and said, "I got two, different names, different addresses," Max felt himself lighten up.

Remedios took time to look at the screen, toggling back and forth between the two Kellys from Pompano Beach. "Both arrested for solicitation." Remedios kept reading, "And both on possession. They real pieces of work, huh?"

"You got pictures?"

"Their booking photos are on here."

"Are either of them white?"

"One is," Remedios said. "That would be Kelly Walker," and Remedios gave an address on one of the streets off MLK Drive. The lieutenant had a puzzled frown thinking about it, saying, "She doesn't really look like your type, though."

LaKelle watched from the kitchen window: watched Darnell fixing the backyard fence with five feet of chain link fence roll she bought at the home improvement store; watched until he got fed up with trying to figure out how to get it around the corner post and gave up. She went to the living room and heard the lawnmower start. Oh well, that was something else that needed doing. That boy, he was trying. She had to give him that. It would've been nice if he'd done that earlier when LaKeisha was awake, but she wasn't going to argue. She had slept through Darnell coming home from wherever he went with Max, the cop Darnell was all of a sudden buddy-buddy with. Car doors slamming, then ten minutes talking in the driveway, LaKelle wondering what they were talking about. Tomorrow's adventure. Then Darnell slamming the house door when he came in. LaKelle wanted to raise her voice then, telling him to mind the sleeping baby, but couldn't. She figured she'd bake him some chicken to be nice for coming home to take care of his chores. Maybe check on LaKeisha and relax a little first. She had some weed around here somewhere.

★ ★ ★ ★ ★

Max got there in time to see a young white guy walking into Kelly's house, a carton of cigarettes sticking out of a plastic bag in his left hand, and thought the address might be out of date.

He walked up, knocked on the door and waited for the guy to answer. No sense in coming all this way and not checking it out. He answers the door, Max asks for Kelly . . . Kelly who? Apologize for having the wrong house and that would be it.

Only thing, a young blonde answered the door wearing a tight tank top and jeans. Okay, it surprised Max a little and he knew she could tell.

The girl had a look like she was waiting for Max to say something. He asked if her name was Kelly Walker and she nodded.

Max told the girl his name and took out his ID. He said, "I was wondering if Darnell Sims came by here last night?"

Kelly nodded. "He came by for a little bit. Brought me a fifth of vodka. I think he wanted to get in my pants, but," she hesitated, "we just ended up talking."

That was interesting. Max stood at the door, thinking she might let him in, but didn't press it. "You mind if I ask what you talked about?"

"I hadn't seen Darnell in a bit." Kelly shrugged. "Just talked about what's been going on. What I been doing, what he's been doing . . ."

Kelly leaned her shoulder against the door, trying to close it a little before Max said, "Darnell tell you what he's been doing lately?"

Kelly turned her head and yelled, "Johnny!" Looking back at Max, she said, "He's the one you want to talk to." She moved away from the door, in time to noise coming from somewhere down a hallway. Max took a step inside, glanced around at bare walls, a mess of clothes thrown on the furniture and a video game console in front of the TV, and looked up.

Johnny walked out from a bedroom, tucking shirt tails in his blue jeans.

"Don't get dressed on my account," Max said, giving Johnny a smile, looking to reassure him.

Johnny gave him a big smile and Max said, "Are you Johnny Stanz?"

The smile was still there, barely, Johnny trying to keep it cordial when he said, "Who am I talking to?"

"You think," Max said, "you could answer a question without asking one?"

Johnny's face changed.

Max got ready for a scene.

Johnny said, "This is bullshit." But it was to Kelly, who gave him a look.

She said, "I'm tired of your friends coming over here unannounced. I can't be doing this sneaking around, trying to lie to this guy's face. I don't need this crap. I got enough problems." She turned to Max. "When you leave, take him with you."

Max watched Johnny turn his back to them. Storm off and pout, giving Kelly some kind of a pose.

Max said again, "Are you Johnny Stanz?" Still not sure.

Johnny nodded, resigned.

"My name's Max and I'm with the ATF."

Johnny asked for some ID and Max showed him.

"How do I know that's real?"

"What do you want?" Max said. "You want to go down to the office and have them make you one? Is that what you want, to talk at my office?"

Johnny shook his head and gave Kelly another look.

"But you and I do need to talk."

Johnny Stanz, turning his head again, said, "Well, we sure as hell can't do it here."

CHAPTER SIXTEEN

Armando Hernandez liked killing people. He was brought over from Cuba in 1985—barely twenty at the time. Arranged for by some of the older Marielitos that had grown up in the drug business of South Florida. Guys that started running cocaine in the early '80s, then moved to heroin later. That's when gangs from places like Honduras and Guatemala started getting involved.

Armando's first kill in *Los Estados Unidos* was of a Honduran immigrant used by one of their gangs to move product into the country. Only problem, it was a lot longer way to Florida from Honduras than from Cuba. Which means some of the boats the Hondurans used had to piggyback the routes Armando's new bosses liked to use. The increased traffic forced the Coast Guard to step up patrols in the Florida Straits, made it tougher for the Cubans to move their own product. Coast Guard cutters were one thing; when they started using those airplanes with radar to monitor air drops and vessel traffic, it pissed the Marielitos off.

Armando remembered it like it was yesterday. Just off the boat, literally. Transferred from a trawler to a speedboat with two hundred pounds of processed heroin all the way from Afghanistan. Didn't come in on some car made to look like a fucking boat, like peasants you see in funny pictures on the evening news. He was delivered.

Still, the men he would be working for had been here for nearly five years, some of them six. Figured they knew everything they needed to know about everything. They had a big fancy house in America. They would make speeches about how to be bad and be successful. See how good their life was? Because they were smart. Bullshit.

He knew what he was to them. No priors here, nobody knew who he was. He fully expected to be handed a gun and they would say, "See that guy right there? Shoot him," and Armando would squeeze the trigger and that would be it.

No, they set up a meeting at the Merrill-Stevens Shipyard on the Miami River. Told the Honduran—Armando never found out his name—that there was an offer on the table for some side work for Armando's Cuban bosses. Make a delivery to a contact in Tampa on his brother's boat. Do it right, there might be more. His own people weren't paying him shit to risk his life, why not get some for his family on his own. Fuck them. After that, who knows?

The Honduran was there first. Armando walked up to him, not a word. The first hit from Armando's pickaxe was at the crown of the Honduran's skull. He was dead then. But Armando put another sixty-eight puncture wounds in him. The *Herald* fucked up the next morning and put a crime scene photo of the guy's body on the front page. They probably should've put his mugshot if he had one or a photo of his body covered with a sheet. But no, a full color shot of his body, blood all over the place.

One of the Marielitos made a comment that the body looked like it had been picked over by scavenger birds. Like he died in the desert or something, all those pock marks in him. That's where Armando got his nickname.

El Buitre.

The Vulture.

Twenty-five years later, Armando had his own fancy American house—or at least a comfortable one on Amalfi Avenue—and learned English.

The gangs? They still had their drug business, it would always be there. Things had changed, though. There was more money and less danger in identity theft and other fraudulent activities. Young kids sitting at a computer ripping decent people off. What kind of a man did that? The fucking Internet was ruining business.

Which is why Armando was glad that his friend Raoul Garcia had called. It told him some excitement was coming his way. Raoul, he still believed in doing some things the old-fashioned way.

Armando was walking east on Calle Ocho, past the persistent click-clack of Domino Park, on his way to El Pub, the red and yellow *gallo* statue in front of him. He would've preferred El Cristo across the street, but Raoul was paying.

Armando walked in and saw his friend at a booth under the big map of his home country on the wall, Raoul's back to him. Armando stopped Raoul from getting up and sat down across from him, shaking hands over the table.

Raoul sat back, almost nostalgia in his eyes, saying, "My old friend."

Armando smiled, his hands flat on the table.

"How have you been?"

Armando nodded his head. "I could use a café con leche."

Now Raoul smiled. "Of course. They have the best here." He called the waitress over, El Pub nearly empty at this time, only an elderly couple at the counter; looking like they were splitting roast pork with a side of black beans and rice and yucca.

After the waitress was gone, Armando said, "How is business?"

"Good. I've had some setbacks lately, but no complaints."

A couple of friends sitting around talking about life, beating around the bush, until Armando said, "These setbacks, this is why you called me?"

The waitress came with their order and left and Raoul smiled. "I just wanted to know your availability."

Armando took a sip. "You could have asked me that over the phone."

"Yes," Raoul said. "But what's the harm in seeing a comrade I haven't seen in a long time."

Comrade was a strong word. Something people he knew back in Cuba would use in their struggle against political oppression. Armando let them have that word, he wanted a fancy American house.

He knew what this was now. An interview . . . an audition. To see if he was still fit, had that look in his eye.

"None at all." Armando shook his head. He felt comfortable enough to say, "Do I pass inspection?"

Raoul nodded. "I apologize, Armando. We haven't seen each other in a long time, you understand? I know you don't work much anymore . . ."

"By my choice."

Raoul gave him that. "Understood. But I do realize you're the best."

"Will you need the best to deal with these setbacks?"

"Yes, I may. I have some people looking into the situation, but I'm not sure how it may work out."

"You have people that you cannot trust? You should get rid of them."

Raoul nodded, thinking seriously about that. "This situation is something that's been tearing my insides for quite some time now. This is a journey that you will take with me, my friend. One that you may not be able to get off once you get on. You and I will see this through all the way. I wanted to communicate this to you, face to face, man to man, so we have no misunderstandings."

Armando sat still while his "comrade" spoke to him under

the black and white map of his homeland, Armando glancing up to find the black circle that marked Matanzas, his home.

The Vulture said, "What kind of journey?" Feeling himself drawn in.

Max sat in his car talking to Johnny, not sure of where they could go. Still sitting across the street from Kelly's house, he said to Johnny, "We have to get you somewhere. There's a lot of people looking for you."

Johnny had a look on his face. "I was fine here before you showed up."

Max nodded, maybe so. He said, "What did you and Darnell talk about?"

"Not much." Johnny shrugged. "I mean, he didn't want to talk. I was downing shots of vodka left and right, trying to get him to do the same." Johnny looked Max in the eye. "He came in and started mouthing off about what he was doing, something about working with the government. You know Darnell, he likes to talk. That was before he knew I was there. But, to be honest, the more I tried to get him to talk, the less he would."

Well, that was something encouraging. Max took a moment before he said, "And why would you want him to talk?"

Johnny shrugged. "I dunno. It was pissing me off. He was trying to impress my lady and he's only there because I let him go."

Okay. "You know a guy named Billy Poe?"

Johnny nodded.

"He was calling your phone after you disappeared. I know because I have your phone. I haven't heard from him since, but he was leaving some pretty dangerous messages."

Johnny had his head down. "You can keep the phone, I don't want it."

Max didn't have the idea of offering it back anyway, but he

understood. "I'm going to rustle up some place for a couple nights. You can't go back to your place and I don't think Kelly's gonna let you back in, just for your stuff maybe." Max grabbed his phone and started out of the car. "Sit tight."

Before Max could close the door, Johnny leaned across the center console and said, "Doesn't the government pay for hotel rooms in situations like this?"

One thing Billy hadn't mentioned, how they were going to get Darnell in the first place?

Lester thought about it relaxing in front of the TV watching Dr. Oz. His mind wandered off to the subject of Darnell again. Dr. Oz wasn't doing anything special right now, him and some other doctors on there explaining what a person's excrement should look like. Can you imagine? Talking about your shit on national TV. What was the world coming to? Maybe if he had a movie star or some of those people from *American Idol,* it would be interesting.

They had a plan and, apparently, a spiffy lodge in the woods to hold Darnell hostage. He couldn't get over thinking of a basement with the bugs crawling around. For some reason, he didn't know. That little shed out back of the hunting camp wouldn't be far off.

Lester didn't know what Billy was doing at the moment, probably somewhere around here, staring out some window. Spooked about the ATF man, Max, coming back. He could have, but they hadn't seen him all day.

There he was, Billy walking in and saying, "Turn that down." Obviously annoyed about something. The man spent his days staring out of windows, how could he not be? He did stop for a second to watch Dr. Oz giving his concerned look to the audience. Not losing his stylishness, hair still in place, when he turned and explained everything to the women in his audience.

"What they talking about?" Billy said. "That looks like a

picture of some turds on TV."

"It is." Lester wondered if Billy was going to sit down and watch, maybe make a conversation with him about it. That Dr. Oz, he was good at that.

Billy said, "You ain't got nothin' to do better than watch *that?*"

Okay, maybe not.

Lester got up, turned the volume down but didn't turn the TV off. "What we have to do right now?"

Something always bothering Billy.

Lester let Billy talk, his voice taking the place of the ones on the tube like one of those kung-fu movies where the voices don't match. Somebody in Dr. Oz's audience was talking, a middle-aged white woman probably telling the world that her poo don't come out the right shape or color, if at all. Until Lester heard Billy say something that surprised him and he said, "What?"

"I said we should try to get Darnell on our own. Not wait for Raoul's go-ahead."

"I was just thinking about that, how we going to find him."

"When? During the commercials?"

The man just couldn't let it go.

Billy said, "You know that ATF guy's coming back."

"So?"

"Any luck, Darnell'll be with him."

"What are we going to do about him? Max, I mean."

Billy looked at Lester when he called the ATF man by name, Max.

He was quiet for a minute, then saying, "Considering all the trouble he's caused, you think Raoul would pay for him, too?"

Max asked Alondra to meet him at the hotel in South Beach, if he could use her room for a couple nights. "I'll pay you back for it."

Alondra thought he had done enough already, but she wasn't going to argue.

They were walking along Ocean Drive, looking for a cross street to head back east, past Collins to where Alondra said she was parked.

"You keeping a dangerous felon up there?"

Alondra was smiling.

"The biggest danger to him is if he wants to go out. I'm not sure he can help himself."

"Is he in trouble?"

"He gets out, he might be. Otherwise, I'd feel better not going into it."

They had walked up Fourteenth and were coming to Collins. Max saw Mac's across the street and thought about asking Alondra if she wanted a drink but passed.

They got to her car, on Fourteenth just short of Washington Avenue. Max opened the door for Alondra as she said, "Where are you?" and Max pointed somewhere off in the distance, in the direction of the Lincoln Road Mall.

She said, "You want me to drop you?"

Max said sure, closed the door, and walked around to the other side.

There was one thing still bugging him, though.

"You have your own place. You're staying at your mom's right now." Max buckled up for the five-minute ride. "If you don't mind my asking, what do you need to keep the room for?"

Alondra turned the ignition and shifted into drive.

"You wanna find out?"

Darnell had been in all evening, flipping through channels while he kept LaKeisha quiet. Nothing on and he was getting bored. LaKelle had gone out. He got hungry and checked the refrigerator around six. Hopefully, she was going to get some groceries 'cause there wasn't shit to eat.

LeKeisha started stirring again so Darnell rocked her, one hand on the remote until he came to a *Star Wars* movie. One of the new ones; he could tell because Samuel L. Jackson was in it. The black Jedi. The *Star Wars* people probably did that to get black people to go see their movies, but Darnell always liked them anyway. Used to get teased about it by his buddies when he was younger, but he didn't care. He kept watching and couldn't tell exactly which movie it was, just that it was one of the recent ones. Long as it wasn't the one with that annoying creature they had made up. That thing comes on, Darnell was turning it.

He watched a few minutes more and no annoying creature. Maybe this was the one where the young guy turns into Darth Vader? Backstabbing his Jedi friends because he was seduced by the allure of evil. Kinda reminded him of Johnny Stanz. What was going on with that guy? Shoot, they grew up together and now Johnny tries to pull weird stuff like that, coming on like Darnell was trying to do him wrong. He'd have to watch out for that guy, a shame.

And there was ol' Samuel L. Slicing up bad guys with his lightsaber. It reminded Darnell of something he read one time in one of LaKelle's celebrity magazines, Samuel L. telling the people that make *Star Wars* movies that he didn't want to go out like a punk; that if he had to die, he wanted it to be worth it.

It made Darnell think, that didn't sound like such a bad idea.

CHAPTER SEVENTEEN

Sensual massage.

That's what it said on Alondra's card. That and a phone number. That was it, no name. Max was curious; and comfortable with Alondra's hands digging into his back on the living room floor of Max's apartment in Palm Bay. He asked and she said her last name was Ayala.

She said, "I think it's Basque, like where some of my ancestors were from."

It made Max think of the Basque separatist movement in Spain. Car bombings and kidnappings.

Max asked how long she'd been doing this, that she was good at it. Not too long, but the money was good. It's not like she knew how to do much else. Alondra said the only trouble was expectations. When the guy expected more, thinking sensual massage automatically meant you were a prostitute. Max said, "Really?" thinking he might think that's what it meant too if he hadn't just been educated on the topic. "A lot of guys expect that?"

She said, "If you want to ask me do I sleep with my customers, ask me."

"Do you?"

"No, I don't. Will I give a guy a happy ending?" She shrugged. "If there's extra money involved. A girl's got to get paid for something like that. But not just because he's good looking. Fact, the better looking they are, the more of a pain in the ass they are, usually."

Max felt hands digging into the middle of his back, just below his shoulder blades. He said, "Your job sounds dangerous," thinking of Tweety as the kind of guy that came to her for a massage. He saw Alondra's head over his shoulder, giving him a look. She said, "You want to protect me?" and Max forgot about Tweety.

Alondra straightened up and started to work on Max's shoulders. "I keep a .22 in my bag just in case."

He thought that was interesting. Not pepper spray, not a small knife or a stick or the kinds of things people find around the house to use as a weapon. A gun.

Max wanted to ask if she knew how to use it, but it came out as, "You ever get a chance to use it?"

He heard her say, "No," among the grunts she made as she dug into Max's back. She said, "How you doing so far?"

Max tried to get words out but couldn't between tugs at his back. They must not have gotten to the sensual part yet. He just nodded and heard Alondra laugh. She seemed happy.

"You're tight."

"Isn't everybody?"

"For the most part. Too much stress in everyday life. I imagine there's a lot of it in your line of work."

Max was in no position to shrug it off, which is what he normally would do. "It's not so bad. I'm like you, it's not like I could do anything else." Trying to find some common ground, hoping that came out right. He glanced over his shoulder and saw Alondra smiling back at him straddled across his back. Still in the game. "Been having some problems lately, though."

Alondra said, "Oh?" Sounding interested. "Anything you can talk about?"

Not really.

Max said, "Just having problems making contact with people, the usual runaround," and left it at that.

She nodded and buried the balls of her hands into an area above Max's shoulder blades. "What's your birthday?" Like it was something she had just thought of.

Max was surprised and it took him a few seconds before he said, "August twenty-nine."

"See? You're a Virgo." Like that explained it. "Your Mercury's in retrograde. You're going to have communication problems."

Oh.

"Don't worry. It should be over in a couple of days."

He was hoping so. "You into all that? Signs and all that stuff?"

"My mother was. Tropical astrology, some sidereal astrology. Moon nodes, primary angles. Guess I picked it up from that. I can tell you that your ruling planet is typically Mercury . . ."

"Typically?"

"A lot of people point to Ceres as the ruling planet for Virgo and Taurus now."

"That's not a planet." Max was wondering if he was saying that right, like it might be to astrology people.

"It's a small planet but has never been recognized, even after the thing with Pluto a few years ago."

Max tried to remember what she was talking about. Pluto?

"What's it mean?"

"You love the Earth."

Max turned his neck. "You mean, like a hippie, dancing around with women that don't shave under their arms?"

"Or join some cult?" Alondra laughed. "No, not like that. Just means that you're respectful, that's all."

Well, he didn't litter and recycled when he thought about it.

"And don't worry, my armpits are shaved."

Max hadn't given it a thought.

Alondra had Max turned over now, on his back. He looked up, watching Alondra run her hand through her hair.

"You want to look, maybe check the rest of my body, too? Just to be sure?"

CHAPTER EIGHTEEN

Eight o'clock at night and Billy said he wanted to go out. They had eaten already so Lester thought Billy was going out by himself and didn't move. Billy said to come on, get up, like Lester was supposed to know.

Lester saw Billy reach into one of the kitchen drawers and pull out a stack of money. He saw Billy counting off bills, mouthing the amount to himself, but never asked how much there was or how much Billy was taking.

Lester said, "Where are we going?"

Billy said, "To get supplies," and they didn't say another word until they were at the hardware store. All the way out to a home store in Sunrise and that was their only conversation.

Billy grabbed a cart and headed to an aisle that had a banner with the word "Adhesives" on it. Billy grabbed some duct tape, glad it was here and he wouldn't have to start looking for it, these places built like warehouses now and you could never get anybody to help you.

When Billy threw two four-roll packs in the cart, Lester said, "What's that for?"

Billy said, "We're going to need something to tape Darnell's mouth shut," and Lester could see what was happening. The details of their master plan starting to come together.

"You need all that?"

"Might need some for the ATF man, too." Billy pushed the cart to the end of the aisle, looking straight up at shelves that reached the ceiling, way up there. Stopping to look like there was something he might need. "You never know what's going to happen, we need to be prepared."

We.

That started Lester thinking: a flashlight; what if they had to go out to the shed in the dark? Rope, some links of chain . . . And he told Billy they should go in that direction, but Billy was busy looking at mixers, appliances used to mix ingredients to make cakes.

Billy said, "You bake?"

Lester shook his head.

"I didn't know. You're always watching cooking shows, talking about cooking something or other. I didn't know how far you took it." Billy put the mixer back—Lester sneaking a look at the little price tag on the shelf, one hundred and fifty dollars—and said, "What were you saying?"

Lester said, "That we should get some rope and look at the chains, you said something before about that." Showing Billy how full of ideas he was.

They found the chain section and didn't know there were that many different types. You could get lost looking. Billy decided on a five-sixteenth-of-an-inch tow chain he liked. Hey, if you could tow a car with it, it should be good enough. For good measure, there was a hundred feet of poly rope he decided on, too. The card on the shelf where the boxes were said "Easy to handle and knot" as one of its main features. Billy had the rope in his hand when he said, "This might be useful," and threw it in the cart. He told Lester to make sure not to lose the receipt, they would return what they didn't use.

They were near the lumber and Lester said, "How about some two-by-fours? It might be a good idea to barricade the door."

Billy told him it was a good idea but they wouldn't be able to fit it in the car. The smallest length was ten feet. Then they started looking at smaller boarding. Oak boards, poplar boards, whitewood boards, but Billy said those weren't thick enough, the guy putting some thought into it.

"Lemme sleep on it," Billy said. "I might have to come back with the Jeep. Take the soft top off so I can fit 'em."

Lester was talking to himself, asking himself what else they might need, when Billy said, "Something to clean up with," like they were thinking of the same thing. Lester was about to ask, *Clean up what?,* but Billy had already taken off.

Lester found him in the cleaning supply section, picking out a mop. Looking at mop buckets by the time Lester made it down the aisle to where Billy was. He said, "Is this for the house?"

Billy was busy hoisting a mop bucket into the cart, trying to fit it in, and said, "No, this is for the operation."

It was an operation now.

Lester nodded, figuring he had missed something.

Billy finished and was looking back and forth, up and down the aisle, on a mission, when he pointed. He told Lester to get two, no three, bottles of bleach and some rubber gloves. Latex ones, too, if he saw some.

Now Lester had to ask, "Why?"

Billy was dead serious except for a slight facial tic, like it was a question he wasn't expecting.

"In case we have to clean up blood. Why else?"

Johnny was thankful he was in South Beach because he was thinking lately of coming down here anyway. If he wasn't staying this close, he'd have to drive down here and there was never any place to park. Thought about chilling out in the hotel lobby, but decided against it. Hey, a free night in South Beach? He needed to take advantage of it.

Stepped out onto Ocean Drive, a breeze coming off the ocean, and headed south. Passed places like Clevelander's and the Colony—tourists getting wasted out front—on his way to a dive bar on Bay Road, away from the neon art deco of Ocean Drive, but ended up stopping at CJ's Crab Shack. A place he liked to hang out where you might run into some locals. That's how trendy it was. You had to look for people that lived there. He sat at a table on the sidewalk to have a vodka tonic and watch the show. A little off the beaten path but still good. Women in their short skirts and high heel shoes walking carefully along the street, on their way to something better. Neon off in the distance that looked like a movie set. To Johnny, some of them looked like they were walking slow enough to be mistaken for prostitutes. Trying not to fall over in four-inch heels but looking like they were streetwalking.

Johnny saw one that he thought he might ask for a drink. A brunette in a black mini skirt and leopard print sandals on his side of the street, a looker. Just stick his arm out and offer her a drink. Make a joke about how hard it was to walk in those shoes, that she needed to stop and rest. The closer she got, Johnny realized it was a guy with a wig and fake tits. What happens when she picks up a guy and the guy finds out she has a pecker?

It was two blocks over and three blocks up where he and Darnell had boosted one of their first cars together, the corner of Ninth and Washington Avenue. At least he remembered it as one of their first. He wasn't sure if it was exactly the first one, but close. Hot-wired it and went for a joyride up and down I-95, dropping it off at a convenience store near their house so they could make it home in time for curfew.

Somebody saw them and recognized Johnny as Rita Stanz's boy. He told the judge that he was sorry because he had to and spent six months in juvie—and never mentioned Darnell's name.

What if he did it again? Johnny thought about it having another vodka tonic. You go up on a street like, say, Meridian, there weren't many people walking around this time of night. Lots of cars parked on the street, too. It could work. He slammed his drink back and started thinking about where he would go.

Just get on the interstate and drive north. Far away from here. After a couple more vodka tonics that he wanted, he'd only a have few bucks left. Maybe a twenty crumpled in his pocket somewhere. Suppose the car he stole didn't have much gas in the tank? Plus, he would have to stay somewhere unless he wanted to sleep at a rest stop. Then, suppose some state trooper gets nosy and calls the tag number in?

Okay, maybe have those drinks and think about it some more. There was bound to be a chick around that he could ask to sit down with him for a while. He looked okay, remembering to grab his good shirt on his way out of Kelly's apartment. An old sports coat, too, although he wasn't sure who that belonged to.

He'd ask a girl for a drink; after that, who knows? Johnny started looking through his pockets, making sure he had enough cash on him.

The minute she said, "You wanna find out?" Max knew they would be in his bed before too long.

Alondra was quick getting undressed. Down to her black bra and panties in no time. Max running a little behind. Sitting down to get his shoes and socks off, standing up to take his pants down. He chalked it up to the age difference, Alondra maybe more than a decade younger than him. It hit him, she was the only person he had met in the last two days without doing a background check on.

Alondra came over and helped Max with his shirt and he forgot about work.

They started with the lamp on, on top of the sheets with the bedspread pushed back. It was nice to see a woman naked again. Near the end of his marriage, Max's wife would bring clothes into the bathroom and come out with all of them on.

Max watched Alondra's hips as she leaned over to turn the lamp off. He hadn't seen a body like hers before. Maybe a model or in girlie magazines, but not in real life. Man.

"I don't want you to look at my eye. The bruising isn't totally gone yet."

He hadn't even noticed.

"You think I'm a hooker, Max?"

Alondra lying flat on her back, flicking cigarette ash into the glass ashtray sitting on her chest.

"Of course not."

Max turned over, moving onto his stomach. He couldn't reach her before she got up. There she was, standing naked, smoking her cigarette.

Max sat up, two pillows behind his back to prop him upright. He watched her standing, staring out of the window through the curtain, smoke curling against the window back into her face. Max could see her, standing there, thinking too much.

"What're you doing?"

Alondra blew smoke. "You do think I'm a hooker, don't you?"

Max shook his head but didn't say anything with it. He knew they shouldn't have done it, had sex, but now it was over and it was like they were transitioning back to real life, back to doing what they did every other day of their lives. He wasn't sure what he could say, or should say, to make her relax again.

Alondra came back to put her cigarette out, the ashtray on the nightstand on her side of the bed now. Max raised the bed sheet while she stood there, deciding, but he watched her turn and go into the bathroom. He knew she might be in there for a while. Max kicked back, hands behind the back of his head. He knew how to tell what people were thinking; he was good at it. But, he couldn't read her mind right now. Women.

The door opened sooner than Max expected. She came out and stood naked over the bed. "I wasn't just looking for a fuck if that's what you're thinking."

Max knew that.

She said, "Or did it for some kind of a thrill, like I slept with a cop or something like that."

It never crossed his mind.

He said, "Why are you mad?"

She came to the edge of the bed, staring down at him. "I'm not." Alondra was sitting on the bed now, legs tucked under her. "I just don't want you thinking I'm some kind of slut. A lot of guys I meet think that, I know it. You just seem different."

"You told me about your work," he said. "What you do and don't do. It's not a big deal."

Alondra leaned in close and started kissing his chest. Her face came up to his; starting to kiss and touch each other again. Max started having that feeling, ready to go again. Against his better judgment, maybe. Told himself, *Aw, what the hell,* and let it happen. She pulled her body back close to his and kissed him again and spoke to Max in a voice barely above a whisper. He had to lean in to hear her when she said, "But I was good, wasn't I?"

CHAPTER NINETEEN

The next morning, Max was in Tom Mako's office at the ATF building in downtown Miami, morning sun coming in through windows facing east. Tom was at his desk, getting back into the groove after a week's vacation. Max looked to a sign on the wall behind Tom that read: *"When you've got them by the balls, their hearts and minds will follow."*

Max thought it was John Wayne that said that, but there was no name behind it.

Max hadn't talked to his partner since he was in the hospital. So he said, "How was the trip?"

"Caught a few redfish. It's a different thing, shooting fish with a bow, you know?"

Max didn't, but he said, "You prefer the bonefishing?"

"Sitting back in a chair, drinking a beer and setting your hook on occasion? It's not a fair comparison, in my mind."

Max thought that did sound good right now. But then heard Tom's voice say, "You work out an assistance agreement yet?"

Max shook his head. "This is the first I've been in the office since it happened."

"That happens. It's hard to get around to all the paperwork, especially in your condition."

"I'm working this unofficially anyway. My original plan, to use him to catch the last of the guys on that Maryland warrant, then I would've done that. This, though. . . . This is for me."

"I know," Tom said. "It's hard for me to figure how that happened. Where you at on that?"

Max couldn't figure it out, either. Far as he knew, only a couple of guys at the office knew he was picking Darnell up.

He said, "I'm having a hard time nailing it down," starting to feel an easiness, the conversation coming natural talking to his partner.

Tom shrugged again. "That can happen, too. It's a bitch. What you got to go on?"

"The head guy's name is Raoul Garcia. Into drugs, who knows what else. I got that name from Darnell. Two guys that work for Garcia, Billy Poe and Lester Long . . . I watch their place when I'm not running around chasing other things. I got another guy in Dade County used to be a part of Darnell's old gang, apparently helped Darnell rob Garcia of some drugs three years back. I don't think they knew who they were taking from, though."

"What's that all about?"

"I was thinking about using this other guy to bait Raoul out in the open but I haven't talked to him yet. I'll let him cool his jets in the can for a bit."

Tom nodded, looking interested. "What'd you lock him up for?"

"Beating up his girlfriend for starters." Max waited for Tom to ask about that. He didn't, so Max said, "I get over there, the guy's closet is a fucking armory. Had a sniper rifle in there."

"You're kidding me." Tom took a sip of coffee out of a mug that had some writing on the side. *I can only please one person a day and today ain't your day (tomorrow ain't looking good either).* The guy liked his little sayings. "What's his name?"

"Alvin Wright," Max said. "Street name's Tweety."

"Sounds like a lot of coals in the fire. You need some help?"

"You'll be the first to get a call if I do."

Tom, shuffling papers on his desk, looked up at Max. "I'm

157

jumping on some kind of operation. Straight from the boss since you're on medical leave. Some guy running in money from Mexico to buy all kinds of U.S. military hardware supposedly being smuggled in from the Iraq War. Leftover now that we're out of there. Don't ask me how, I haven't been briefed yet. Supposed to be a sting, that's what the young guy running it said. A sting."

"They love saying that. Young guys dying for a big collar. I bet he gave it a name, too."

"Operation Prime Time."

"Guy sounds like he wants to be in rock 'n' roll, not government service."

"We were like that once."

Max shifted in his chair. "That was before my six-pack turned into a forty-ounce."

Tom got a phone call and Max watched him answering questions, not being able to say much, giving a lot of uh-huh's and yeah's then hanging up the receiver. "Operation Prime Time. The boss wants me to watch over the kid, be his mentor."

"Have fun."

Tom got up and hooked his sidearm on his belt. "The offer for help still stands, partner. You sound like you got your hands full."

"I know." Max got up and started for the door. "I can't wait to get back to work so I can rest."

It was ten in the morning by the time Max got to Darnell's. Darnell wasn't outside waiting this time, so he parked. Walking to the house, he could hear voices coming from inside. Not raised voices, but loud enough to where both people were making sure they were heard. Sounded like two women. One being LaKelle, the other Max couldn't place but it sounded older.

Max was at the back door. The women were in the kitchen

area near the back of the house. Max could hear them. He hesitated and finally knocked, but it was Darnell who answered.

Darnell opened the door and said, "About time you got here."

"Yesterday you told me I was too early."

"Yeah, but my momma wasn't here yesterday."

Max made a mental note to check first from now on. He let it go and heard Darnell say, "Jesus Almighty, they been going at it since she got here."

Max stepped inside and the voices stopped. It got quiet. Max said, "How you doing, Miss Delores?" Darnell's mom nodded and gave Max a smile, the kind of smile you get from a cute grandma.

The smile disappeared, Delores still looking at Max when she said, "I had to take a cab over here."

Darnell motioned for his momma to be quiet, not to start anything more . . . which got him nothing but a look from her. He was gone for a minute, leaving Max to make small talk with Delores about the weather. She wanted to talk about how the humidity made her ankles swell; LaKelle in the kitchen making noise emptying the dishwasher. Darnell came back with LaKeisha and that got his mom's attention.

Darnell put LaKeisha in her grandma's lap and was straight out the back door, not a word to LaKelle. Max followed him out and couldn't help but smile. "Having a rough morning?"

"Sh*iii*t."

"I thought working with you was bad enough. I bet living with you is probably no thrill either."

"Hey, man," Darnell had his eyebrows up. "I ain't done nothing wrong. LaKelle wants to go out for the day, do what she do for daily activities. I dunno what that is, but it's something. I tell her I'm going out with you, that I got some important business. I see we gonna have a problem so I call my mother. I'm trying to co-ord-i-nate."

159

"Yeah, well," Max said, "coordinate this . . . you and I are going to talk to Johnny Stanz. I got him at Alondra's hotel room."

Darnell looked at Max. Something going through his mind, taking a minute to put it together. "How'd you find him?"

"You think I don't check up on you? I found him at your girlfriend's. . . ."

Darnell looked over his shoulder.

"Don't worry," Max said. "LaKelle's still inside. Anyway, she doesn't want him there anymore. I had to get him somewhere."

"What about Alondra?"

"She's somewhere else."

Darnell let it go at that. "You know, I done talked to Johnny. I don't think he's going to want to see me again."

Voices started from inside again.

Max said, "You rather stay here, it's up to you."

Max heard Johnny Stanz through the door. Saying to someone in there with him, "Get dressed . . . I don't know, just get dressed . . . I'm sorry, baby, but you're gonna have to go."

Max and Darnell stared at each other in the hallway. Darnell shook his head. Must have disapproved at what he saw as Johnny's irresponsible behavior. The door opened and a blonde came out in clothes she had on the night before. She looked at the two of them and walked away, stopping down the hall to put her shoes on.

It looked like Johnny didn't have a problem making himself at home. Darnell kicked some clothes out of the way. Look at this place: a half-empty case of beer, imported, resting on the dresser, bottles from the case all over the place, a box of rubbers sticking out from under the bed. Darnell shook his head again, judging. He looked up at Johnny, caught him staring at Max like he was about to wet himself.

Max looked for a chair and pulled it next to the bed. He told

Johnny to sit down, the bed was fine. Johnny could see Max wasn't in a good mood and started to speak; wanted to apologize, the man so nice put him up in this nice room keeping him out of harm's way. That was before Max said, "I got a shit-all investigation here. You're running around, sticking your dick in whatever looks your way."

Darnell thought she was cute.

Max said, "I trusted you, but it looks like you thought about running on me, couldn't help yourself. You do that, I'm gonna be back where I started. That's my problem, what's yours?"

Johnny was caught off guard, but could give Max a few if he was thinking correctly. Maybe if they were sitting down and having a beer together. Instead, he looked across at the mop of blonde hair, broad shoulders, and elbows resting on big legs— the man looked like one of those people from Sweden—and had nothing to say.

"Look here," Max said, "you're going to sit here and answer my questions about Raoul Garcia, Billy Poe, anything else I can think of. We didn't get much of a chance to talk before, that wa my fault."

Johnny waited.

"Start," Max said.

Johnny began when they picked up Darnell. Billy left house without saying what they were going to do. He was told to wait; a little brick ranch number in Lake Park. Joh said he could take them there if they wanted.

Max paused but didn't say if he wanted to go or no said, "So you weren't there? Didn't know anything about

"No. I had no idea what was going on."

"You're telling me you weren't in one of those cars?"

Johnny shook his head. "Honest."

Max wasn't sure, this coming from a convict. "I car you to stay in for the night, keep your pants zipped

think I should believe you now?"

Max sat up in his chair, not looking like he was expecting an answer. Johnny thought that was a good sign. It was silent and Johnny looked at Darnell until he saw the ATF agent lean into his elbows again.

Max said, "You're at the house alone. What happened next?"

"It was like three hours before they came back. It was Billy, a buddy of his named Lester, a couple other guys I didn't know. I see they come back with a colored guy with something over his head. I don't know its Darnell at that point. They didn't tell me until later."

Johnny stopped for a second and Max jumped in. "Why you think they had you there? Especially if they didn't even take you with them?"

"I guess it's because I know Darnell. I guess they wanted to see if I could talk to him."

"About what?"

Darnell tensed up.

Johnny shrugged. "I never found out."

"When were you going to find out?"

Johnny told Max what his instructions were: get in the car and start driving. He was supposed to get a call, tell him where to go and what to do. That was it. He said, "But I let Darnell go before I ever got the call. I just wanted out."

"So you don't know where you were supposed to go or what was going to happen?"

Johnny shrugged.

"How about Raoul's place, could that have been it? You know where that is?"

Johnny shook his head. "Times I met him, it was always someplace public, like a parking lot or something like that. He's pretty careful about that."

It was giving Max a headache. "How long you know Raoul?"

He paused. "You run drugs for him, do some odd jobs?"

Johnny nodded. "That, set up meetings with people I know. That's about it, really."

Max took a moment to stare. "Yet he picks you for this."

It didn't sound like a question, but Johnny said, "I think it was because I know Darnell, I'm just guessing."

Max took a deep breath in. It sounded like bullshit, but he'd heard worse. "How'd they know where I would be?" He said, "I only told a couple people and they were on me like stink on shit. You hear anything about that?"

"Man, I didn't hear anything. I was so nervous, I was trying not to listen, you know?"

Max stared ahead, didn't say a word.

He got up and pulled Darnell aside. In a whisper, he said, "That sound about right to you?"

That was nice. Telling Darnell that he trusted his opinion on this.

Like they were partners.

Armando Hernandez asked one of the old Marielitos if they knew someone who wanted quick money. Who didn't? He said it needed to be somebody in jail. The Marielito asked which one. Armando said, "My information has this man at the Metro West Center."

Armando always liked the idea of killing somebody in jail. The guys in there were crazy. They were already locked up, some of them never getting out; what did they have to lose? They would do anything to prove their dedication. The Marielito on the other end of the line told him there was a friend in the Texas Syndicate that could get the job done. Armando knew the Texas Syndicate to be a prison gang but didn't know why they kept the name if they were as far away as Florida and they started in California, Folsom Prison.

The Marielito asked if it was okay for a Cardinal to do this, what the Texas Syndicate called a new recruit. Armando said that would be even better, he would be eager to please.

It was The Vulture coming out in him.

The Marielito said, "How much are you willing to pay?"

Raoul had given Armando the figure of fifteen thousand dollars. He said, "I'm authorized to give them five thousand dollars."

There was a silence before the Marielito said, "I take half. They can divide the remainder how they see fit." Another silence. "This is acceptable."

When he said the word "acceptable," it sounded to Armando like the Marielito was practicing his English.

The Vulture thanked him, then said, "You make twenty-five hundred dollars for making one phone call. You see how lucky you are to live in the USA?"

CHAPTER TWENTY

Lester came back from the fast-food joint with burgers and chocolate milkshakes. Had to go by himself because Billy didn't want to go out right now. But complaining because there was nothing to eat. Turning in the driveway, Lester saw envelopes sticking out of the mailbox. Tried to balance the shakes on his arm, leaving a hand free to carry the mail. Mostly junk, catalogs. What was Billy doing that he couldn't walk out and pick it up? Probably staring out the window while Lester did it.

Lester set the food down and sifted through the mail. Hoping for a government check; sometimes they came for the previous tenant and Billy figured out a way to deposit them in his account. A girl he knew at the bank. If she wasn't working that day, he had a buddy that worked at a check-cashing place in Hollywood Hills. They used to smoke weed together. He would do it.

Nope, no check. Lester took his burger and shake to the TV. Didn't look at Billy, but knew Billy was staring back. Thinking, why didn't you bring mine?

Billy made a face and gave Lester some noises to go along with it. Huffing and puffing to show Lester he was displeased. Billy stood over the counter looking at the mail. Lester would hear rustling, Billy digging into the paper bag from the burger place. Then chomping, Billy deciding to eat standing up. Lester leaned his body over and saw Billy, Jesus, stuffing the whole thing down his throat while browsing through an IKEA catalog.

That was for the previous tenant, too. Then slurping the chocolate shake, making that annoying sound trying to get every bit of it out of the cup. Driving Lester crazy.

"You ever get tired of sitting around?" Lester said.

Without looking up from the catalog of home office desks and portable closets that you had to put together yourself, Billy said, "I'm getting tired of eating this fast food, that's for sure. It's giving me indigestion."

What did that mean? He had seen Billy eat fast food—burgers, tacos, chicken—every day as long as they had known each other. Now the man was popping Rolaids like they were candy, chasing it with a swig of Pepto-Bismol.

Billy said, "Next time, go to the Pepper Pot," a Jamaican and Indian food joint near their house that he thought would make a difference in how he was feeling.

"It's the grease," Lester said. "I can try and cook something if you want." Trying to understand.

"What the hell you gonna cook? Something you saw on TV?"

Billy went back to reading his magazine, maybe trying to decide if a loveseat and chaise lounge modular sofa would look good in here. Lester had glanced through the catalogs before on occasion. Still, Billy hadn't answered his question and Lester could feel the air going out; their big plan going kaput.

Until Billy said, "We're still in business." Looking up now. "Soon as I hear from Raoul, we finish our plan, we'll be in the money."

Lester wondered what Raoul had to say that was so important if they were doing this on their own.

"When's that gonna be?"

"Two or three days at the most."

Lester said what he was thinking. "What you need to hear from Raoul?"

"Man has his way of finding out information. Information that could be helpful to us."

Lester shrugged. Okay. "What're we going to do until then?"

"That ATF man and the nigger shows up, we may have an opportunity to move ahead of schedule."

Lester figured Billy would know first, he'd be looking through the curtains.

"You look like you watch a lot of TV, so you can hang around." Billy was rounding the countertop that separated the kitchen from the living room, weekly circulars folded under his arm. "Soon as I finish up in the bathroom, I'm gonna take a nap. After that, I need to get out and see me a woman."

Eleven-thirty, Tweety finally got on the bench press. He had planned on getting to it earlier but was asked to play a pickup football game. No pads, both sides in prison whites so you had to know who the guy on your team was. Guys hitting hard because they could and the C.O.s let them. On offense, everyone wanted to be T.O. if they were young or Jerry Rice if they were older; on defense, they were whoever it was happened to be the big hitter in the game right now. Tweety heard a couple of Pittsburgh Steeler names. It lasted longer than he thought, the guards letting them play an extra half-hour before everyone had to file in a single-file line for noon chow.

He had, quick, done three sets with forty-pound dumbbells, wanting to get what he could for his biceps. Looking at them while he was doing it, thinking if he ever got that Darnell's skinny neck wrapped in one he would suck the life out of him. They were big enough to handle that white man, the ATF guy, too. He gets out of here, somebody's gonna pay.

Tweety sat on the bench press and ripped off a set. Ten reps at two-forty-five. He sat up, catching his breath, and watched a basketball game going on. A white guy going to the hoop got clotheslined. No foul, keep playing. Running up and down the court, no ball movement, everyone heaving up jumpers or driving the lane, trying to put on a show. Except the white guys, apparently. The ones who played football were bikers, with the size and balls to play the line, pancaking each other onto the ground then using their fists to keep their guy down. Basketball, the white guys were smaller, no bikers; young guys, newbies doing time for drugs, that called home every afternoon.

Tweety laid down for his second set, no spotter, concentrating on his motion when he felt a body straddling him. He started to say he had it, that he didn't need help with the weights, when he felt a sharp pain in his chest. He managed to replace the barbell and felt two more stabs, then slumped back, prone on the bench.

The young Latino guy backed away and looked around. He decided he had time to cut a gash across the man's thigh, he heard people bled out from there. That would be his calling card for after he was out of jail, a cut on the left thigh to let people know it was him.

He ran away, wondering if he was going to be a hero to his gang and what they were serving for lunch.

CHAPTER TWENTY-ONE

Max was looking at the little house in Lake Park. Looked a lot like Billy Poe's house, just stucco instead of siding. He pressed his face up to a window on the side of the house, into a hallway that ran to a kitchen. The kitchen separated from the living room by a little dining-L. He guessed there were bedrooms and bathrooms beyond that on the other side of the house.

Max called Johnny Stanz over to point out to him where things were happening: where he was when they brought Darnell in, where they kept him. There, that little bedroom in the back, the one they were just looking at through the window. What were you doing while this was going on? Nothing, sitting on the floor of the living room, listening to Billy's bullshit. For how long? Johnny shrugged.

Max sent Johnny back to the car. Some help. He kept looking around. Looking for something, anything, that he could use as a reason to get inside. Because that's what he wanted to do. Get inside the house and look around.

From the car, he heard Darnell say, "I could get inside if you want. I got a little feeler pick on me."

Max looked at him and shook his head. Glancing around to see if a neighbor was outside.

But if it was a kidnapping, what was the score? Just revenge? Was that what it was for LaRon, Darnell's cousin? No one was going to find out now.

Outside of street gangs, Max had never heard of a kidnapping for straight torture. Foreign countries, maybe, to make a point. But not here. So, maybe it was a P.R. thing for Raoul. Going back to his roots. Here, it was always money.

Max left the house in Lake Park feeling he was missing something.

Alondra spent her day along the South Beach art deco hotel district, on both Collins and Ocean Drive. Looking for prosperous young gentlemen on vacation, those she could pick out that weren't gay, but it was getting harder to tell. Handing out her *sensual massage* cards. Some were interested, some glanced at it and never changed their expression, one guy wanted to talk to her about the Lord Jesus Christ. The next guy after him said sorry, handed the card back to her right before his girlfriend walked out of the lobby of the Loews hotel on Collins; one guy said, yeah, and dropped it on the ground right in front of her.

Walking along the strip of hotels between the Loews and the Royal Palm, her feet were starting to hurt even though she wore flats on purpose today. What if she went by the Clark, relaxed for a bit in her room? That guy Max was putting up was still there, probably for a couple more days. She'd have to talk to Max, see how long a couple days would be.

She could go up and he'd want to make conversation. Oh, you're Max's girl, huh? Let her know what a cool guy he was and how he and Max were buddies. She'd see what a mess he's made of the place and he'd ask what she did for a living. She wouldn't answer and ask him how long he was going to be here. He might take it as a come-on.

Alondra sat at one of the sidewalk tables outside of the Essex House trying to take a load off. Watching people passing by on cell phones or staring at their iPods, looking down at her *sensual massage* card and thought, hell, she should change that to *massage specialist*. Place an ad in the *Herald* or *New Times*. She'd

have to call and see how much they were. That way it would
look more legitimate when she'd walk into the hotels and try to
leave them with the hostess at the door. Do you have a price
list? Maybe add *Serving South Beach for 5 years.* Make it sound
official. She knew some of the hostesses; they'd help her out. Of
course, some would touch it like it had anthrax on it and drop
it on their podium or straight in the trash. You couldn't work
with those people.

Or what if she went looking for that money LaRon told her
about. The money that him and Tweety took off a drug dealer a
couple years ago (Darnell might have had something to do with
it, too, she wasn't sure). What she did remember was LaRon
telling her that he could never spend it, it was too dangerous.
Then why take it in the first place? Well, once the guy, the drug
dealer, was dead or something similar, then it would be okay.
What was "something similar"? She assumed LaRon meant if
the guy was in jail, but he didn't say.

But LaRon was passed away now and Tweety, well, Tweety
was in jail and hopefully never coming out. Alondra thought
LaRon said the money was buried in Tweety's backyard, just
sitting there.

What was the harm in getting it out now?

She thought there could be some harm: she didn't know this
drug dealer, for one. If LaRon was so scared, maybe he had
reason to be. What if he had some way of knowing if she took
it? It was a long shot, but could happen. Second, what if Tweety
came out of prison looking for the money? He went in for beating her up but, really, how long would he stay in jail?

If she had somebody she could get the money with. Somebody
she could trust. Not use the person; she'd give some of it to
whoever it was. Maybe not half, but some. It would be more to
protect her just in case.

Relaxing back in the little wrought-iron chair, Alondra
wondered if Max was that person.

171

★ ★ ★ ★ ★

The minute Max heard the phone ring, he had a feeling.

It was Dan Remedios calling, Max was quiet listening to details of Tweety's stabbing. Dead before they got him to the infirmary. Multiple stab wounds; the one to the heart was what finished him off. Sliced the femoral artery in his leg for good measure. Max found a convenience store parking lot and pulled in, just through questioning Johnny Stanz at the Clark Hotel. He asked if they had any idea who did it.

"Not yet. We got a lockdown at Metro West right now, looking for contraband. We could shake something loose, but I can't give you a timeframe."

Max told Remedios, "Keep me informed, will you?" Knowing he would. "I appreciate it, Dan."

Max hung up thinking it could've been jailhouse B.S. Guys squaring off, making decisions that could mean somebody's life. Nobody wanting to back down.

He could think of one way to find out.

Max reached across the seat, opened the glove box, and felt around for the .38 Airweight he kept in there. Checked the magazine and handed it to Darnell in one motion.

Darnell said, "What's this?"

"I thought you wanted to work for the government?"

Look at him, trying to be a smart-aleck. Darnell felt the .38 in his hand and looked at Max. "Yeah, but you hand me a gun all of a sudden, it makes me curious."

Max backed out and started out of the parking lot. "We're going by Billy Poe's house, ask some questions. You're gonna come with me, all right?"

Asking, but really telling.

"You're going to be my backup." Max was concentrating on traffic, surprised Darnell was quiet long enough to let him get on the Julia Tuttle before he said, "I'll do the talking. You stand there. Long as you don't point that thing at me, we'll be fine."

Max knew it wasn't smart and had the idea of staking out Billy Poe's house one more time, see if anybody came or went; but, was getting fed up running around and wanted to find out if Billy knew anything about what happened to Tweety.

He saw it as he was approaching, driving towards trash scattered in the yard and the Buick on cinder blocks in the driveway of Billy's neighbor . . .

The orange Camaro popping out into the street and going in the opposite direction. One head in the car.

They drove east, going at a slow pace. Keeping the Camaro in sight but not getting too close. It was hard to lose in this traffic, the thing looked like a great big pumpkin in the middle of ordinary cars.

The Camaro turned onto Unity Boulevard, maybe heading for the interstate. He does that, they'd lose him. Max knew it and thought about cutting him off but wanted to give Billy a chance to take them to Raoul.

Darnell watched the Camaro speed up to make a green light and felt Max do the same, changing lanes and getting around a Camry to make it; Darnell's eyes wide as softballs going through the intersection. No telling where they were going, making circles for all they knew. He read Max's mind about pulling Billy over if it went on too long or they found that Billy was just going to get something to eat. That would ruin their element of surprise. He just hoped that Max didn't want to get into that high-speed chase shit, though. You could end up dead doing that. Or severely fucked up, end up on *World's Greatest Police Chases* on TBS at one o'clock in the morning.

But something happened because the Camaro started picking up speed on Unity. Max's gold Impala behind Billy must have become something more than a couple guys driving around, happening to be going in the same direction. It must've become an unmarked police car, a couple of guys driving around wanting to know where he was going.

The Camaro got smaller as Billy gunned it and made a left onto Northwest 22nd. Max hit the accelerator, but his Impala didn't have the horsepower to keep up. He made the same left and saw Billy make another right.

Max found the Camaro on North River Drive and watched it keep straight for about one hundred yards before Billy started weaving in and out of lanes again. Made a hard left turn at Northwest 31st, cutting a car off and nearly getting t-boned by a Chevy pickup.

Max was late getting to the intersection. Not able to move between traffic as easily as Billy but it didn't matter. Soon as he made the corner he saw it: the Camaro sitting outside a machine shop, smashed head-on into a trash bin.

Billy sat in the driver's seat, trying to wake up and remember what happened. Came to and realized, first, that he was still alive. Second, that fucking gold car hadn't caught up to him yet or else the ATF man would be yanking him out. Probably throw him out onto the pavement in front of all these people and make a scene.

He squeezed past the air bag and stood up; caught sight of his skid marks through people starting to crowd around him. Shit, big marks in the middle of the road before he jumped the curb. It must've been the car. It didn't handle as well as he was led to believe.

Billy didn't answer questions about whether he was okay. No time if he was going to get away before the gold car showed up.

He reached inside for his cell phone and some cash in the middle console. Left the car there and went to get laid.

Billy was gone by the time Max parked and he and Darnell got there. Darnell looked in the car while he heard Max talking to some of the machine shop guys. Asking where the driver went. A couple people said he started walking down the street before they lost sight of him.

Max pulled Darnell away from the car and they started walking that way, north on 30th. Max asked Darnell if he had his gun. Darnell said no. The only other thing Max could say was, "Keep your eyes open."

They looked in alleyways and business storefronts, stopping in a couple to ask if anyone had seen a man matching the description Max gave.

Ten minutes passed and Max had an idea. He'd have to make a decision quick: hang around here and get involved in the accident report or, with Billy gone, get back to the house and see about talking to Lester.

Gloria finally got to meet one of them, Lester; one of the guys she heard about and talked to Raoul about, but never met. When they came over, Raoul made her stay in the bedroom, man talk, but she managed to listen anyway.

They were in the living room: Raoul, this Lester, and Ramon, one of Raoul's lieutenants from their native Puerto Rico. Gloria thought the word *lieutenant* sounded old and Ramon looked young, maybe in his early twenties.

She heard Raoul questioning Lester when he came in. Asking where Billy was, the other one she heard about and didn't think much of. Lester shrugged and Gloria snickered, expecting as much. "How do you not know?" Raoul said and Lester said he wasn't a babysitter. That's what this Billy was, Gloria thought, a baby that needed watching.

Raoul said, "I've been calling him for an hour," and Lester

remembered Billy saying something about going to find a girl, but didn't mention anything about it.

In the silence, Raoul said, "Why are you so late?" and Lester said, fuck, he didn't know he was on call. If he would've looked out the window he'd know why, Lester had to take a cab over here. Billy hadn't left him with the keys for any of the vehicles.

That got Raoul asking questions Lester couldn't answer about his car, his new Camaro. Jesus, you could've sworn it was a custom-made Rolls the way he was going on.

Lester said, "What are we doing?" hoping to change the subject.

"Oh, now you're interested in working? First, you're not on call, now you're interested."

Lester had asked because he could see Ramon pulling out guns and bullets and putting them on the coffee table, getting ready.

Like he hadn't even asked a question, Raoul looked past Lester at Gloria and said, "We'll be back in one hour."

Driving away from the accident, Darnell had said, "You sure you just want to leave?"

Max was looking in his rearview mirror at cars starting to stop; traffic starting to back up in the other direction, a crowd starting to gather. He said, "What do you want to do there?"

"I dunno, there might have been clues in the car."

He had a point, but it made Max smile, Darnell playing amateur sleuth. Max said, "Maybe, but with Billy not around, I want to get back, see if we can get Lester at home by himself. He seems to be the easier of the two to talk to."

"You mean interrogate?"

If that's the way he wanted to put it.

CHAPTER TWENTY-TWO

On the way over, all Raoul wanted to know was, "Where is Billy?"

"I don't know," and Lester had to tell him that Billy talked about going to get a girl, that yes, he left in the Camaro. What else could he tell?

Raoul knew that would happen, Billy using his car to get girls. No man that grotesque could have a woman somewhere on his own without the material trappings of a fine automobile. He called Billy four times while they were on the road; each time he hung up telling himself to be patient, the man was practically a Neanderthal.

They got off the interstate—it was a quick on and off—and Raoul was telling them how they'd work it. They would walk in and be polite. Raoul would ask questions, Lester wouldn't open his mouth. As soon as Raoul found out where his drugs or his money was, start shooting. Telling Lester to point and squeeze if it had been some time since he handled a sidearm.

Lester looked around; shit, he couldn't figure out where they were. Somewhere in Liberty City. He had to say, "You wanna shoot some drug dealer that pissed you off, that's your business. I'm not doing this."

"Don't worry," Raoul said, "they're not expecting us. That's when you do it, catch them off guard."

"How many are *they?*"

Raoul ignored Lester and started giving directions to Ramon.

They were creeping down a street, Lester didn't catch which one, when Ramon cut the headlights. It was overcast out. In front of a little pink house that looked more like a shed than anything, Raoul turned to Ramon and said, "Leave the motor running."

The second the door opened, Lester expected to hear gunfire even though Raoul said they would talk first. A white guy answered the door, no shirt, skinny, dreadlocks. Lester could see he was surprised to see Raoul at his door, even through the thick marijuana smoke wafting outside.

Raoul brushed the smoke away from his face and said something to the guy. Lester was too nervous to hear and busy looking past the guy, intent on seeing how many others were in there, but did hear Raoul call the guy by name, Barry.

Raoul said they would talk, but it didn't last long.

Raoul: You thought I forgot about you, didn't you?

Barry: What are you talking about?

Raoul: You still owe me ten thousand dollars.

Barry: I thought we settled that.

Raoul: We didn't. We are now.

There was a silence, Barry, the white guy, searching for words while Raoul raised a .45 and fired. Barry's body, skin and bones, jumped backwards, legs kicking out and hair flying.

Lester followed through a kitchen—scales and adding machines on the table—down a hallway to the bathroom where Raoul lifted the lid on a toilet tank and took out a wad of bills wrapped in a plastic bag. He said, "Barry was always so predictable," and told Lester to count it.

Lester did that while he heard shuffling through the rest of the house, stopping at first in case there were other people, then assuming it was Raoul looking everywhere he could for other money.

178

When the noise was over, Raoul came back to the bathroom. All he wanted to know was, "How much is there?"

"Thirty-two hundred, all hundreds."

That was it.

Lester followed Raoul back through the kitchen, man, wanting to get out of there *right now*. On their way out, Raoul fired again and Barry's body jumped.

Raoul paused, so Lester did too, waiting to see.

Lester, nervous with a plastic bag of money in his hand, said, "Is he dead?"

Raoul fired a third time. Lester could almost see the bullet going in. He had never been this close.

Raoul looked for two more seconds and said, "He is now."

When they got back, Raoul took some bills for himself and told Lester to keep the rest; that there wasn't enough there for him to wipe his ass with and some other smart comment that Lester couldn't make out.

"What is this?" Lester said. "Money for me to buy groceries?"

Raoul turned to Ramon, who was on his way out the door for a cigarette, and said, "Do you believe this?"

Lester wasn't sure Ramon understood, that it might have been too much English for him.

Ramon answered in Spanish, but Raoul didn't say anything back. He said to Lester, "I give you, by your standards, a large gratuity and this is the thanks I get?"

"Gratuity?" Lester said, looking down at the bag in his hand now. "You mean like a tip?"

"What do you think a gratuity is?"

The patio door closed behind them, Ramon continuing outside while Raoul and Lester spoke.

Lester stretched out his arm, the bag in his hand at the end of it. "You can keep it," he said, "I don't want it."

Raoul put his hand on Lester's and guided it back to his chest, saying, "It's for you, you keep it. Consider it a gift."

Lester shook his head.

Raoul said, "Consider it a test of loyalty, then." Tests were one thing Raoul liked. "You will keep it." Raoul's voice was a little stronger that time. He said, "There should be twenty-eight hundred dollars of my money left. If any of it is spent foolishly . . . well, remember today."

Lester wasn't sure what that meant. What was foolish spending? Sometimes, the man said things that didn't make sense. Either way, he didn't really see the loyalty test part of it.

Alondra got back to her mother's and was tired. The smell of food coming from the kitchen kept her up for a while, but she was dozing off before long.

She would wake up to images of Tweety standing over her, his arms flailing at her; at first like he just wanted to scare her. He did a good job. After one of them connected, he must've figured, why not? She remembered asking him to stop, calling him by name, Alvin. That must've pissed him off more. Alondra remembered him saying something right after that, but she wasn't sure what it was. She was too busy trying to protect herself.

Now, walking around pretending like she was interested in giving massages to tourists with expectations. She knew some girls—if they decided to make it a sexual encounter—that could make a couple thousand a day. Fifty or sixty thousand a year working part-time, but that didn't cover rent on a decent place in South Florida. That just wasn't her thing. Her mom would always say, "If you don't like that, try something else," with her mom voice, showing genuine concern. Like it was that easy. If she had done better in school or tried harder or studied more, m*aaa*ybe. She knew it was her fault, nobody else's, and she would have to get over it.

A half million dollars would help anybody get over anything. She would fall asleep and wake up—on and off to smells coming from the kitchen—remembering Tweety and LaRon and Darnell and all the trouble that money caused.

Lester was home now, on the sofa, high on Billy's weed. Some he found in a blue duffel bag in the back of the closet. Billy didn't know Lester knew it was there. Billy would take the bag out when he got back, to check. He might raise a fuss about it but screw him. He's the one who took off. Right now, Lester was more worried about what Rachael Ray was doing, showing you what kind of dinner you could make in half an hour.

He had an idea that he could find something to cook for him and Billy. If the guy was going to complain about greasy fast food. Look at Rachael, she made it look easy.

Like it was ESP, Lester saw a car pulling up in the driveway. It didn't look orange, the color not bursting through the sheer curtains hanging over the living room windows. Lester got up, moving like he was in slow motion.

He recognized the gold car. But, it couldn't be, could it?

It had to be the weed talking.

Chapter Twenty-Three

Max sat talking to Lester in the living room. Darnell hung back, wanting to listen without looking obvious. He would pace from the dining-L to the living room and back again. Then back again, glancing at the big screen TV, and swung around when he heard Max say to Lester, "Are you high?"

Lester looked up from the sofa. He said to Max, "Hey man, I wasn't really expecting visitors," and thought about offering a hit to Max. Could be asking for trouble but, shit, he knew—for a fact—that some of those law enforcement types toked every once in a while. Assholes knew they could do it and get away with it. A guy like him does it, they run him in.

Lester wondered if that's what this was.

Max started with the same questions Darnell heard him ask Johnny Stanz not two hours ago. How do you know Raoul? How long have you been working for him? Things like that.

Max got into the day of the wreck, calling it the "incident." Just like Darnell did. He knew Lester was there and didn't ask him if he was. Max said, "How did Raoul know where to find me?"

Lester shrugged and mumbled to himself.

"I didn't catch that."

Lester said, "I don't know anything about that. They called me and I showed up," and watched Max stare ahead in silence. "They told me where to go, what to do, and I did it."

"They told you to point a weapon at a federal officer? You

were in the Camaro, weren't you?"

Lester didn't answer *that* but did say, "I didn't know you were a fed." He shrugged. "He didn't tell me that. As far as I knew, you were somebody like me." Then, subdued, "We were after him," pointing to Darnell.

Max kept asking himself the same question: Why?

That could wait. Instead, he asked Lester, "How much you get paid?" Not that it mattered, but he was interested.

Lester blew out of his mouth. It took a minute for him to answer, Les taking his time to lean back into the sofa and stare down at his hands. In a soft voice, he said, "Hadn't been paid yet."

Maybe it was interesting after all.

Max shook his head. "Looks like you been fucked, Les. Real good, right up the ass."

"Why's that?"

"Attempted murder on a federal officer." Max hated to use that word again, but liked the sound of it to make his point. "I can't seem to get hold of Billy or Raoul. You're left holding your dick in your hand, my man."

He could see Lester thinking. The wheels turning, imagining the rest of his life in prison. Wondering if it would actually be him holding his dick or if it would be somebody else.

Lester popped up, a friendly look on his face. He said, "Oh, I know where you can find Raoul. It's not a problem."

Like they were old buddies now.

"He lives off Tamiami Trail. Yeah, we went south off the Dolphin Expressway, at the LeJeune Road exit. I remember passing the dog track on Flagler, you know the one?" Lester didn't wait for Max to answer before he said, "You turn right onto Tamiami and it's on the second street on the right. Second Street, I believe it's called too. You gotta go down five blocks, hang a right onto 31st. It's the second one on the right."

Max was following the directions in his head, knowing they were close today, sort of near where Billy Poe crashed. He stood up and said, "Get dressed."

"For what?"

"You're gonna take us to Raoul's."

Lester shook his head. "Unh-unh. Bad enough I'm talking to you now. I'm high, I let my guard down, and you took advantage of me in a moment of weakness. I'm staying right here."

Max didn't want to get into it, waste time arguing with a stoner. He had the directions straight in his head and thought about taking Lester into some kind of custody. Alondra's place was already taken. He couldn't imagine LaKelle taking kindly to Darnell bringing a stranger home. What could he do, stick him with the child molesters under the Julia Tuttle bridge?

"What are you going to do?"

"I told you. I'm staying right here."

Max offered protective custody anyway.

"Nope," Lester said. He got up off the sofa and found himself looking through the front window curtains. "No one's seen you, so you were never here. I never saw you, you never saw me. You find Raoul, you did it on your own. You're a fed, you have your ways."

Max thought the high might be wearing off, Lester sounding lucid and doing his best to make sense. He offered his card. A second one in case Lester lost the first.

"I don't want that." Lester held his arm away from Max. "Somebody happens to see that, I'm dead for sure. He looks dirty, but Billy likes to do laundry. He might go through my pockets before putting my pants in the wash, looking for money."

He waited.

"You want to stay here, that's up to you. Call the office if you need me, we're in the book. If Raoul's place doesn't check out, we'll be back." Max turned to Darnell and headed for the door. "I just hope we get to you before Raoul does."

Lester watched from the window, Max and Darnell getting into their Chevy car, getting ready to leave. The car looked too small for a big guy like Max.

If Billy knew they were here . . . Lester was thinking. He'd have a fit. Their big moneymaking scheme—the kidnap and ransom of Darnell Sims—just walked in and out of here without so much as breaking a sweat. The way Lester saw it, it wasn't his fault. He'd just been through a traumatic event. Killing random people and rifling through their house for money wasn't something he cared for. He needed to relax, calm down. That was another thing, Billy's weed, that he would be pissed about. He could lie about the Darnell thing. It didn't even have to come up. The weed would take some explaining, that he was cleaning up and ran across it.

Where was Billy anyway? Fuck him. He was off getting some while Lester got stuck watching some guy's nerves jumping from multiple gunshot wounds. Lucky he wasn't running for his life right now, they were in that house so long.

What if Billy found out he told them where Raoul lives? Crooked government man, he took advantage of him on that one. Asking him important questions like that while he was stoned, that wasn't right. What if they apprehended Raoul, then what? Who would pay when they kidnapped Darnell?

Lester started to get nervous, then relaxed, thinking, *What if they took Darnell and asked the government to pay?* Did they do that? Shit, maybe he should've taken Max's card. No, Max said to call the office if he needed. That sent Lester to the kitchen looking through drawers for a phone book.

We're in the book.

Lester would have to remember that.

★ ★ ★ ★ ★

Raoul said he had to go out for a while, no further explanation, so Gloria made her and Ramon vodka tonics and sat down in front of the TV. After a few minutes, Ramon said, "I wouldn't mind sitting outside. You wanna sit outside?"

"I could use some sun."

Ramon didn't think so, but watched Gloria strip off shorts and her t-shirt, a string bikini underneath. She pulled a lounge chair over and angled it to where she thought Ramon would sit at the outdoor table. Ramon watched her turn over to lie on her stomach and looked around for tanning lotion, but didn't see any.

Gloria said, "I need to get rid of my tan lines."

Ramon was noticing them, white diamond shapes on her butt cheeks showing today, which meant Gloria normally had a full bikini bottom on when she sunbathed. But it was different today.

Ramon wondered why.

She said, "You know where he's going?"

Ramon shrugged. "You know as much as I do."

Gloria was propped up on her elbows, able to take a drink. She said, "Could be to meet a woman for all I know."

Ramon thought maybe she was trying to get answers out of him. He knew Raoul slept around, so what, but didn't say anything. It wasn't a big deal but the last thing he wanted was to get started on that.

So it surprised him when she said, "It doesn't bother me anyway."

"Really?"

Everything he knew about Latin women, man, the one thing you don't do is step out on them.

"It's not like we're living together anyway. He drops in. He might stay a few days, but I know he does the same thing with other girls." She said, "It's sort of a version of Arafat, except his

186

version is *not too many* nights in the same place," and could see it went over Ramon's head; that the guy was too young for the reference.

She looked at Ramon's glass, just ice left in the bottom, and said, "Let me get you another one."

He liked it, the way she looked right at him saying it instead of at the glass. Ramon watched Gloria pick it up off the low wrought-iron table, bending over further than she had to—and making a show doing it—but that was for his benefit, he could tell.

She went inside and he waited, wondering what an Arafat was. It wasn't too long before Gloria was back and held the glass at his eye level, her hips, waiting for Ramon to take it. When he did, she said, "How long have you been working for Raoul?" but knew the answer.

He said, "Since I came here," meaning the United States, not just Florida. Ramon had to stop and think about it. "Almost eight years now."

"You did some odd jobs for him when you were a child, right? Before all of you came here."

That surprised him, how she knew this. Ramon took a sip from his second vodka tonic, just right.

Gloria said, "I hear things. Raoul doesn't think I do, but I do. Like that guy Lester, the one you met today . . . Raoul's got a big deal going on with him and another guy. His name's Billy. They were here yesterday. I'm not sure what it is yet, but it's something."

Ramon was wondering where she was going with this. "Does he realize you know all of this, his personal information?"

That shut her up.

For a minute, until she said, "I'm just worried and I've told Raoul that. Those guys are fuckups. The one, Billy, he breathes heavy through his mouth and always has dirt under his fingernails. You can't trust unhygienic people."

"Did he ever talk about using someone else?"

Gloria shook her head.

And Ramon started to think; think about what kind of money might be involved in this "big deal." He wondered if Gloria could be more specific, but didn't say anything.

She said, "You have the time?"

Ramon glanced at his watch and told her.

She said, "He'll be back soon," throwing her head to the side, wiping hair out of her face. "You think you're up for a quick fuck?"

CHAPTER TWENTY-FOUR

Billy had himself a whore in Miami Lakes so it wasn't too far from his accident. At least he wrecked on his way, not going in the opposite direction so he'd have to double back and pass the accident scene.

He let himself in the front door with a key he had that he put on Raoul's key ring for the Camaro. He'd planned on taking it off when he gave the car back, but now what?

First thing Billy did when he walked in was ask if Simone could fix him something to eat. Told her that his stomach had been acting up from all the fast food lately. Simone microwaved him a TV dinner and went into her room. Billy figured she was in there for the night, thinking Simone wasn't working this evening, and sat down to find a ball game on the tube. Billy had a thought that he might be here for a few days, so he went into Simone's room and asked her if she wanted to fuck. Show her that he wasn't here for a free meal, that he was an understanding guy.

After that, it was a different woman that appeared in front of Billy. See? Show a woman how nice you could be, realize that she has needs too. It was no big deal. Now, Simone was in a g-string doing her go-go numbers, topless. He was following her butt, hips moving side to side while she danced over him on the bed. She wasn't too bad looking for a dancer, a word Billy knew meant hooker most of the time. Skinny arms, straight limp hair, some of her teeth starting to fall out from the drugs. Track marks between her toes so they wouldn't show up on stage in her bare arms. Right there, he saw some as she started moving up on him, rubbing her beaver in his face as if she was dancing. Like he figured, she wasn't working this evening. He guessed she was dancing to keep in practice. Simone was nice enough to let Billy smoke chips from her rock of crack cocaine. Cut a hole in a beer can and used a straw when she realized she had misplaced her bong.

"God, I love this," she said. Billy was hoping she meant his dong but they were past that now. She had to mean the crack. Billy heard Simone say something like doing crack was like coming into the world for the first time. How could she know what that was like?

"You staying a while, baby?" Simone said it at the same time she put the beer can on her night stand. What did she mean? He told her he might be here a few days. Right before they went to bed.

Billy rolled over, his body jumping between coughs. Not as young as he thought he was. Problem was, no sooner was he up than he was coming down again. He hated the way you did that on crack, that's why he preferred marijuana. You could at least stay chilled out for a while.

The crash landing got him thinking about Raoul's car. The man was going to have a fit. Billy felt he had to explain it in a way that wouldn't get the man upset. That was the key. Billy had his head on the pillow, turning on his back to see Simone lying there. He wondered if Simone was her real name or one she used on stage. Maybe she didn't bother to tell him her real one when they first met and he's been calling her that all this time? That would be mean. On her part, not his. She caught him staring at her titties. They were big ones.

"They're real." She was looking at him right in the face.

"I figured that much." Enough light to see little blue veins, something he didn't think you would see on fake ones. "You ever think about a boob job?"

Now she was staring at them. "Never. I like them natural, don't you?"

He sure did.

Billy tried to remember what he was thinking about.

Oh, yeah. Raoul.

Billy got out of bed, didn't say a word, and went out into the living room. Dug around in his pants pockets for his phone and went out onto Simone's patio.

What a shitty view. A fucking salvage yard across the street. Workers must line up when she lays out. Billy saw her tan lines, some shading on her chest too. Means she takes her top off sometimes, lets them get some sun. He could imagine nothing getting done at that time. Whatever. Okay, so, Raoul. Yeah, he'd be pissed but so what? Him and Lester were about to do their own thing, what did they care about Raoul's car?

Still, it would've been nice to let Raoul do his thing about finding the colored guy, Darnell. But they were bound to come back by the house again. That could take care of that. From there, Raoul'd have to be paying *them*. He could see the man trying to haggle with him over the cost of the car, though. Try to take seventy thou off the top, something like that.

Okay, break it to him, try to be nice about it. Hell, it was the ATF man's fault anyway for following him. He had to know something like this would happen.

He decided to leave that part out.

Something must've happened because Billy's phone rang just then. He looked down at Raoul's number. It got Billy jumpy and he said, "You ain't gonna believe what happened," before Raoul had a chance to talk.

"Tell me."

Billy said, "Somebody wrecked your car."

★ ★ ★ ★ ★

Max and Darnell followed Lester's directions right to a hacienda-style house on 31st. Only difference was, Max believed it was quicker to zip back down North River Drive, take Tamiami Trail under the Dolphin Expressway and find his way from there.

Either way, they were watching a dark blue Hummer in the driveway. Headlights on, they could see the shadow of somebody's head behind the wheel. Looking like he was waiting.

Darnell was speaking to himself when he said, "What's going on here?"

It surprised him when Max pointed to the glove box and said, "There's binoculars in there. Grab them and gimme the tag number."

Shit yeah, something to do. Max finally seeing his potential for law enforcement work. He read off the plate number to Max. The guy was out of the truck by now. They could see him as a young guy, almost like a kid except for that bulge under a suit jacket. The door to the house opened for a moment and they saw a woman's head poking out. It closed again. The guy stood there until a man came out.

Max said, "Thanks," into his phone, then said to Darnell. "That vehicle belongs to somebody named Ramon Diaz. I never heard of him, but he's got some priors."

Darnell didn't think that meant too much. He had some priors and look at him.

Max took the binoculars from Darnell. He said, "That might be Raoul," staring at the man coming out of the house. Couldn't tell much in the shadows of a porch light without his night vision glasses. Passed them back to Darnell and said, "You recognize him?"

Darnell had them on the second guy when he shook his head. Older than the driver, he could tell that much; a little thicker around the mid-section, but not what he would call fat. Maaaybe a little chubby. He said, "I never saw the guy. We took our stuff from one of his runners, just we didn't know it at the time."

The second guy, the chubby one, was standing in the doorway of the house. Talking to the woman inside until she poked her head out. She was closing the door as he walked towards the Hummer, but not closing it all the way until the Hummer backed out onto the street. Going east on 31st, away from Max and Darnell.

Max put the Impala in drive. "I'm curious to see where he's off to."

They followed the Hummer back to Tamiami Trail, where it took a left and headed west on Flagler. Turned north on Le-Jeune, over the river and onto Okeechobee Road. Off that until they ended up at an empty parking lot in Mango Hill.

It was quiet until Darnell said, "Where the fuck are we?"

"Goodlet Park is somewhere around here," Max said. He pulled off and looked around, no cars behind them. He pulled ahead and parked off the street. "Other than that, we're in no man's land. I hope he didn't make us."

They waited in the silence for a minute before headlights showed up behind them. Getting bigger in the rearview mirror until it turned off, heading towards the Hummer.

"Something's going down." Max reached under his seat for a nine-millimeter and told Darnell to be ready.

"The fuck you mean, 'be ready'?"

"Don't freak out, just follow my lead."

Don't freak out? Okay, sure. "What you gonna do? Walk over there and arrest somebody?"

Max shook his head. His gaze on the Hummer a block away from them, he said, "I wanna see what's going on. I'll bet it's dope or some shit like that." He would've preferred it was guns, but wasn't picky. "You mentioned stealing from one of Raoul's runners before. It wasn't some setup like this, was it?"

"This?" Darnell shook his head. "No, it wasn't like this. This scare the shit outta me. No, we caught the guy at a stop light and rushed him."

"How'd you know what he had with him?"

Darnell shrugged. "That was LaRon's deal. He called me, I was in the middle of fucking. He said he needed another man, I showed up." He turned to look across the street and pointed.

Two guys got out of the second vehicle, a Land Rover, and walked towards the rear of the Hummer, which was facing them. The guy driving the Hummer walked that way, too. Max and Darnell could see the Hummer driver hold his jacket open in the Land Rover's headlights.

"You see that?" Darnell said. "He just showed him a gun."

Max had his binoculars out again, trying to make something out. "He's just setting a boundary, making sure everybody stays cool."

"You think those others have 'em too?"

"I'd bet on it." Max brought the binoculars down, they were doing more harm than good. His night vision glasses were probably in the trunk, back there with all the rest of his stuff. He said, "Nobody wants trouble, don't worry. They just want to make sure the other guy knows it."

It was over quick. A duffel bag exchanged for what looked like an attaché case. Yep, drugs for money. Max was sure of it. Then there was standing around for a moment. Max was guessing that they were telling each other how good it was to do business together.

What happened next was strange. The Land Rover sped off, but the Hummer with Raoul in it stayed there, parked with its lights on and the engine running.

Raoul said to Ramon, "You see that car over there? It's been there since we got here, the same time as us. I first noticed it when we were on Flagler."

Ramon looked in his rearview mirror, a gold car back there. Uh-huh. The old man could be sharp.

"You think they're cops?"

Hmm, more than that. That fucking government man and his black sidekick. No doubt about that. Billy wrecks his car and now this? Some fucking coincidence. He told Ramon to stay here while he made a phone call, get rid of Billy forever. There, it was done.

Ramon said, "What do you want to do?"

Raoul thought about it and said, "Drive back the way we came. I'll tell you where to go from there." He had a thought to stop in a self-service storage unit off Unity Boulevard where he kept some guns.

See what happens.

Darnell said, "Somebody's getting out."

Max could see that, down the skinny path of concrete between rows of storage lockers, the Hummer parked in the middle. They had left Max's car at the road and hopped the fence; surprised there was no razor wire on top, people keeping property valuable to them in here. Max had a feeling the guys in the Hummer knew he and Darnell were here. What they did was stand by the SUV, baiting Max; the young guy, Ramon, sliding one of the storage locker doors open. Waiting for them. Fifty yards away.

"Don't move," Max said to Darnell. "Don't do anything unless I do it first."

They waited, heard noises coming from the direction of the Hummer. The storage locker doors closing. Silence after that.

Then a quick burst from an automatic weapon and Max ducked his head behind the storage unit row and pulled Darnell back.

Max brought out his nine-millimeter and fired off two quick rounds with his left hand. Another burst of automatic gunfire from the Hummer. Shit. Max moved across the space between rows of storage units after it was over. Hoping to get a better angle with his right hand.

He said to Darnell, "See what you can do, just point and squeeze."

Darnell said okay, he'd try. He looked at the gun in his hand, one of Max's leftovers. He wasn't sure what kind it was, but it looked like a shitty little gun.

Max peered around the corner and squeezed off a round. Looking straight into a fucking darkness, he couldn't see a thing. More gunfire coming from that direction and Darnell getting off some shots.

The Hummer's engine roared and Max saw it coming straight for them. He yelled for Darnell to get down, quick, and fired off a round as the Hummer sped past them. Max got on one knee and heard glass shatter, knowing he got something. Maybe Raoul was hit, maybe not. He heard return fire as the Hummer moved past them; had to be going fifty by the time it hit the chain link fence and busted through. Disappearing into the night after that.

Max got up and shook the cobwebs out, looking across the concrete pathway to see if Darnell was still alive.

As they were speeding away—clear of the scene, the storage complex in the distance through the Hummer's rear glass— Raoul said, "That was the ATF agent and the black one. Did you see that?"

Ramon did. He nodded, but wasn't entirely sure what Raoul was talking about. Raoul turned to face forward, slapping

Ramon on the back and telling him what a good job he did under that pressure; telling Ramon what a valued asset he was.

Ramon said, "How do you think they ended up on us?"

"They followed us."

That was obvious. Ramon tried another way, maybe his English wasn't so great. He said, "Yes," sounding understanding, "but how did they know to follow us?"

Raoul stared, squinting at him. "What do you mean?"

"They found us somehow. Who knows how long they've been watching us. We need to figure out how they knew."

"So it doesn't jeopardize my future plans."

Again, Ramon wasn't entirely sure what Raoul was talking about but he wanted to know more.

He said, "There are only so many answers."

Raoul kept squinting. "What do you think they are?"

"Well," Ramon said, making rights and lefts in no particular direction, "there are only so many people that would know to communicate information to the ATF man."

"That's exactly what I was thinking," Raoul said. "It's like you have a gift."

"What the hell just happened?"

Darnell had his head down, rubbing his skull, looking over his body to make sure all the parts were still there.

"You okay?" Max said it watching Raoul's Hummer moving down the road. Waiting for them to double back.

Darnell nodded as Max looked over to him.

Max took a walk down the aisle of storage lockers, people's personal belongings on the other side of the doors. Some of them bigger than others, you could store some spare furniture in those. He got out a small flashlight attached to his key chain. Except this one, N35. One of the big ones, but Max bet there weren't end tables or bedroom sets in it.

Darnell walked up to him and said, "This is it?"

"I believe so. I'd love to see what's in there."

"You an officer of the federal government. Bust the damn lock and look inside."

Yeah, Max thought about that too. But he was here with a civilian. Starting to think of Darnell in those terms, a civilian. Not *convict* or *felon* anymore. Plus, this wasn't an official investigation. He could get around that if he wanted to, but it was messy.

They could ride around and come back. See if Metro P.D. showed up responding to shots fired. He could call later, talk to somebody about what they found inside.

Chapter Twenty-Five

Heavyset.

Bald except on the sides. A goatee.

Dresses like a lumberjack.

A look on his face like he had to take out his driver's license to tell you his name.

That's how Raoul described Billy Poe to The Vulture.

The Vulture was sleeping when Raoul called, about ten o'clock. It woke him up, Raoul's incessant rambling about Billy Poe. How dumb he was; how dumb Raoul was for trusting him, that you couldn't do that anymore, be kind-hearted enough to give someone an opportunity. In his sleep, The Vulture thought Raoul said something about Billy and his car, a new Camaro.

The Vulture went to the address he was given looking for a lumberjack. Except the man he could see through open windows didn't look like that. This man was thin. Not much hair, but not bald. He wasn't sure about the look on the man's face, he was watching TV. Everyone looked the same watching TV.

The Vulture put his latex gloves on and walked around the side of the house. There was a chain link fence with a gate that he opened softly, waiting for creaking as he did it. He stopped to wait again, this time for a dog or neighbors' lights to come on.

There was nothing. The Vulture found the back patio door that Raoul said was there. He had an angle to see what this man was watching. A cooking program, a white man telling you how to make Salvadoran *pupusa*. He watched the skinny man put a cigarette out and disappear into a hallway and tried one of the back patio doors. It opened in his hand and The Vulture had to quick reach for his gun, a .22. What he brought in case of a surprise.

He preferred to do it quietly. He liked the word *intimately*. It was more personal that way.

There was the sound of a toilet flushing and he could see this man coming back into the living room to watch more cooking programs.

The Vulture thought he could fit into the space between the sofa and the wall. Look at that, even for his age, he was thin enough and flexible enough to crouch down for a few moments. Back there, he felt the man fall back into sofa and get himself comfortable.

How should he do it? He could shoot straight through the sofa, a stained, rent-to-own model with upholstery tearing with its age. He could tell the man was sitting upright, not lying down. But the gun was no fun and loud. It would be difficult to turn his body and bring his knife, a Smith & Wesson SW960 with a 440c six-inch steel blade, down in a stabbing motion. The kind of thing that earned him his nickname.

What The Vulture did was rise up and pull his knife across this man's throat, right above the Adam's apple. There was some kicking, this man's eyes moving up while he clutched at his throat.

You want to look at me? The Vulture stared back and put the point of the blade against the man's chest, right where the heart is, and shoved it in. The man stopped moving. The Vulture moved to the front window, closed the curtains, and stood listening for sounds, voices, general activity. No light coming on down the street. There was nothing.

He tilted this man on his side, touching places where there

was no blood, and reached for a wallet. He was curious.

The driver's license told him this man was Lester Long. That was a funny name, The Vulture couldn't remember ever killing someone with such a funny name. He would have to ask Raoul who this man was. This was the address given to him. He wondered if he would have a difficult time collecting for this. He could say it was dark, Lester Long jumped out from a hiding place. You don't have time to ask for somebody's identification in that situation. Yes, that would work.

Now his mind was elsewhere and he began looking around this house, a dump, until he came to a utility closet. Inside was a yellow slicker suit, both the jacket and pants. He put it on and decided Lester Long didn't look quite right. He would need more stab wounds.

The Vulture knelt on Lester and got started. He had a reputation to uphold.

Billy Poe sat in the living room of Simone's house drinking beer out of an aluminum can. He preferred bottles, longnecks if he had his way, but cans was all the woman had. Jesus, the woman used her empties in the event she misplaced her bong, how could Billy expect to find bottles here?

She kept asking what he went out on the balcony for. To use the phone. Who were you calling? My boss. What's his name? It's Raoul, but mind your fucking business from now on.

Billy waited for the next question, this woman didn't seem to get the hint, but Simone said, "I used to date a guy named Raoul . . . before he got sent to Raiford."

He didn't want to get into it, there were a lot of correctional institutions in Raiford. FSP, where Ted Bundy was executed . . . the West Unit, others. She might not know which one.

But he was curious about one thing. "For what?"

"He killed a guy. The guy was mouthing off, trying to start

something in the parking lot of some club. The guy pulls out a knife, a little switchblade. They roll around on the ground, Raoul gets cut across his arm. He gets the knife away, starts stabbing the guy, one goes into his heart. Raoul says he meant to stab him in the stomach but the guy jerked at the last minute. Sounds to me like it could happen."

"I guess it didn't sound like that to a jury, huh?" Billy said. "Did he get life?"

Simone shrugged.

"You didn't talk to him after that?"

"Not after his arraignment."

"Never went to see him?"

Simone shook her head.

It got Billy thinking. "How old's your Raoul?"

Simone stopped like she was thinking about it. "He'd be about my age, maybe a year younger."

Okay, different Raoul.

Simone moved closer to Billy, on all fours crawling towards him with a smile on her face. "Now, we're together. You don't have anything to worry about, baby." She made a space for herself and cuddled under his arm. "This is where I wanna be."

That was nice of her, really. Only thing, he had to get moving. Set his plan in motion for the abduction of Darnell, the nigger hostage. There was money to be made. Shit, he didn't have a car. That was a whole other problem.

Billy started to run his fingers through Simone's hair, pet her head a little, and he could see her getting comfortable. He said, "I know, baby. You don't have to think about him anymore . . ."

"Or anybody else. I told you, we're together now."

"That's right. You're mine now."

He could hear her making noises, little sleepy noises, like she was starting to drift off. Her little snores would be coming next.

He had to hurry up.

Billy passed a hand through Simone's hair again, then ran it down the side of her torso while she moved in closer, about to fall asleep.

He said in a whisper, "Baby, where your keys at?"

All Raoul wanted to talk about were dead people.

How did it go with Billy Poe? He called Billy a cocksucking motherfucker with a hint of his P.R. accent.

The Vulture said, "I was hoping you would call me about that."

Raoul stopped. A *Yes, he's dead* was good. *I was hoping you would call me about that* meant something went wrong.

"The man I killed did not match the description I was given."

Raoul said, "What did he look like?" and waited.

"This one was thin and with hair. Besides that, there was nothing distinguishable about him. I confiscated his ID. His name is Lester Long. You know this man?"

"Yes, I know him. You're certain he's dead?"

"Quite certain."

"And you left nothing behind that could identify you?"

The Vulture told Raoul no, there was nothing left that could incriminate him, and again, yes, that he was sure Lester Long was now deceased. He felt like going into details to prove his point, tell Raoul that he stabbed Lester eighteen times, counting to himself as he did it. This line of questioning was annoying and unnecessary. He was a professional.

Raoul stepped away from the living room. He was at a woman's house. A woman named Ariel that he kept at a townhouse in Hialeah. A young woman he found wandering the streets, up and down Calle Ocho some nights. He'd watch her, looking to see if she was in the business of propositioning men. He stopped her one evening, hoping to get asked for sex; Ariel said she didn't have anywhere to go. That was it? He took her off the street and had her living in a nice home, a safe place for her to stay and that Raoul could store guns at temporarily. Put shoes on her feet, clothes on her back, and a roof over her head.

Raoul stepped around clothes lying in the living room, more in the hallway leading to the kitchen. In exchange for the niceties he provided, Raoul demanded sex. She gave him her pussy because she was grateful, but the woman could not keep a house.

Raoul was outside, closing a sliding glass door as he said, "Yes, killing him is fine with me. He was as useless to me as this fucking Billy Poe."

The Vulture waited.

"I'll pay you the fee from Billy Poe for Lester's death."

The Vulture was relieved. It saved him the trouble of having to inquire about it.

Raoul said, "But I still want Billy Poe dead."

"I understand. Do you know where I can find him?"

"Not at the moment." Raoul looked off in the distance at the neighborhood beyond the back patio fence. "Give me some time. I'll let you know." Raoul turned his head back to the house, like he was checking if the girl was listening. "I have others for you as well. One of them is a colored. I want him brought to me beforehand. Afterwards, you may do as you wish."

The Vulture waited, listening closely.

"The other works for the government. Will this prove difficult for you?"

"What does he do for the government?"

"He works for their Bureau of Alcohol, Tobacco and Firearms. Have you heard of this organization?"

The Vulture said he had. "It will require more planning. There is the possibility of greater scrutiny considering his position."

"I'll triple our usual fee arrangement."

"It shouldn't be a problem."

CHAPTER TWENTY-SIX

Max let Darnell talk him into leaving the storage unit, not hanging around to watch Metro P.D. investigate. They had made the block in Max's Impala and saw two cruisers arrive less than a minute after they parked. Crime scene tape going up, okay, Max knew they showed up and could call somebody later about it.

Darnell said he wanted to get home and lay down with his baby girl after all this excitement. Maybe LaKelle too.

Max needed a shower. He called Alondra, asked if he could come over, asked if she had taken a shower already. It seemed like a perfectly legitimate question to him. He needed one, he wondered if she did. He could hear laughter in her voice when she said, yeah, she did already, knowing what he meant.

He went straight to the shower when he got to her place. Alondra surprised him by jumping in there with him: "I thought you took a shower already?" She said, "I felt a little dirty after you called." They finished in there, took a few minutes, hopped into bed, and did it again. Did it with the bedspread up, Alondra didn't dry her hair and she didn't want to get her sheets wet.

It was nice. Max surprised her by being more gentle this time. Taking his time with her. After it was over, they lay in bed. Alondra was smoking. She wanted to say things to him. Like, how would you like to have, say, fifty thousand dollars? A finder's fee. Is that was he was to her, a finder? She thought about what their relationship would become after she said something like that. She wouldn't be able to take it back, pretend like it never happened. For the time being, he was quiet so she was quiet.

Until he said, "Tweety was killed in lockup."

That got Alondra sitting up. "What happened?"

Max took in a breath and cleared his throat. "He was stabbed. It could've been some prison yard bullshit, who knows. It probably was. Either way, they haven't caught the guy who was responsible."

"Where would he go? They're in jail."

She wasn't understanding, but it was okay. He said, "It's not a matter of physically catching him. There's a code in there. You do something like that, you keep your mouth shut. It's not all that different from the outside, really. But in there, there's nowhere to run. You admit it, your crew is going to take *you* out."

Oh.

Max said, "It could be related to that thing him and Darnell did. People around that situation seem to end up dead."

Alondra wondered if Max slipped in saying that, relaxing in the afterglow and not thinking.

She said, "Having any luck with that?"

It surprised her when he said, "Some. The guy we're after is a Puerto Rican named Raoul. I'm thinking he might be the one who had Tweety killed, I just can't prove it."

Saying it out loud made Max think about it again: how would Raoul know about Tweety being in jail?

Alondra was grinning at him. "You sound like you're getting close."

He looked over to her and said, "Yeah, we got pretty close tonight." He didn't elaborate, but said, "We'll get him soon enough."

Alondra didn't want to sound too obvious. Max was getting quiet again, so she would too. *We'll get him soon enough.* Yeah, she'd let that happen before she thought about touching that money. If this Raoul could get to somebody in jail, he could get to her, no doubt. He might even know who she was, she couldn't be sure. If he was dead or locked up, that wouldn't matter. She'd take it and head to Spain, Mexico, shit, anywhere. Alaska, it didn't matter. Let somebody tell him then.

How about asking Max to come with her? Right now, she was using him. It's not like she felt she was, she was. He was a good guy, they could get to know each other. She wondered if he had relationships, or if that came second. Look now, it was almost eleven by the time he got here. Didn't he say something about being married before? Maybe that was it, she came second. Alondra told herself that kind of thing didn't matter to her, she wasn't sure about marriage anyway.

If Max wasn't the person she could trust to get that money with her, she didn't know who was.

Billy threw up when he walked in the house.

This was some sick shit here. Lester's blood all over the damned place. His body . . . Billy couldn't even begin to describe it. Eyes bulged open, skin turning color in spots. A zombie.

The cops would be here soon if somebody saw, somebody would be reporting the smell. He'd have to remember to watch the news to find out.

Billy had come here to take a shower, relax, because he lived here but now he didn't want to go any further than this. Somebody could still be here for all he knew, no telling. He turned around, shut the ceiling light in the kitchen off, and walked out, back to Simone's junkyard Celica sitting in the driveway.

Poor Lester. He would've loved that camp with the satellite TV.

This morning Max stopped by the office, ran into Tom Mako, and his partner brought up the subject of when Max was coming back to work.

Max said, "A couple more days. I have one more doctor's appointment for my head. I'm guessing Monday."

"What are you doing here then? Man, you should be at the beach, getting drunk . . . anywhere but here."

Yeah, he should. It was nice out, one of those days. Sunny, a breeze bringing in clouds every once in a while to give some relief from the sun. Max could see himself relaxing under a blue beach umbrella nursing a drink.

He said, "I'm trying to run down some information real quick. It shouldn't take long."

Tom sat down at Max's desk, the chair across from him. He said, "You still after that accident? Trying to figure out what happened?"

"Man, it's all I think about. I think I've just about got it, but there's something not right. I put a guy who I think was involved in Metro West for something unrelated . . ."

"I remember."

"He turns up dead. That could be a coincidence, but I'm not counting on it. That makes two people dead from a three-year-old robbery of twenty grams of coke? That doesn't seem logical."

Tom sat back, as if he was thinking about it. "No, it doesn't." He waited, then said, "Wasn't there supposed to be a third guy?"

"Darnell Sims. I'm working with him now. He's a good kid, I'm just trying to keep him alive. I got another guy stashed at a hotel in South Beach. I can't keep him there forever, though."

"Which hotel?"

"The Clark."

Tom nodded from side to side. "That's an okay place. You paying for that?"

Max nodded.

"Must be getting expensive."

"Why you think I need to get him out of there? This is the kind of guy, he's not gonna stay cooped up forever anyway."

"What's his name?"

"Johnny Stanz. It's nobody we've ever busted."

Tom shook his head. "Doesn't ring a bell." He put his cowboy boots on the corner of Max's desk.

It relaxed Max a little and he kicked back and asked, "What's the name of that thing you're on?"

"Operation Prime Time."

"Yeah, Prime Time. I love those names. You remember Grass Roots?"

"That's the one with the convenience store owner . . . selling cigarettes without the tax stamp? A Lebanese national?"

"I think they got Grass Roots because he was sending the proceeds to buy military armaments in his home country, support terrorism. Somebody said it was low-tech but effective, like a grass roots movement."

Tom leaned back, hands clasped behind his head. "They traced it all the way back to his village. I hope they waterboarded the shit outta somebody over there."

Max said, "It's the same way with Prime Time? They following that back to some shithole?"

"I do believe they will be." Tom craned his head to watch one of the file assistants—Deborah, just out of the criminal justice program at U of M, hoping to be an agent—walking past Max's office to a ladies' room down the hall. "Man, I like her ass."

"I know. I think she's in her thirties. Was doing something, I don't know what, and went back to school."

"Her ass looks like it's in its twenties, maybe late teens. Of legal age, at least."

A minute passed and Deborah came out. Back past Max's office, giving gents fifteen years older than her a smile. It made Tom ask, "You seeing anybody now?"

Max wasn't sure seeing was the right word.

Ten in the morning, Darnell was waking up to the sound of LaKelle cleaning. Not cleaning in the bedroom, but he could hear her out there, heavy footsteps walking around. Letting him know she was ready for him to get out of bed.

He was wiping his eyes when his phone started buzzing on the nightstand. Max Bradford. Jesus, the man never stopped. Darnell didn't feel up to answering it, still recovering from his near-death experience last night. That's the way he told it to LaKelle. A near-death experience.

Max left a message saying he'd be there in half an hour.

They were going to swing by Lester's, talk to him again.

CHAPTER TWENTY-SEVEN

Johnny Stanz spent part of the morning in the Clark lobby, checking out tourists, middle-aged and younger, walking in and out. Ten in the morning, some of the younger ones just coming in from their night out, he could tell.

He sat back, a red leather chair that was supposed to look cool instead of be comfortable. But he liked it, the way it made him feel. Cool, like it was supposed to. Johnny caught sight of his reflection in a window looking out to Ocean Drive and the ocean beyond that; he turned his head this way and that, checking himself out at different angles.

He remembered coming here, two years ago, this exact hotel. It was for one of those TV shows that has people having a pool party. Shit, he remembered now there was a pool on the roof. He'd have to check that out later. Either way, the chicks were getting drunk and trying to get on TV, so they'd grab a guy and start making out, get the cameraman to turn their way. One girl grabbed him, didn't ask his name, and starts kissing him.

Man, it made him feel like a teenager again. This chick couldn't have been more than twenty, twenty-one. When the camera turned away, she kept going at it and he knew he was going to get lucky. They got back down to her room—she took a while to remember which one it was—and started getting undressed. Johnny remembered worrying that he drank too much and was going to have trouble getting it up. They lay down and she ended up passing out while he was on top of her and he had to roll her over when it looked like she was going to hurl. He was a gentleman and held her hair back while she went on her pillow. They couldn't make it to the bathroom. He left her on her side so she wouldn't choke if she had any of it left over and got out of there thinking he was a nice guy. Imagine if he wasn't there, she could have died.

Still, they had a good time. He'd have to find another one like her. Get further than second base this time.

What'd the ATF guy expect him to do, sit in his room all day?

The first thing Max noticed was the smell. It was coming from outside Lester's house, strong enough by now to make it down the street. Darnell said he was getting queasy and headed back to the car.

Max had an idea what the smell was.

The shades on the front windows were closed. Max banged on the carport door before deciding to walk around back. That's when he saw Lester, starting to bloat; skin turning color; that stiff look to his limbs telling Max that rigor was setting in. Bloodstains down Lester's shirt onto the sofa under him.

Max didn't go in, looking at the scene through the back patio door. He felt for Lester. The guy might've been part of the crew that ran him off the road—tried to kill him, really—just that something told him Lester Long wasn't that bad of a guy. Maybe in over his head here, like he wanted to be doing something else. It was a hunch.

Max couldn't see Billy doing this either. Another hunch, Billy didn't have this in him. This was personal. He could see several puncture wounds in Lester's chest. He wasn't completely sure, looking through a glass door, but Max didn't see defensive wounds. None that were obvious.

No, this wasn't Billy. This guy had fun.

★ ★ ★ ★ ★

Outside, in the car, Darnell said, "What's going on?"

Max said, "Lester's dead," and turned the ignition. "I'm going to call it in to a friend at Miami Metro, let them handle the initial investigation."

"What're we gonna do?"

Max was backing out, starting back east. He said, "We're going to see Johnny. I'm going to have to move him, I don't know where to yet."

The Impala was moving forward, Max heading back to the main thoroughfare. It was quiet while Darnell listened to Max talking to a friend in the police department.

When he hung up, Darnell said, "What'd he look like?"

Max glanced over, not surprised by the question but not really wanting to answer it either. He let it go for a few moments while he decided, then said, "He looked pretty bad."

Darnell said, "He's dead, I know that. What's that mean, 'he looked pretty bad'?"

"Whoever did it took their time."

Now Darnell was turned in his seat, his body almost fully facing Max's.

"*Took their time?* Are you serious?"

Max was coming to an intersection, looking at oncoming traffic to make his right turn and head south. He said, "Yeah," and nodded. He didn't feel like taking it any further than that.

Darnell did. He said, "You think it's Raoul?"

"Not him," Max said, "but somebody that works for him, probably. I can't see him taking the chance to get personally involved. After last night, he knows we're onto him."

"What about Billy?"

"What, a roommate quarrel?" Max shook his head. "I gave it a thought, but it doesn't fit. Worst case, a roommate quarrel ends up in a quick shooting, a crime of the moment." Max made his right, on his way back to the Airport Expressway now. "This is somebody different."

Darnell shrugged and said, "You got me. I dunno all these people's business . . . And if you think Johnny gonna tell you, you wasting your time. He's knee deep in pussy right now, which is where I ought to be."

Ramon was able to get away; this time, telling Gloria to meet him at one of the love motels on Calle Ocho. Gloria told Ramon that still might not be safe, Raoul had a habit of cruising through there. She knew for certain he had picked up girls there, *streetwalkers* she called them. Ramon said he would be careful, there was a small parking lot in back where he could leave his car.

They got to it right away, feeling as though they were getting it out of the way. Gloria doing her best to show that she was into it; moaning, calling him *papi,* running fingers on his chest. After it was over, Gloria lay on top of the sheets, no clothes on, while Ramon put his men's bikini underwear on, and she talked about Raoul.

How she wasn't even sure his family was full Puerto Rican. She said she thought his ancestors were from the Dominican, a little town named Paraiso, somewhere on the Pedernales Peninsula.

"Does it matter?" Ramon said, trying to get comfortable. Thinking about going to sleep right now, the romance over for the time being.

"It's just one of his things," Gloria said, some annoyance in her voice. "How he puts on a show, a big deal about being Puerto Rican. It's s*ooo* important." She dragged the last part out with a hand gesture.

Ramon said he didn't know what she was talking about.

"Ramon," Gloria said, rolling the r hard, "sometimes I think he's a phony. And if he's using Billy to get his money back, he

214

might be as stupid as Billy is."

Ramon said, "I wouldn't go so far as to say that. The other one, Lester . . . He's dead, you know."

"Only after you were chased by the ATF. I can't go back to the house. I have to stay with my cousin. I hate my cousin."

Ramon started to believe that's what this was about, Gloria being inconvenienced.

To change the subject, he said, "He got rid of one, he'll get rid of the other," and watched her stare until he said, "What?"

"Lester's only gone because whoever he hired killed the wrong guy," Gloria said. "It's Billy he wanted dead because Raoul was pissed about his car being totaled."

The woman had a knack for knowing things. Ramon decided to see if she knew this: "How much money are we talking about?"

"Five hundred thousand, give or take," Gloria said and watched Ramon's reaction. "Supposedly, the black one and others like him stole it from Raoul some years ago. He wants it back . . . or whatever he can get his hands on."

Gloria moved closer, watching Ramon stare at the ceiling before he said, "It's that much, huh?" and she grinned at him, not sure why but it was coming naturally.

"And what has he told you about it? I had to. As soon as it's over, you know he's going to have you kill Billy. After that, who knows?"

"What are you saying, that I shouldn't trust him? Shoot him before he shoots me and take off with the money?"

Gloria wanted to say yes, but don't forget to stop by, we can meet here, in this room.

"We have a change in plans," Raoul said to The Vulture. "Another name that has been brought to my attention, Johnny Stanz."

"Who is he?"

"To the world, he's nobody. To me," Raoul said, "he is someone who has betrayed me that I would like eliminated."

The Vulture loved words like eliminated.

They were alone in a small parking lot off Martin Luther King Boulevard in the Brownsville area, the elevated Miami Metrorail tracks in the distance.

The Vulture said, "Can you tell me anything more about him?"

Raoul said, "Yes, I apologize," dropping his head and smiling, almost as if he was laughing at himself for overlooking details. "He won't be a danger to you . . ."

"But this man had the temerity to betray you. Can you be sure?"

"From what I've been told, he's a buffoon. His disrespect towards me is more out of stupidity than hubris. He's the man responsible for this mess, he's the man who let the colored one escape."

The Vulture looked around at cars passing, noticing that Raoul had a duffel bag with him. A navy blue bag in the back seat of his SUV, windows rolled down. He said, "What about the lumberjack?"—what he remembered Raoul calling Billy Poe—and saw Raoul's expression change, almost to a grin.

"I'm reconsidering my plans for Billy. I need to speak with him before I move forward with anything else. He may have information that is valuable to me."

Raoul could see the disappointment on The Vulture's face and patted him on the back, leaving a hand on The Vulture's shoulder as he said, "I'm sorry, my friend. I know you were looking forward to that."

The Vulture gave him a shrug.

"Ah, my old ally," Raoul said, "you've always been so understanding."

"Could the other two still happen?"

Raoul knew he meant Darnell, the colored one, and Max, the government agent. He said, "It's quite possible. Right now, I need you to concentrate on Johnny Stanz."

The Vulture glanced again into the back seat of Raoul's SUV, the money bag resting there. That helped him concentrate. He said, "Where can I find him?"

Raoul looked one way, then the other. He said, "It's my understanding that he's at the Clark Hotel, one of the hotels on Ocean Drive. Do you know this place?"

The Vulture said he'd heard the name and could find it and Raoul started describing Johnny Stanz.

The Vulture said, "Has he worked for you?"

Raoul shook his head. "Outside of helping my organization locate and confine the colored one, he has no historical connection to me whatsoever. Lester did work for me, but the association was tenuous. That could have been someone from his past, a former associate holding a grudge."

The Vulture nodded. "That happens."

Raoul got home, it was quiet except for scrubbing noises coming from a downstairs bathroom. Ariel cleaning again. The woman had been cleaning since Raoul surprised her with his bags and Ramon following him in. She was obsessed with it— cleaning to please him—which was commendable except that she hardly stopped. He couldn't so much as ask for a simple blow job without her claiming she was exhausted from cleaning.

Raoul looked around for Ramon, glancing through French doors leading outside; calling throughout the house, checking a downstairs spare bedroom.

He found Ariel on her knees in the guest bathroom, cleaning the space behind the toilet, and could tell he'd startled her. He asked where Ramon was and she shrugged at him, big eyes looking up at him as if she were scared.

 Raoul started dialing, calling Ramon's cell number twice in a row before hanging up. The middle of the day, where could he have gone?

CHAPTER TWENTY-EIGHT

There was a restaurant on Collins where The Vulture liked to go. Cuban locals looking him over might see the kid coming over, the thug, in a boat. Packed in like sardines with other thugs. What did they know? Maybe that was their circumstance, not his. They might see the box-cut leisure shirt hanging out of his trousers and think something else, an immigrant bum coming here to find work using someone else's Social Security number, sending money back to his family. He didn't have family.

But other locals would come in and see him as just another part of the South Beach culture. He could be Armando here. Look, it's a Cuban guy, this place must be authentic. Bringing in their shopping bags, they'd give him a smile and walk right past, happy with themselves. See, he was a good guy, concerned with making people satisfied with themselves. He let them enjoy their ideas, sitting down with his *arroz con pollo*.

The happy shoppers were usually the women, sometimes a group of them together; sometimes with men much younger or older than themselves. Today, though, it was a male, a kid, came up to him and asked if he was Cuban. Armando smiled and told him yes, that he was from the barrio of Las Lajas, near Guantanamo.

He could see that meant nothing to this boy, maybe as young as a teenager, getting away from his mother for part of the day. Armando could see the boy had a picture on the front of his t-shirt from the *Scarface* movie, Al Pacino as Tony Montana.

Armando said, "This is what you think Cubans are like? This is why you want to take a photograph with me?"

The boy had a look, he wasn't expecting that.

"So you can tell your friends that you took a picture with Scarface? You want to be a gangster?"

The boy started eating it up, giggling, not understanding what Armando was trying to say.

So he said, "You want to be a gangster, you need to go grab one of those good-looking girls out there, drag her into an alley, beat her senseless. Steal her purse and bring me the money. Prove to me you are a gangster."

The boy said, "You serious?" A different look on his face, the stupid grin gone now.

Armando made his face look annoyed.

"No, I'm not serious." The kid started to move away. "Go back to your momma, suck her nipple some more until you grow up, boy." The kid was on his way out the door now, grabbing his buddy's arm as he went. "Or stay and have some black bean soup and *ropa vieja,* it's wonderful here."

So much for being Armando.

He finished his rice, stabbed the last two pieces of chicken, and sat back. Thinking about the one Raoul told him about: Johnny Stanz. His idea was to take this mental description to the Clark Hotel and wait in the lobby. Perhaps sit down with a copy of today's *Herald* and blend in with the tourists. He was curious to see if his murder of Lester Long had made it in there.

Armando left his money on the table, always leaving thirty percent when he appreciated food from his home, and walked out onto Collins. More people with shopping bags along the sidewalk and traffic full of automobiles. People going about their routines. He crossed the street and headed east on Seventh Street towards the ocean.

★ ★ ★ ★ ★

Max had tried Johnny Stanz's number three times, no answer. He hung up and concentrated on the road, finding his way onto the Airport Expressway before ending up on the Julia Tuttle Causeway.

Darnell said, "You should've known Johnny ain't gonna just sit in that room and watch television. He my friend and all, but he ain't the smartest guy you ever met. No telling what kind of monkeyshines he getting into."

Max was busy driving, thinking about other things, when he said, "I guess I didn't explain the gravity of the situation well enough, how much danger he could be in."

"Gravity . . ." Darnell blew out of his mouth. "You not kiddin' about that. Man, these dudes are trippin'."

Yeah, but about what?

Raoul decided he needed to talk to Billy Poe before he was dead to clear something up. Apparently, Billy had done *something* before he wrecked Raoul's car. What was it? Perhaps he had found out some information about the federal agent or the colored one called Darnell. Raoul started thinking back; yes, that's what he and Lester were supposed to be doing.

He would ask Billy how things were going, if they had found anything out. Casual. Like nothing out of the ordinary had happened. My car? It can be replaced. Your loyalty cannot, Billy. If the subject of Lester's death was brought up, Raoul could easily act surprised. Really? I wasn't aware. What happened? Meet me somewhere, we can talk about it.

He left a message on Billy's phone and waited.

Pissed off, Raoul jumped on Ariel about picking up this house. Told her she needed to vacuum, what she was doing wasn't good enough. "How can I be expected to live in such filth?" He brought Ariel to the kitchen by the arm and was pointing out grease spots on the stove top. As he said, "How long has this been like this?" he wondered how the stove top got that way in the first place. Best of his knowledge, the woman didn't cook or even know how. He felt like asking her, "How come you never cook for me, my dear?" Soften her up for sex; but he knew he didn't have to. If he told her to undress, she would, for the privilege of being off the street. Occasionally, Raoul would have to say, "Would you like to go back to the street?" or some other threat. Sometime he did it because he wanted to, for fun. Not today, though; look at her, on all fours cleaning up spaces between the kitchen tiles, Ariel aiming her butt at him. So much as telling him she wanted to go to bed.

For her age, she was extremely adept at pleasing a man. Raoul was curious where she acquired these skills and sometimes wondered to himself if she was lying when she said that it was just that she didn't have anywhere to go.

Raoul was getting undressed, starting with the buttons on his shirt. He could leave it on the kitchen countertop before retiring to the bedroom, Ariel was cleaning anyway. This was obviously what she wanted, what with how she was enticing him with her flirtatious ways while cleaning. As Raoul got to the buttons near his mid-section, he heard a phone ringing in the living area.

He picked it up and a voice said, "Who is this?"

Raoul recognized the voice as Billy Poe and introduced himself. He had called from the house phone, knowing Billy wouldn't recognize the number.

Billy: "What do you want?"

Raoul: "Billy, we have business to discuss."

Billy: "Like what?"

Billy's voice was monotone, like he'd rather be doing something else, but Raoul was surprised he had not hung up yet.

Raoul: "Have you learned anything about that ATF agent?"

Billy: "That's what you called me about?"

Raoul: "Yes. Why, is there something else?"

This caught Billy off guard. Was he serious? Billy decided to try it.

Billy: "What about your car? I know you're pissed."

Raoul: "These things happen. I wasn't thrilled, but it can be replaced." He waited and said, "You cannot."

This wasn't the Raoul Billy was used to. He said, "Lester's dead."

Raoul put on a show, telling Billy how sorry he was; that he knew Billy and Lester were friends. Took a minute and asked if Billy knew how it happened.

Billy said, "All I know is that I showed up at the house, his body's cut up all to shit."

"Billy, that sounds terrible. Have you seen anything on the news or in the newspaper about it? I don't recall having seen anything."

"I haven't had a chance to look yet."

Raoul said, "Who do you think could have done such a thing? I never knew Lester to have any enemies."

Billy said, "Me neither. He was a bit annoying sometimes, but Lester was a good guy."

Raoul waited, giving himself time to prepare. Hoping Billy would continue to talk, give him time to rehearse his tone of voice when he said, "Billy, this could be serious. Perhaps Lester was involved in some enterprise that you were unaware of. It might not be safe for you. You should come in, let me protect you."

What was this, Billy thought. Okay, now it was getting weird. Raoul was sounding almost touchy-feely that time. Maybe he had changed, seeing things a different way. One of your guys dying might do that to you, Billy didn't know.

223

He said, "I don't know. I think I'm pretty safe, nobody knows where I am."

Raoul took a moment, then said, "Billy, I made contact with you by mistakenly calling you from a number you didn't know and you returned my call. Everyone can be located. Whoever this person is, they may have resources beyond mine to find you in a similar manner. Working together, we can trick this person and avenge Lester's death."

Billy waited, unsure.

Raoul said, "Lester deserves justice."

The Vulture sat in the lobby of the Clark Hotel, holding open a copy of the *New Times* in front of him. There was no copy of the *Herald* or even the *Sun Sentinel* lying around on the lobby coffee tables. He passed the time reading about arts and entertainment news instead of an account of Lester Long's death.

Several youngsters, on their way in or out, stopped and asked if he was okay, did he need some juice or his pills.

Which he thought was nice, considering the disrespectfulness of the young boy that wanted his picture because he thought Armando was Scarface and it would be cool. The Vulture moved the *New Times* copy he had thrown on the seat next to him, gathered it up so a young woman who looked at him like he didn't belong here could sit.

He sat back and crossed his legs, arms folded over that, and tried to be Armando again, the nice guy who would take a picture with you or move papers out of your way. Armando glanced to his left, past lobby furniture and through a wall of glass windows that looked out to Lummus Park and the Atlantic Ocean. Watching tourists sunbathing and revelers heading to the beach.

He looked closer, wondering if somebody matching Johnny Stanz's description was out there. If Raoul was correct, he could be out there. Enjoying himself with no idea of what was about to happen to him, either out of ignorance or complete disregard. Probably a little of both. No matter to Armando, it was another few thousand dollars for him.

He started thinking. Even for a seasoned professional such as himself, it would be difficult for Armando to single out a person in this mass. Look at them, there must be hundreds out there. Thousands by nightfall. He could go out to the park and relax, sit back for a couple of hours. Waiting was a big part of it, but some hotel person might come ask him what he was doing here all day.

It wasn't until the girl next to him got up that The Vulture felt his luck start to change. He watched her walking across the lobby, stopping to put her sunglasses on and try to look like a starlet, then noticed two men walking in past her. The white one was in blue jeans and a blazer over a button-down shirt. Cowboy boots. A giant, he had to be six-one, six-two. The other . . .

The other was a black. *Un negro.* In baggy jeans and a t-shirt, that streetball look they like to wear.

The Vulture watched them stop, the white one looking like he was going to the front desk for something. He watched some more and saw them disappear towards the elevators at the far end of the lobby.

As he watched the elevator doors open and the two men step inside, The Vulture had a fleeting thought that they didn't belong here either.

Darnell said it was a waste of time coming up here if Johnny wasn't even going to be in the room. Max told him he tried to call. "You saw me," he said. "I tried three times on the way over here." Darnell said, yeah, and we should have gone to Lincoln Road, to one of those restaurants. They could've gotten something to eat, drink some Bloody Marys and wait.

Max tried to make himself sound annoyed or like it was his fault when he said, "I guess I wasn't thinking."

Darnell said, "Well, how about now?"

Armando tried to be casual about watching the elevator floor indicator, whatever you call that electronic gizmo that told you where an elevator stopped. He had gotten up and walked the fifty feet or so from his chair when the two men he saw earlier got in.

This one said the elevator stopped on two.

He decided he would wait. If they were up there too long, Armando figured it meant that they found Johnny Stanz and were speaking to him. If they came down quickly, that meant he wasn't there and they would wait too.

Several scenarios went through The Vulture's mind. If they were all up there, should he storm in, waving his knife. Cut them all, a bloodbath. Ooh, he liked that word, *bloodbath*. But it was impractical. The federal agent was probably armed.

What if they all ended up waiting together? Armando frowned. That would be awkward. At least that would tell him Johnny Stanz was not in his room, Armando could step outside and wait for him there.

What if the white man and black man walked out of the hotel alone? Should he wait? Raoul did mention he would triple the usual fee for the white man and, surely, the *negro* was worth more than a common thug like he was led to believe this Johnny Stanz was.

Decisions, decisions . . .

Darnell had talked Max into waiting outside. Not outside like in the hallway, Darnell told Max that would be lame. He meant *outside* outside. He meant hang out in front of the hotel. Darnell

226

asked again about breakfast and Bloody Marys—"The government's gonna pay you back, right?"—but in front of the hotel was the best he could get. Max said he didn't want to miss a chance if Johnny happened to walk past them.

They came back down the stairs, different from the way they went up. It gave Darnell time to think about what he wanted to eat and drink. He didn't know if he could get away with drinking in public. Dangit, that's why he wanted to go to one of those outdoor cafés. Why was Max treating him like this? Of course, a cop comes up to him, he could look at Max, who would show his badge. Darnell decided he'd think about it.

They walked across the lobby, tiles squeaking under Darnell's sneakers. He looked around: damn, some good-looking women in here. Hanging out across the street would be a show. Shit, he could be home right now, LaKelle telling him to raise his feet so she could sweep under him. Telling him not to go into the kitchen, she just mopped.

Instead, he was here: people getting drunk in the middle of the day, people having a good time, gorgeous women walking around. See, there was one over there—a young brunette adjusting her bikini top in the lobby, one of those sarongs hanging from her waist. Being dramatic about it, making sure people were watching her. Even that old man, sitting in a chair near her, was watching.

Hold up. That guy looked familiar.

The girl was done fooling with her bikini and now the guy, the old man, was staring back. Looking straight at Darnell looking back at him. The old guy didn't move. Darnell turned, the way you do when you think somebody's staring at something behind you. There was nothing there. It was weird.

Darnell took one more look at him, trying to remember where he'd seen that guy's face before.

CHAPTER TWENTY-NINE

Johnny Stanz said, "You sure you're legal?"

Her name was Vanessa, she nodded her head. Johnny couldn't remember her last name, one of those names that ends with *ski*. Polish or something along those lines. She said she was from somewhere in Michigan but didn't get specific. Down here for some rally or protesting something . . . No, that wasn't it. One of those love-ins, hippie get-togethers where everybody sits around hugging each other. That's where Johnny found her, in Flamingo Park, in a group hug with four other people. They weren't sitting around naked—it wasn't the '60s—they were just hugging. There were all kinds that came to Miami for one thing or another.

Johnny watched from across the street for about fifteen minutes before walking over. Hairy people with tie-dye t-shirts, piercings in weird places. Most of them needed to bathe and wash their hair. He moved through the crowd trying not to get hugged, but they couldn't help themselves. One girl told Johnny, "I love you," but he knew she didn't mean it in any way. It was just what they did, flash peace signs and love their fellow man.

Eventually, he saw Vanessa, looking like she was about to hug a nearby tree. She was staring at it and Johnny wondered how far they took this hugging thing. Look at that, the guy next to her started climbing up. He might be there all night; maybe he was protesting something—oil, tobacco companies, who knows. Johnny wondered how they could protest either one. He bet they chain-smoked cigarettes when they weren't putting their show on and all those thirty- and forty-year-old vans parked up and down Twelfth Street had shit mileage.

Johnny grabbed Vanessa before she had a chance to follow her tree-climbing buddy. This time, he asked to be hugged. He wanted to be hugged by her. Yeah, she needed to wash her hair too, but what the hell.

It wasn't long before they were back at her place.

A small two-bedroom on Euclid, ten minutes from the park. Vanessa said they found it on the Internet, a thousand for three days. A bargain if they split it eight ways. Eight ways? Johnny understood what she meant when they walked in, half a dozen more hippies inside, dosing on acid.

Johnny followed Vanessa through the living area. These guys didn't get up to hug, too far out there to make the effort. Johnny glanced outside and saw three more people, tattooed bikers with beer and pot stretching out in the backyard.

The bedroom was empty. Johnny walked in and had a seat on the bed, a hint, but Vanessa's head disappeared into a duffel bag. Rooting around in there for something. She came out with two tabs and asked Johnny if he wanted one.

"What is it?"

"Ecstasy," Vanessa said. "You've never done it? It'll make it a lot better."

Yeah, he'd heard that, maybe what made it so easy for these people to love everybody. Like that one guy up in the tree, what was he on? Johnny popped it in his mouth and looked around, letting the tab dissolve. Vanessa sat down next to him, lifting her shirt off. Johnny was looking for hair under her arms but didn't see any. The way he was starting to feel, it might not have mattered. He was warm inside, the drug starting to come over him.

Vanessa still had her bra on, a little skinny but not a bad body. She asked him, "You feel it?" and they started to fool around. That's when Johnny asked her if she was legal, the last sober thing he figured he'd say for a while. She smiled, nodded, and started undoing his belt.

He lay back on the bed, letting her do the work. The room started spinning and he was starting to see strange things. He wouldn't be any help anyway. This felt more like LSD than Ecstasy, maybe she got them mixed up. Vanessa had his belt off, not having any trouble with it, she must've been used to the drugs. Johnny heard noises from outside but didn't pay much attention. It could be anybody, there were about, what, twenty people out there? Shit, now the noise was getting louder and it was starting to get to him. He'd start thinking about that and not be able to perform. He wanted to get up and go out there, flash his teeth that looked like movie-star teeth compared to what he saw in the living room and ask them to calm down, if they could respect his privacy.

Before he could do that, the door opened and a hippie couple, a boy and a girl, burst in, laughed, said they were sorry, and disappeared back into the hallway.

They left the door open.

Shit, they weren't going to get any privacy here. These people were all about group love or some weird shit like that. He wasn't looking to roll over and see some guy checking him out.

Wait.

What was he doing *here*? He had his own room, at a nice hotel not too far away.

He wondered if him and Vanessa could get there in this condition.

Darnell had to settle for a bottle of soda, Max wouldn't let him drink alcohol while they were supposed to be working. Max gave him the money and sent him to the nearest convenience store he could find. Darnell knew there was one on Sixth Street.

Max gave him a twenty. Darnell figured he'd keep the change, that Max never said anything about giving it back.

He came back to the park, a bottle of water and orange soda with him, and found Max in the same spot when he left. Darnell twisted the top off his bottle and looked across the street. Yep, that guy was still there. It was quiet between Max and Darnell, Max busy looking through crowds of tourists for Johnny Stanz and trying to call him again, so it gave Darnell time to think . . . think about where he'd seen that guy before.

At some strip club Darnell was at, getting titties rubbed in his face?

By the looks of him, Darnell wasn't sure the man's heart could take that kind of excitement.

How about a fast-food place near LaKelle's? With his age, he looked like he could be a manager. Probably not, how many faces of those do you remember?

Somebody he robbed?

Darnell thought about it. Maybe. He wasn't going to pretend to be an angel, but he didn't go around robbing random people either. Stick 'em up, I have a gun in my pocket. Nothing like that. Maybe when he was younger, a couple robberies starting out. With concealed carry laws now, you get your head blown off pulling a stunt like that. The other guy could say it was self-defense.

Darnell sat back, relaxing on his elbows, grass underneath him. Moving an arm every once in a while to grab for his soda. Max still working the phone, looking for Johnny. Darnell shook his head, that was a waste. He tried telling the man, no telling what old Johnny was doing with himself. He could be up in the room right now, passed out and unable to hear Max's big bear hand pounding on the door, that cop way of knocking.

Somebody he robbed.

For some reason, that kept coming back to Darnell. He

231

wasn't sure why. Like he told himself, he hadn't robbed many people, he could count them on one hand. Oh well. He took another sip and glanced around with no particular agenda. He liked where he was, between a strip of fancy art deco hotels and the ocean.

Somebody he robbed.

He liked where he was, but that was ruining it. It was annoying him now. The only real robbery he'd ever done, face to face, was Raoul. And even that was planned. He remembered LaRon, his cousin, spent every afternoon for a week watching Raoul, following his routine. He called it recon. That was short for something, but LaRon couldn't tell him the real word, he didn't remember it. Tweety would go too when he had free time. They decided to bring Darnell along one day, it was a Thursday, when they knew they'd need a third guy.

That was it. The day Darnell went. They saw Raoul standing on a street corner, Dixie Highway and Douglas Road in Coconut Grove, with this guy. He remembered it because LaRon kept talking about it, how it was strange, the only time Raoul had done that all week. Met this one guy. Yeah, Tweety wanted to find out who he was; if he had money, they could jack him too.

Darnell never heard if they found out who he was.

It was the scar that set Darnell to thinking. The guy had a scar running down the left side of his face, from his cheek to his jaw. A thin one, like someone had swiped a knife at him and nicked him. Darnell looked back towards the hotel, trying not to be obvious; it had been a few years but, yeah, he could see that being him. Hmm, it's a small world. What was he doing here?

Max said, "You think he saw you?"

"We looked right at each other," Darnell said. "I mean, the

man was staring hard. At first, I thought he was queer. I thought he was gonna start making goo-goo eyes at me, like he wanted my meat."

Max glanced over. They both did. The guy sitting in the lobby probably doing the same thing when they weren't looking. Everybody looking without trying to look like it.

Max said, "How sure are you that it's him?"

Darnell took a sip of soda, unfazed now, staring right at the man before he looked at Max. "Before, I wasn't sure. The more I look, the more positive I get."

"You have to be certain."

"I am."

Max nodded, that was good enough for him. "You said he knows Raoul, right? You saw them together one day."

Darnell nodded.

Max wanted to play devil's advocate, trying to consider other possibilities. "Maybe he just likes to relax down here, people-watch. Lots of people hang out in the hotels they don't stay in."

Darnell said, "Yeah, if they pimps." He took another look, knowing what Max was trying to do. He was trying to be a cop, do his job, ask questions. Darnell had one: "What if he's meeting his buddy Raoul down here?"

Max didn't see how that was possible. It was too much of a coincidence. Then again, so was this.

He said, "We'll just sit here, see what happens. Least we can grab Johnny before he goes inside. We're in a good spot."

Max and Darnell sat silent, watching. Darnell noticed Max did a lot of watching. Watching cars, watching houses, watching hotels. It must go with government work. They sat and watched, making small talk at times. Not always about the job. Darnell asked Max what he liked to do outside of work. Max said there wasn't much time outside of work. Darnell said, "C'mon, man, you can't tell me you work all the time. There has to be *some*thing. We getting to know each other here." Max made it sound like a chore coming up with something and Darnell teased him some more about it. Max told him he liked to watch football and go fishing when he had the chance. Max said where he grew up in Alabama, it was fishing in ponds and streams. Here, it was more open ocean, fish like marlins. Darnell said, "That's the ones that jump in your boat?" Max said sure, they could, but he'd never seen it. Darnell said, "I seen that on TV," and shook his head, definitively, like you would never catch him doing that. "That shit is scary, a big fish like that. That's like some kind of monster."

Max asked Darnell if he'd ever been fishing. Darnell shook his head and told Max that black people don't fish all that much, outside of fishing in creeks and streams on the side of the road. Little bodies of water small enough to where he figured there weren't many fish in them. But, yeah, you drive north of here, out past Twenty Mile Bend to the Glades, around Canal Point, you'll see black people up and down the road. Sitting on ten gallon buckets turned upside down, a cane pole in the water, sweating their ass off. "You ask me, they crazy," Darnell said. "You just as soon pull a gator out of there as a fish. You do that, you dead. You ever seen a gator run, their little legs pumping? They run, like, twenty miles an hour." Darnell repeated the last part. "That's like Olympics speed."

Well then, Max asked what Darnell liked to do in his free time.

Darnell shrugged, thinking about it. He thought about it some more and when Max thought he wasn't going to say anything, Darnell said, "I like to get blow jobs," that look on his face you have when you can't come up with anything else.

Darnell happened to look up in the direction of the Clark Hotel. "Check it out."

The old guy was getting up. Stretching out his old bones

after sitting for a long time. They were watching him, hands on his back, arching backwards to limber up when Max said, "He's trying to throw us off, make himself look like he's just one of the crowd."

Darnell liked Max's tone. Like Max took what he said as the truth, he didn't have to work to convince him. Max said, "You didn't see Johnny go in, did you?"

Darnell shook his head. Max didn't either, confident even though they had been talking, discussing fishing and blow jobs. He'd kept an eye out.

The old guy, some kind of Latin American descent but Max and Darnell couldn't decide which one, appeared on the sidewalk in front of the hotel, on foot going south on Ocean Drive. Max had to bob his head a little to follow him in the crowd until he said, "I'm going to follow him for a bit, see if it goes anywhere."

"What you want me to do?"

Max took a few seconds making a decision then said, "You stay here and watch for Johnny. He comes back, you call me. Don't go up there by yourself, you understand?"

Max slipping back into official mode now.

He said, "This probably won't take long anyway. He could be going for lunch, for all we know."

That got Darnell thinking. "I'm getting hungry. And it's hot out here, I'm bound to get thirsty. You think you could leave me some money?"

Chapter Thirty

Max approached Ocean Drive, stopping to look at traffic in both directions. Cars creeping by at no more than five or ten miles an hour. He darted through a gap when some of them were stopped at a red light. He had to work to keep up with the guy, focusing on the bald spot in the sidewalk crowds. Lucky for Max, the guy was taking it easy, strolling down Ocean Drive; stopping to look in cafés, making small talk with one tourist couple. It was more like a saunter.

Max started to wonder if he had the right guy. Yeah, he might know Raoul, but that was Darnell talking. Right now, he didn't look like an associate of a known drug dealer. The guy looked like just another guy, enjoying a stroll on a nice day. What Max thought about doing was going up to him and starting a conversation. Make up a story. Excuse me, how do I get to the Jackie Gleason Theater? That he wanted to take a picture of the statue in front, it was famous. A mermaid. He couldn't think of anything else. He couldn't ask how to get to the beach, it was right there. Anything to get the guy talking, learn more about him. One thing Max didn't like was the way he was dressed, blue jeans and cowboy boots. Everyday wear for the office, his unofficial uniform. It didn't look too good out here, though, in come-as-you-are South Beach. If the guy made a comment, Max would say he was from Texas, that's how they dressed, and hope for the best.

Max was going to do it when the guy turned at Fifth Street.

Max saw the Wave Hotel in the background before the bald spot disappeared. Max made a slight jog, slowing up before he got to the corner and found the guy crossing the Fifth Street median, heading towards Collins Avenue. Then saw him through a crowd taking a left onto little Ocean Court Alley. Max thought about what he was going to do, found a quiet place to pull his nine-millimeter, racked the slide and slipped it back into the holster inside his blazer. Who knew what the guy was doing, he could round the corner and the guy could be there waiting for him. Max wanted him to be heading for the marina, an elderly gent, a retiree, looking at boats, thinking about retirement.

But he wasn't. He was a figure in the alley, open space between the rears of business establishments.

Coming Max's way.

Look at that, just like he told Max. Darnell saw Johnny walking back into the hotel with a girl. They looked like they were stumbling, not walking, holding each other up. Cutting up about something Darnell couldn't make out. Darnell looked at his watch and nodded. High or drunk or both this early, it was a shame.

They were having some trouble right at the hotel entrance. Having a tough time negotiating the door. Jesus, how wasted were they? Darnell watched them giggling about it. The girl was young and Darnell was surprised, she didn't look at all like Johnny's type. He liked them all tits and ass. Big ones on both counts. That's how they met after not seeing each other for five years, ran into each other at a strip club in Pompano Beach on White Night, when they let white guys come in to watch pole shows and go to the VIP Room. The girl was flat and Darnell couldn't tell what her butt was like in baggy jeans, but she didn't look bad.

Darnell wanted to cross the street right now, cut through the crowd and surprise Johnny. Ask, "How you doing, man?" and see the look on his face. But then, he thought about what Max said. Not to go up to the room alone, call him when Johnny came back. At any rate, Johnny and his girlfriend would have hotel security on them in a minute if they kept this up, making spectacles of themselves. Darnell didn't need that, a guy in a sport coat and necktie giving him a hard time.

He looked at Johnny again, a hundred or so feet away, Johnny making it inside now. Give him another five minutes to make it up to his room, Darnell decided he was going to go up.

Max's voice was in his head, telling him to call. He was busy, finding out about that old fella. Who knew when he'd be back?

"Are you the one named Max?"

As the guy spoke, Max was telling himself to pull his nine-millimeter. Get it out of his holster, show it to the guy, let him know not to do something dumb.

The guy stopped short, some distance between them. Ten feet or so. If the guy came closer, then Max would take out his weapon. Max was a little surprised being called by his name, but didn't answer the question. Instead, he said, "Who are you?"

The guy looked like he was going to say something. Maybe he did, but Max didn't hear it, noise coming from busboys coming out into the alley through a service entrance. Max's head turned, his hand going inside his coat on instinct. He felt the handle of his pistol and looked back, ready for the guy to make a move.

It didn't happen that way, though. Max looked up and the old guy was gone, around the corner of the alley and down the street, just like that.

Darnell had followed Johnny into the hotel and stayed on him. It wasn't hard, they were stumbling all over the lobby. It was almost embarrassing for Darnell, having to stop so Johnny wouldn't notice him; he could feel stares, like what's this black guy doing hanging around in here? He smiled and nodded at anyone who looked his way.

They took their time, laughing at some stupid shit along the way. Darnell was getting fed up with this foolishness. They reached the door of Alondra's room and took some more time while Johnny fumbled for the room key. It wouldn't surprise Darnell if he couldn't find it. He could see that happening and Johnny deciding they were going to sit in the hallway. Maybe that would happen, until Johnny took out the key and swiped it in the door lock. Got it right on the first try and Darnell moved out from the stairwell, came up from behind them, Johnny and his girlfriend too far gone to notice what was going on behind them. Darnell let them go in and stuck his arm in as the door was closing.

That finally got Johnny turning around. He took a swing out of instinct at the black figure he couldn't make out. Darnell dodged it without much effort and caught Johnny's body into his on the follow through. By this time, the girl was starting to back away, yelling obscenities as she ran for the bathroom. That bathroom was a popular hiding place. Johnny started to fight again, as best as he could in his condition, until Darnell wrestled him onto the bed. Sat Johnny down and gave him a second to calm himself. He let Johnny settle and have a look at him, let him realize there was no danger.

Johnny looked up, that blank look on his face that he still wasn't aware of what was going on, until Darnell told him, "Hey, it's me," then Johnny said, "What're you doing here?"

"I wanted to talk to you. Time I saw you before, we didn't get a chance to talk."

Johnny said, "About what?" but was worrying about something else. He heard Vanessa in the bathroom and went over there, telling her it was okay through the door, that that was his black friend. "I thought y'all were accepting of everybody, that the color didn't matter?" Darnell didn't know what that meant, but okay. He couldn't be sure, but it didn't sound to Darnell like she believed Johnny. Darnell believed she said some curse words and the door stayed closed.

Johnny started knocking on the door, banging on it with his fist, and Darnell told him not to do that, that he was making the situation worse. Johnny had that pitiful look on his face looking over at Darnell from across the room, who told him to come on, sit down, cool down some more. Darnell said, "She'll be all right, let her chill out in there. She'll be okay."

Johnny sat on the bed and took a deep breath. He looked at the bathroom door, then back at Darnell and said, "Man, you really ruined my high."

It was weird for Max. It was like the guy *wanted* him to know he was out there. He had to be connected to Raoul, no doubt about it now.

He walked to the end of the alley, didn't run, and looked both ways down Fourth Street. He was ready, his hand inside his blazer, but the guy was gone.

Max stood there for a second, trying to figure how the guy knew his name and, two, what the guy was doing there. He retraced his last several days. No, he didn't remember seeing the guy. Darnell would've brought it up if they had seen him, like he did today.

Darnell. The thought reminded Max to call, warn Darnell that the guy might double back. No answer. Fucking Darnell, he could've been telling some girl he was a rapper right about now. Max needed to get back.

Max walked back the way he came and decided to make a call to Miami Metro and ask about Raoul's storage unit. See

240

where that was at. He was forwarded to a duty sergeant who told him, "Our guys show up with a search warrant and a locksmith, this is about seven this morning. The only way we figured it out was where the tire tracks started. We picked the one where the driver started peeling out. We thought we were lucky because that's pretty thin, but the judge was in a good mood. Anyway, somebody on our end fucked up because the place was left alone for a couple hours."

Max said, "Whaddya mean 'left alone'?"

The sergeant said, "Our guys had to respond to another call, a homicide about two blocks away."

Max let him go on.

"We open it up, it's empty. We were lucky once, we can't go back to the judge without something more concrete."

Max didn't say anything, about to hang up when the sergeant said, "You're from the ATF, right?"

Max told him he was.

There was a silence and Max could hear the guy flipping papers over. "There's no name, but the notes say you're the second ATF guy to call about this. Hmm, that's odd. Must be something pretty important."

CHAPTER THIRTY-ONE

Max went straight up to Alondra's room, right past the entrance when he didn't see Darnell. It didn't occur to him that the reason Darnell wasn't outside was because the old guy had come back and Darnell did something. It was more along the lines of Darnell being off somewhere, grab-assing.

He went upstairs and banged on the door with an open hand, loud. A few moments passed and the door opened. Darnell was on the other side.

That didn't surprise Max, either.

He said, "I thought I told you to call me," looking at Johnny but talking to Darnell.

"I knew you'd be busy. I was trying to help out."

"You were supposed to let me know. You call me, I probably would've told you to follow him up here."

"I know," Darnell said. "That's why I did it."

"But you didn't call first."

" 'Cause I knew you'd let me help you."

Maybe there was a miscommunication. Darnell talking in circles, back in his convict manner. Max let it go. He said, "Anyway, your friend is definitely bad news. He knew my name, which probably means he knows yours, too."

"What did y'all do, sit down and talk?"

Max said, "I bet there was a whole lot more talking going on up here," and gave Darnell a look.

Darnell gave it back and started to say something. Max cut

him off and said, "Whatever it was, I hope you said your good-byes. Johnny, you need to get out of here, it's not safe anymore."

By now, noise started coming from the bathroom again. Max said, "What is that?"

Darnell said, "That's Johnny's piece of ass for today. That's what he's out doing when he should be in here, cooperating with our investigation."

Okay, that one made Max smile a little. He walked past Johnny to the bathroom and knocked. A soft one, knuckles tapping on the door, and identified himself.

The door was still closed when Vanessa said, "Let me see your ID."

Max told her to crack the door open and he slid it through. Ten seconds later, the door opened and she said, "Thank God you're here. I was fearful for my life." She pointed at Darnell and said, "You should arrest that guy for breaking and entering."

Max took his badge back and told her he would take it under advisement. Then he asked, "Are you okay, ma'am?" She nodded and he told her, "Good. You need to go. Get back to wherever you came from right now. Take your things, you're not coming back."

They waited while she scooped up her purse and flip-flops, not taking time to put them on, and walked out of the room barefoot.

Johnny still had a look on his face that he didn't understand what was going on.

Max said, "Get dressed. This place isn't safe anymore."

"Where're you moving me?"

"I'm not. You just need to go. Hit the road and drive."

Johnny hunched over, cradling his head in his hands. "This is crazy."

Max nodded, knowing what Johnny meant. "I'm sorry it happened this way. You still have your phone? I've been trying to call you."

Johnny looked up and nodded his head. "I had it off, seeing as how I was in the middle of something."

Max said he was sorry about that too. He didn't mention that he told Johnny not to leave. Instead, he said, "You okay to drive?"

"I am now."

"We can't be seen leaving together in case somebody's still hanging around, but Darnell and I are going to hang around. We'll watch you until you get in a cab. After that, you'll have to get out of here."

"With what? I don't have any cash."

Max didn't hesitate to get out his wallet and give Johnny what he had on him.

He turned to Darnell and said, "Give him the change off that twenty I gave you earlier."

Raoul said, "I've been calling you, check your phone," and Ramon did. Eight missed calls from Raoul's number. As Ramon was doing that, Raoul put his hand on the face of Ramon's cell phone and said, "I need to be able to reach you. Where have you been?"

Ramon moved away, mainly because Raoul's hand on his phone was annoying him. He said, "I was out," and kept checking his calls, looking for Gloria's number so he could erase it.

"What if there was an emergency?"

Ramon erased three calls from Gloria, all last night to arrange their tryst this morning, and looked up. "Is there?"

"Not at the time." Raoul sat down on the couch, made a scene stretching out, rubbing his head like he had suddenly developed a headache, and said, "Since then, I've talked to Billy. He's coming over."

This surprised Ramon and got him interested. It was working the way Gloria said it would. He sat down across from Raoul and asked why he would want Billy Poe to come here.

"Because we need to speak to him," Raoul said. He was sitting up now, the headache apparently passing. "Billy may have information that's important to us, it's to our advantage to have him around as long as possible."

Ramon was sitting up on the edge of a chair, saying, "Then why try to have him killed?"

"That was my mistake," Raoul said. "That decision was made in emotional haste, a mistake I urge you not to make, my friend."

Ramon sat still, hearing the familiar voice of a mentor.

Raoul saying, "There's a lot of money at stake here, Ramon. And the decision to have Billy killed was an error in judgment that I hope you can learn from." He said, "You will make a lot of money from this as well provided we use any information Billy Poe has available. You like that, don't you?" and saw Ramon smiling. "After we've completed our journey, who knows? Until that time, he's valuable."

It was the *who knows* part that had Ramon thinking, the same words Gloria said in bed less than two hours ago. He wanted to talk to Raoul about Gloria, but decided to ask questions about Billy.

He said, "Do you trust him?"

"I never have," Raoul said. "From the moment I met him, there wasn't much in the man that inspired a great amount of respect. He's an experienced operator and has some marginal talents, to be sure, but I've made mistakes along the way entrusting him with too much responsibility."

Ramon was starting to realize why Raoul had him around— why he was so upset at the missed phone calls. A critical time like this, Raoul needed someone he could trust, someone to fix Billy Poe's messes. Raoul talking to him the way he and

Ramon's father used to talk, about trust and loyalty in business, getting Ramon more involved.

If that was the case, Ramon said, "So, what happens to Billy afterwards?"

"After we get the money?" Raoul said, wanting to be sure.

Ramon nodded.

Raoul leaned back into the couch, looking as if he was thinking about it. "I may have a colleague eliminate him, I'm not certain yet."

"That's risky," Ramon shook his head. "There's too many loose ends right now, too many people out there that know what's going on." Ramon took a chance saying it, maybe Raoul would call his "colleague"—Ramon wasn't sure who that was—and have it done immediately.

"With great reward," Raoul said, "comes great risk."

So much for Ramon's idea. If Raoul wanted *him* to do it, so be it. The only thing he was concerned about still was the timing, if it would happen the way Gloria predicted.

Raoul continued. "I know I can't trust him, but I need him a bit longer . . . until this is done. That's why I have you around, for my protection."

Ramon stood up, feeling he had to with his mentor's confidence in his abilities to protect him from the dangers that Billy Poe presented. It was touching to him, a big moment. Inspired, he said, "I would never betray you."

Raoul stood up and hugged him—their bond complete—two comrades vowing protection to each other, Ramon feeling he was considered Raoul's equal for the first time.

Ramon sat back down, wiping a tear away from the corner of his eye, his indiscretion with that lying bitch Gloria coming to mind.

He would have to do something about her. Too bad, she was an excellent lover.

★ ★ ★ ★ ★

Darnell said, "We need to talk."

They were outside the Clark when he said it, watching Johnny get in a cab and on their way back to Max's car. They had crossed Collins by now, on side streets away from the crowds.

Max didn't like the way it came out of Darnell's mouth. He had gotten over thinking of Darnell as someone he picked up, a scumbag, and was seeing him as a good-natured guy, a guy who cared about his kid through all the attitude. Max asked him what it was, get it out of his system and move on. Darnell wasn't as quick with it as he had hoped. Darnell said, "Look," like he was about to admit something, "I think I know why Raoul is so dead-set on catching up to all of us, why he's driving so hard." Max said okay and asked him again, trying to stay optimistic. Darnell said they did steal drugs and did okay, that he made a few grand. He remembered LaRon giving him five thou for his trouble, but that his cousin and Tweety did most of the work and took more. He said people thought moving drugs was easy, but it wasn't unless you knew what you were doing. Anyway, there was a lot of confusion at the moment they stopped Raoul, ambushed him while he was waiting at a red light at an intersection in Homestead.

Max told Darnell to get to the point.

"We grabbed a lot of stuff," Darnell said. "You got to understand, I was young and naïve."

Max did the math. "You were twenty-seven."

Darnell disregarded what Max just said, telling Max, "I always heard LaRon and Tweety grabbed about half a million in cash."

Whaddya know? He said it like it was something that just happened to take place, an afterthought. Darnell said he never saw any of the cash and Max asked, "Then how do you know?"

"You hear things."

Max didn't doubt that. It happens. He said, "All this time, you were never curious? You never wanted to find out?"

Darnell said, "Curious? I got a baby that needs food. Hell yes, I'm curious. My cousin and his knucklehead friend have five hundred grand sitting around, I'd like to know. I risked my life, too, I think I should get a cut." He waited then said, "At least a nick."

Max wasn't as upset as Darnell thought he would be. He was thankful for that. He watched Max rub his chin and his face; watched him stare off in the distance, at little row houses on Meridian Avenue, like Max was thinking about his next question.

Which was, "You say 'sitting around'? What makes you say that?"

"I mean," Darnell said, "I never saw LaRon with anything too flashy. At least, not flashier than he already had. I don't suspect they were saving it in the bank. I just think they were scared."

"Of what?"

"Spending it. See, they knew Raoul was a big score for them. Way bigger than anything they had done up to that time. They start buying expensive cars, you never know what information Raoul's gonna find out. Look how it's going now. You ask me, they were in over their heads."

"You were too."

"Me?" Darnell said. "Shit, I was just helping out."

It made Max remember Darnell's comment about deserving a nick. He thought it over: LaRon and Tweety didn't spend the money and they were dead now; they didn't look like the type to do anything smart with it, like a trust; and, Darnell didn't have it, he wouldn't be here if he did.

"When you were robbing Raoul," Max said, "did you see anything that looked like a case, anything like that?"

"We just grabbed a bunch of gym bags from the back seat." Darnell shrugged. "That's how he was carrying it back then. That's Raoul's fault for being so haphazard with it. I gave mine to Tweety after it happened. I never even looked inside."

A gym bag. Considering the denominations, large bills, it was more than possible.

Max went over it again in his head and believed it could happen. Three guys surprise a car at an intersection, they've been watching your routine for a week. Happens to normal people all the time, just without being followed and not with cash and drugs in the car.

Max looked at Darnell and felt an excitement come over him. A jolt, he had some information Raoul would find valuable. It almost made him forget everything that had happened up till now. Not quite, but almost. He still had some questions but, for now, there was only one thing he could think of.

"You have any idea where that money might be?"

While he was out, Max swung by the office and left Darnell in the car. He heard Darnell start to complain about it, slammed the door, and headed upstairs.

He stopped in Tom Mako's office, hoping to catch him in there. Tom looked up from his computer, reading glasses on, humming a song, Tom's head bouncing around to it.

Max said, "Tom, I need a favor."

Tom closed the window he was looking at on the screen and turned towards Max. He said, "What's up, buddy? How you feeling?"

Max stopped to answer him but was in a hurry. "I'm doing okay, better every day." He said, "Your ex brother-in-law's still on Miami Metro, right? I can't remember his name."

Tom nodded without giving a name. "We still talk. I'm closer to him than I ever was to Darlene."

Max said, "Long as y'all don't have kids together," and Tom laughed. "Way I remember it, he was a pretty stand-up guy."

Tom listened to his partner laying it on a little, waiting for the favor.

"I need this one close to the vest," Max said. "There's a body in a house on Jann Avenue in Opa-locka. I need to see what they have on it."

"That's pretty serious." Tom sat back. "You saw the body?"

Max nodded. "He's a guy I was watching as part of an unofficial investigation . . ."

"That's this Darnell thing?"

Max nodded again. "Yeah, he was one of the guys involved in my accident. I talked to him a couple of times. I might've been the last person to see him alive."

"And you don't want to tell Don until you have more information." Tom was looking at Max when he said, "I'll run it by him, see what comes up."

"I'd appreciate that, buddy."

Max was turning to leave when Tom stopped him. "Max, if you need some help, my door's open."

Max said thanks, then stopped, remembering an odd question he had from before. "What was that song you were humming when I came in?"

Tom looked up. " 'Take This Job and Shove It.' " He smiled. "I heard it a couple months ago and haven't been able to get it out of my head since."

CHAPTER THIRTY-TWO

"You don't have time to meet me in private? You have me sweating my ass off in the middle of this heat? The humidity is wrecking my hair."

Ramon didn't have much time and told Gloria that on the phone; that he wouldn't have time for another round of love-making. She said, "What, you daddy has you by the balls? Did he cut them off?" Driving him crazy with her nagging, it was a lot of attitude out of nowhere, but to be expected. He had come to realize what a conniving woman she was, his eyes opened to her infidelity.

They were in a parking garage at the corner of Unity Boulevard and Southwest 7th, aisles empty of cars at this time of the early evening.

She said, "What is it?"

Ramon told her about the discussion with Raoul, telling her he was convinced it wasn't going to happen the way she said. "He's trusting me with additional responsibility. A man in his position needs people he can trust. Why would he do that and betray me in the way you suggested?"

Gloria shook her head, a grin on her face. "The only one in a position is you," she said. "Bent over and taking it up the ass. You really believe him?"

He didn't say anything.

"Ramon," Gloria said, irritating him with the way she rolled the *r* in his name, "you keep up this blind faith, you're going to end up in your grave."

He listened to squealing tires, looked around, and realized that it was coming from the other side of the garage, a ramp for cars to go up and down levels separating the two sides.

"I feel sorry for you, I really do," she said. "It's like you need someone to hold your hand. Like a child, someone to wipe your little *beee*hind when you make a mess in your pants. Otherwise, Lord knows what you're going to do."

"Please don't say anything else."

"Or what? Huh, *Rrrr*amon?"

Doing that on purpose now.

"I'm asking you nicely."

"What are you going to do, hit me like a big, tough man? Is that what you're going to do, *Rrrr*amon?"

He heard the car behind him turning but didn't turn around; heard the engine noise getting farther away as it left the garage and heard Gloria going on over that. She was raising her voice over the noise, still rolling her *r*'s to annoy him. Ramon looked over the low garage wall, not staring but long enough to see dozens of cars down there at intersecting streets.

Gloria was telling Ramon what a loser he was, wasting his time playing wet nurse to Raoul, still talking while Ramon reached inside his waistband for a Smith & Wesson Raoul kept in the Range Rover glove box. He thought the sight of his hand going around to his back would shut her up, but it didn't. *Ay Dios,* so much as daring him to do it. So he did. *Bam.* Saw her body shoot back, bounce off her car, and land on the pavement. It was loud, the echo bouncing off the concrete walls the way sound always did in garages. Thoughts of her ugliness and nagging went through his head, so he shot her again, telling himself because he wanted to be sure she was dead.

But it felt good too.

★ ★ ★ ★ ★

As soon as he was home, Ramon made a point of finding Raoul. Sitting on the patio, talking to himself, going over things in his head. Ramon joined him out there and asked where Billy was.

Raoul said Billy was coming over and they would go for a ride to sort things out. Saying it wouldn't be long before they left, Ramon came back just in time. That made Ramon think Raoul was out here rehearsing, imagining what he would say to Billy.

Ramon wanted to get to it right away, break his big news. He said, "Can I ask you a question?"

Raoul nodded, still silently mouthing words to himself.

"Do you trust Gloria?"

Raoul's mouth stopped moving. His eyes moved from the sky, staring somewhere up there to concentrate on what he was saying, to Ramon, sitting in a deck chair across from him. "Why would you ask that? Is she trying to pit you against me?"

Ramon stared.

"You don't have to tell me," Raoul said before Ramon could answer. "I know the woman. I always suspected she would eventually turn on me. I thank you for telling me. I'll deal with her before she has the opportunity."

Ramon was kind of surprised it wasn't a bigger deal than that. He said, "I already have."

Raoul turned again to look at him.

Ramon could feel some pressure now. "She tried to convince me not to trust you . . . to double-cross you before you did the same to me. She got really ugly with me when I refused."

"So what happened?"

"I shot her," Ramon said. "Twice."

"Where?"

"In the chest."

Raoul looked away, saying, "I mean, where at? What location?" without looking back.

"You know the garage off the boulevard, near the expressway overpass? She's on the third floor."

"Did anybody see you?"

Ramon shook his head. "I'm certain."

Raoul didn't say anything.

Ramon was quiet for a minute, letting Raoul think about it. Eventually, he said, "She wanted me to split the money with her, run away forever."

"How did she know there was money involved?"

"She spies on you."

Raoul didn't say anything.

Ramon said, "She was an evil witch."

"Did she tell you how much money is involved?"

Ramon shook his head. "She never said a figure," he said, hiding that fact. "She just knew there was some involved."

Raoul shook his head slowly.

Ramon almost wanted to apologize for doing it, especially without talking to Raoul first, until Raoul said, "If you had to do it, then you had to do it."

That made him feel better.

Raoul said, "It would've happened anyway. The woman had a way of sticking her nose in places it didn't belong." He leaned back in his chair and thought of her. Her nice body . . . the way she looked in lingerie . . . the ways she would pleasure him . . . her lack of sexual inhibition.

Then thought of the times she would feel like she had to give him advice . . . give him tips on how to handle his business . . . tell him what she thought of this person or that one, like he was concerned about what she thought.

Raoul was staring at the sky, about to continue rehearsing his speech to Billy Poe, when he said, "You're sure she's dead, right?"

The first thing Raoul said to Billy was, "Let me tell you how sorry I am for Lester's passing." Like it was from old age or natural causes.

They were riding in a Range Rover that Billy wasn't sure who it belonged to. Somebody was in the driver's seat that Billy recognized but couldn't remember anyway until Raoul said, "You may have met Ramon previously, I'm not certain." Billy nodded, but wasn't sure if Ramon saw it or not. Raoul said, "Ramon is one of my most trusted associates," and Billy thought back to when Raoul said that about him and Lester a long time ago.

"Ramon's father and I grew up in our homeland of Puerto Rico," Raoul said. "Have you ever been to Puerto Rico?" and Billy shook his head. He'd never been further than Punta Gorda unless you counted that time he spent in FPC Pensacola on credit card fraud. He didn't because he was forced to go there, in the back of a Bureau of Prisons van, and he was sure Raoul was talking about a vacation.

Raoul was smiling when he said, "Pedro, that's Ramon's father . . . We were inseparable. Running the streets, doing mischievous things that young boys do. When Pedro couldn't find anyone to watch little Ramon, he would come along. A cruise ship would dock at San Juan, Ramon would ask a vacationing couple if he could carry their bags while they strolled Old San Juan Street, looking in storefronts . . . the woman's handbag, a knapsack, whatever it may be. They would give him a few dollars and he would follow most of the day. When they weren't looking, he would be gone, bring the belongings back to us." Raoul stopped in the middle of his story, looking ahead like he was reminiscing. After that, he said, "I knew that he was a special young man."

Ramon was driving through the suburbs, going south, already

passing South Miami Heights on his way to Leisure City and Homestead. His eyes were straight ahead and Billy noticed Ramon didn't appear to be paying attention to Raoul talking about him.

"When Pedro passed away," Raoul said, "I invited Ramon to come to the United States and live with me. He was seventeen at the time, a difficult age, but Ramon was always a dedicated boy. When Ramon first arrived here," Raoul gestured with it, "he fell into a bad crowd, hooligans. They talked him into robbing dwellings, a person's home. Being the foolish children they were, they didn't give Ramon any gloves to wear. All the rest of their gang had gloves to mask their fingerprints, but they neglected Ramon. He was sentenced to three years, did eight months, and never said a word." Raoul raised his voice. He said, "He's a wonderful young man."

Billy saw Ramon looking back at him in the rearview mirror.

Billy said, "That's a great story," and stared out the window. "What does it have to do with me?" Feeling like he made a bad decision, that he never should have agreed to this.

The smile talking about Ramon was gone from Raoul's face. "I'm telling you how valuable loyalty is."

Billy watched Ramon staring at him in the mirror and Raoul said, "Ramon could have tattled on his friends. New to this country, the only friends he had to that point. They treat him like shit, as good as piss on him, and he acts like a man."

"I thought he had you? Weren't you his friend?"

"I'm more like his uncle," Raoul said. "Children are so impressionable at that age, they value their friends more than an older family member."

Billy thought Raoul had his answer right there, but didn't think it through and wouldn't after all these years. Instead, he said, "Okay, he did his eight months, great."

"Look," Raoul said, "I know you've been a good soldier, but

I don't need a tone of voice. I think maybe you need a lesson in what loyalty is."

Raoul said it and Billy recognized it. Saying he didn't trust Billy. Not as much as he did his golden child, anyway. Billy felt no control over the situation, two immigrants talking down to him, taking over.

"It's just that this is a long story," Billy said. "You're the one who called me and you want to talk about this? You want me to hear about the old days?"

"My point is that in light of Lester's death, your loyalty is important to me." Raoul's expression didn't change when he said, "If there's something you're not telling me, it's between you and whomever. I've offered you that chance already."

"So what're we here for?" Billy said, staring out the window again at strip malls and apartment complexes.

"I want to know what you've been doing since I saw you last. Have you found out anything on this government agent or his black accomplice?"

Billy shrugged. "I never found out where they lived if that's what you're talking about."

Raoul sat back, almost in a resignation, and said something to Ramon in their native language that made Billy glance towards them for a moment.

Billy said, "Is there something you want to tell me?" imagining what they might be saying about him. Billy, sitting in Raoul's eighty-thousand-dollar SUV in torn blue jeans, muscle shirt, and black doo-rag, acted offended, for what good it might do, saying, "I thought *we* were having a discussion."

But he knew they weren't. Figured as much when he stepped in the car and knew it for sure now.

Raoul said, "I'm the one doing all the talking, Bill. I ask you a question, you have no answers." He said something to Ramon again that Billy didn't understand, then turned back. "Do you have any information for me whatsoever?"

Billy shrugged, that pitiful one when you know you're caught and won't get out of it. He said, "What do you want to hear?"

"Whatever you want to tell me, Bill."

Billy took his time to make Raoul wait. He hated being called Bill. He said, "Max, that's the ATF agent, has come by the house a few times . . ."

"A few?"

"A couple." Either Raoul wanted to interrupt him or hear what he had to say. He waited until he thought Raoul was done before saying, "But I never told him anything."

"So you talked to him?"

"A little, yeah."

Raoul sat back, wanting to ask what they talked about, but didn't. He waited for Billy to continue and Billy said, "The first time I saw him, he found me and Lester at Johnny's house."

"This is Johnny Stanz?"

Billy nodded.

Raoul made a call and ignored Billy for a few minutes, busy on the phone. He wasn't speaking English, but every once in a while Billy would pick up on a word like *Johnny* and he thought he heard *ATF* at one point.

Billy was looking out the window, watching high rises and parking lots pass in the distance, signs of civilized life that were getting more sparse the further south they went until he could feel Raoul hang up and say something to Ramon.

Then he got Billy's attention by asking, "So, you know where Johnny Stanz lives?"

"Sure," Billy said, like he thought Raoul did too but was surprised to hear that he didn't. "Lester and me did some jobs with him before. You just run into guys, learn things about them like where they live, little things like that."

Raoul said, "So you can direct us to his house?"

"Yeah," Billy said. "But we got to turn around. It's in the opposite direction."

"You see, Billy," Raoul said, "you thought you wouldn't have anything to contribute."

CHAPTER THIRTY-THREE

Johnny got home and started throwing things in a bag, not wasting time, not stopping to fold anything or check if it was even clean. He used the money Max gave him on a cab back to his house. Thirty-five dollars, he had some left over. Enough to fill up his car sitting in the driveway, a white '93 Beemer with no air conditioning, and get out, go anywhere. He had two credit cards, one from Kelly that he took after Darnell showed up and one in a fake name.

He stopped to take a cigarette out of his shirt pocket and think. He hadn't packed his bathroom things yet, a toothbrush and things like that. He could do that before he left. He needed that cigarette right now, a single he picked up somewhere and didn't know the brand. Maybe it was Vanessa's.

Johnny found his lighter in a kitchen drawer and paced across the living room. Long draws while he looked outside, watching for anything suspicious. People in their yards, sitting in their sofas on front porches, kids playing in the street, it was normal. He stepped away from the window and thought about what he might be forgetting. Nothing that he could think of and took one more drag, about to put his cigarette out, when he decided to look outside one more time.

Shit. Billy Poe on the sidewalk. What's he want?

Johnny looked up and down the street good then, expecting to see Raoul. But he wasn't there and Johnny was staring all the way while Billy turned into his driveway and came up to the front door. Johnny tried to think where his gun was, a .38, and remembered he left it at Kelly's. Fuck. Billy knocking on the door now, his big paw shaking Johnny's screen door. Billy still knocking while Johnny tried to figure out what Billy was doing here. Johnny told himself to relax, it was Billy, nobody else. By themselves, they could talk.

Johnny let him in and closed the door.

Billy started by saying, "How you doing, Johnny?" as he walked in, a deadpan expression on.

Johnny said, "What're you doing here?" and liked the sound of it coming out of his mouth. Didn't think it sounded like he was annoyed, more like surprised to see him without it being overdone.

Billy said, "You didn't think I was going away, did you?" and Johnny could feel the mood change.

Johnny, trying to deal with his nerves, said, "I always wanted to explain what happened."

It was right then that Billy started acting like a hard-on, getting close to Johnny, saying, "Raoul would like to hear that."

Johnny tried that surprised tone again. He said, "He's here?" looking around Billy like he was interested.

Billy didn't turn around or look away.

He said, "He's not far."

"That's great." Johnny started to move, making like he was ready to go, anxious to tell his side of the story. " 'Cause I'd really like to explain things to him. Let him know what happened with Darnell. I didn't mean to let him go, he's got to know that."

Billy put his hand on Johnny's chest as Johnny tried to move past him and said, "You will get a chance to make amends."

Darnell told Max he wasn't certain where the money was. Where do you hide that kind of money anyway? Most people would put it in the bank. Darnell could tell you LaRon wasn't most people. If he was, they were fucked.

Max said you could stash that anywhere. Pick a spot in your house, something as small as a crawl space. Darnell said yeah, reminding himself it was in a gym bag. Max was going to ask, but Darnell volunteered that LaRon's baby sister was living in his old house, a rundown piece of shit shotgun shack in Liberty City. He said, "Calling it a shack might be generous," as if that was something Max wanted to know.

Now they were both silent, windows down on Max's Impala, a breeze blowing in this afternoon. Getting on 95 and going north, Max said, "Lemme think about the best way to do this. That money's been sitting there for three years, twenty-four more hours aren't going to kill anybody." He glanced left, checking the lane for oncoming traffic. "If it's even still there."

"There ain't that much to think about." Darnell pictured them in LaRon's house, LaRon's sister in Darnell's face about why they were there. "Either way, you gonna be rummaging through a dead man's belongings."

On his way to drop off Darnell, Max got a call from Don. He told Max to come into the office and bring his friend.

Max knew that meant Darnell.

The minute they walked in Don said, "He doesn't leave this building," pointing at Darnell. "His ass is mine now."

Darnell started to say something. Max could see it and stopped him.

Don walked around them and closed the door. Slammed it, making a scene for the rest of the office's sake. Max knew Don liked to do that every once in a while, show everyone he was in charge.

"What the hell're you doing with him anyway?" Don said. "He should've been in custody the minute you saw him."

"He needs protection," Max said, "not incarceration."

"What the fuck are you, some kind of prison reformer?"

Max said, "You stick him in some jail, he's liable to end up dead."

"Like that guy in Opa-locka, Lester Long?"

That caught Max off guard.

"You didn't think I knew about that, did you?"

It wasn't surprising, but he was wondering now.

"I hear it's connected with your horseshit investigation," Don said. "Who did it?" and waited. "The bad guys?"

Max nodded and Don said, "Who the hell is that?"

Max didn't want to, but felt he had to say, "A drug dealer named Raoul Garcia. He's the guy behind all this."

"Drugs?" Don said. He was over his desk now, palms down on the desktop like he was steadying himself. "That's not even our jurisdiction. Turn him over to the DEA."

Max said, "Not now," and knew he shouldn't have.

"It's not a request."

"I've come too far with this," Max said. "I'm not about to turn this guy over."

"What," Don said, "you got a hard-on to help your little convict buddy here?"

"He's been busting his ass, Don. If it wasn't for him, we'd be nowhere. How'd you like that with this internal affairs inquiry coming up?"

Max could see that stopped him, gave Don something else to consider he wasn't thinking of.

Don couldn't let it go. He pointed at Darnell, saying, "He's a piece of shit that deserves to go to jail."

"Fuck that," Max said. "This kid's got more guts than most of the guys I've worked with."

"So now your buddy's got guts, huh?"

"You're damned right," Max said. "He's gonna finish this with me."

Don picked his hands up off the desk, standing straight up and arching his back. "That's cute, Max." He was smiling, a fake one. "You two grab-assing around town."

They were doing anything but that and Max thought he made that clear. He didn't say anything back to Don. He didn't know what a response to that was, really. He had already decided what he was going to do.

Don paced back and forth behind his desk, either waiting for Max to say something or thinking about what he was going to say.

Don stopped pacing and said, "Metro P.D.'s handling that situation in Opa-locka." Like he was getting it together. "We're gonna let them." Don tugged at his waistband. "But you've got a review on Monday." Don stopped fidgeting long enough to say, "All the dots better be connected. There better be a pot of gold at the end of this rainbow."

Outside, walking to the car, Darnell said, "Max, are you going to be in trouble?"

Max was leaning on the car roof. "I don't know yet. More than anything, he wants his ass covered." He looked across the roof at Darnell. "He's counting on me to do that."

"I heard you talking about some internal affairs thing. I seen that on TV shows, that sounds pretty serious. Is it really that bad?"

"It can be."

"What they do to you? Put you in jail?"

"No," Max said. "They question you. It can be serious. Sometimes, it's just to show you who's boss, how tough they are."

"Sounds like the kind of people I got to deal with."

Max thought that wasn't far off.

"One thing that bothers me," Darnell said. "You really think I'd be dead if you hadn't found me?"

"It's a good possibility."

Max could see it happening, the same thing that was happening to everybody connected with this. He said, "You need to stay close, it can still happen."

Darnell eyes got big. "You serious?"

"Everyone connected to Raoul has turned up dead. What makes you think it can't happen to you too?"

"You think it's a bunch of coincidences? I mean, look what you just said, everybody connected to Raoul is dying."

"No," Max said. He didn't, but couldn't put a finger on it. "I don't know how or why he's getting a jump on all this. Until I do, you're about the only person I can really trust."

That gave Darnell a strange feeling, almost like he felt good hearing Max say that. They got in the car and Darnell remembered a question he had, saying, "What'd he mean about a pot of gold? What was all that about?"

Max turned the ignition and said, "He means this better be resolved."

Max could see the look on Darnell's face that he didn't understand. So he said, "Either the bad guys get caught or you get turned in."

Max dropped Darnell off, then called Alondra and told her he was coming over. He wouldn't stay late, but he needed to talk to her. She asked about what, trying not to sound defensive, just curious, and he said he didn't want to discuss it over the phone.

She hung up, kind of nervous thinking what it might be about, and poured herself a drink. She kept the vodka out, on the kitchen table with a bowl of ice nearby, hoping Max would see it and want one. Geez, lighten up the mood from that phone call.

In the moment she opened the door and saw Max's face, that crooked little Max grin on it, Alondra felt her nerves start to relax. Okay, he didn't look mad, that was good. She said, "Is everything okay? You sounded upset on the phone."

He said, "No . . ." not sounding sure about it, and gestured to come in. "Busy day, that's all."

Now she was interested.

But then Max said, "We should talk for a minute," like something was going to happen after they talked and she felt an uneasiness again.

"About what?"

"Your room at the hotel."

That couldn't be *that* bad. She asked about it and Max said, "No, it's in okay shape, outside of needing to be straightened up."

Alondra was moving from interested to curious. She felt like Max was beating around the bush about something and said, "What is it, then?" with a tone.

He said, "The guy I was keeping in there, I had to cut him loose. Somehow, that location was found out. You won't be able to go back for a while. It's not safe," and Alondra breathed out.

She sat down on the sofa, inviting Max to do the same and putting her hand on her chest like she was relieved. "I thought it was gonna be worse than that."

"I'm sorry about this," Max said. "You're not angry?"

Alondra shrugged, starting to concentrate on pouring drinks instead of whether the hotel room bed needed making. The vodka was on the kitchen table, but she forgot the tonic water in the fridge. She went in the kitchen and came out with a bottle in her hand and kind of an excited smile, saying, "I was thinking of getting rid of it anyway."

Just like that, she didn't make a big deal of it.

Max watched her, checking out her butt as she was slightly bent over making their vodka tonics. He sat back, relaxed, and asked if she was serious.

Alondra glanced over her shoulder and said, "Yes. I need to be doing something different, further along with my life. Giving tourists massages in a hotel room and then having them expecting a handjob isn't exactly a promising career."

He watched her lay their glasses on the coffee table, a glass tabletop, and looked for coasters. He made a comment about it and Alondra was on her way to get some, her butt standing out in pajama shorts. Max liked the way she looked in her lounging-around clothes, just right.

She came back and he said, "You have any idea what else you're going to do?"

Alondra said, "Nope," sliding coasters under their glasses, "but I've always thought doing business in that room is dangerous. I had some cards made up and passed them around at the hotels, for what good it did. You give a massage in your client's room, they're a lot less likely to try something. There's a record of who's in that room, with their name on it, not mine."

Max nodded. Thinking about it, it sounded right. There's an incident in a room, they'll look it up, see who it belongs to. It's gonna be some guy's name comes up. A lot less potential that way.

He said, "You ever thought about a gun?"

Alondra was sipping when she shook her head. She brought the glass down, saying, "I get nervous around those things."

Max thought about asking if she wanted him to leave his in the car.

She said, "I have mace, but that's it."

"You ever have a problem?"

She shook her head and said, "Nothing serious."

They had gotten off the subject now and there was a silence, the two of them sipping at the same time. She didn't want to appear too forward, but had to ask, "You mind telling me what happened to make my room *unsafe?*"

"Can we just leave it that the guy in there was discovered to be staying there?"

"By who?"

"The bad guys."

Oh.

Max said, "No one has any idea who you are, so you're in the clear. But it'll be some time before you'll be able to go back."

Alondra listened and nodded. She wondered when she'd go back to steady work. She had just told Max she was thinking about getting rid of the room and was serious. Until then, it was like her office. How long was "some time" going to be?

Max said, "I hate to tell you that and I'll help you out where I can, but that's just the way it's gotta be right now."

That was it, the end of their conversation and Alondra was willing to let it die out. She stared at him over the rim of her glass and she wanted to talk about something else.

Max did too and he tried to make small talk. Anything he could think of: the weather . . . she said she had dropped off business cards at hotels, he could ask which ones.

Before he had a chance to ask any of that, Alondra stopped him and said, "I don't know about starting over. I'm not sure what I'd be able to start over with."

"There's always college or some kind of trade school," Max said. "You have nice hair, if working in a salon is something you'd be interested in."

She understood what he was trying to say and smiled. She took a moment thinking about it and shrugged. "I don't know." She said, "Everything costs something. It's overwhelming, you know?"

He did. Max went through college on the G.I. Bill, but knew not everybody was ready to do that, make that kind of sacrifice for a better life. Or compromise, or whatever the word was he was looking for. He decided to ask, "Is there anything else you think you might want to do?" with a genuine curiosity.

When Alondra didn't answer right away, Max started telling her good things about herself. Things he'd noticed since they met. Not that he felt he had to, but just to encourage her.

While he was speaking, Alondra said, "What if you could get a half-million dollars, what would you do?"

Max paused. It was an odd question, considering. He said, "If I was you?" playing along.

It might've sounded like that's what she meant, but Alondra said, "No, *you*. What would *you* do?"

Watching, waiting for Max to answer.

Max took his time. "I'm not sure what I would do. It depends." It really didn't. "If it's part of an investigation, no way. It's not worth it. What, so I can buy a house or a boat? I'd be looking over my shoulder the rest of my life."

"What if it wasn't that? Five hundred thousand just sitting around?"

There was that number again and Max was starting to get curious.

She was serious.

"I don't know," Max said. "There's got to be a catch. Somebody's always going to miss that kind of money."

Alondra said, "That's why they never spent it," and waited.

"Who?"

"LaRon and Tweety."

Max paused again. "Are you talking about some money from a robbery three years ago?"

Alondra was nodding and smiling all in one motion by now.

Max said, "Are you telling me you have it?"

"I don't, but I might know where it is. Back then, they'd never shut up about it."

Except around Darnell, apparently.

Max was staring at Alondra, waiting for more, when he said, "Are you going to tell me?"

He said it and she tried to gauge the reaction, figure out what Max was thinking from his tone of voice.

She decided he was noncommittal.

"Max," Alondra said, "I'm not sure you ever answered my question."

That stopped him, she could see it.

"Which one?"

"If you could put your hands on a half-million bucks, would you?"

What she meant was, would he answer different knowing what he knew now?

CHAPTER THIRTY-FOUR

As soon as Johnny was in the car, Raoul got right to it. Questions about Darnell: how did he get away? Why did you let him go? . . . *why did you let him go,* not giving Johnny the option of saying he didn't.

"You see, John," Raoul said and Billy looked back, that real annoying habit of messing with people's names. "I've been speaking to Bill about the value of trust and loyalty. That said, surely you see my disappointment that you've failed me on both." Johnny was in the backseat, smushed between Billy and Raoul. The two of them on either side of him, close, acting like assholes trying to intimidate.

Johnny smiled at Raoul, a crooked smile, like he wasn't following what Raoul was talking about. Shit, like his words went in one ear and out the other.

He felt compelled to say, "I wanna explain." Christ, it was awkward the way they were sitting. All three of them facing one direction, Johnny having to turn his head constantly when he spoke. He didn't recognize the one behind the wheel. He said, "Darnell overpowered me. Hit me in the back of the neck, right at the base." Johnny turned slightly to show Raoul, on his right, exactly where. "It stunned me. Then he wrapped his hands around my neck. That little space between the tie wraps was right on my Adam's apple. I was about to pass out, I had to pull over."

All that and all Raoul did was nod, almost smiling.

Johnny turned to see Billy, still with his nothing expression, a blank stare. He turned back to Raoul, the man's grin widening a little. It looked to Johnny like he thought it was funny.

Raoul was the one that said, "Then what happened?"

"Darnell escaped. He was running like a wild man through a crowded neighborhood, attracting attention."

"And you drove away?"

"I didn't want to get caught."

Raoul said, "How about after that?"

What, after that? Johnny wondered if he missed something.

Raoul leaned against Johnny and said, "Why didn't you contact us, let us know what had happened?" with a look on his face like he was expecting an answer.

Johnny didn't give him one and he knew, *knew* Raoul had already made his mind up about what happened. He knew because Raoul didn't pursue it; didn't press Johnny on what really happened. The only thing he asked was where Darnell lived.

It was a quiet twenty minutes before they were in front of the little pink stucco house in Oakland Park, LaKelle's house, where Johnny knew Darnell would be. Raoul looked around, the sun beginning to go down but still a lot of activity. He told Ramon to drive around the block, he was interested in seeing the house from the back.

Raoul took that time to make a quick phone call. Johnny looked at him, wondering what he was saying in a language Johnny didn't understand.

Raoul switched back to English, saying, "It's too early, let's go back," and Johnny had a sense of relief but got nervous again when Raoul said something to the driver—the guy Johnny didn't recognize—speaking in their native language.

What Raoul said was, "We still need to do something with this one," and nodded towards Johnny.

Darnell had come home and gone straight to bed, still in his clothes. Lying in bed awake now, LaKelle was lying next to him, and he waited for her to complain about his tennis shoes being on her good comforter.

She said, "LaKeisha's sleeping. You wanna fool around?"

She could see it surprised him.

"You using birth control?"

"What's that supposed to mean?" LaKelle said. "You got one beautiful little girl, you don't want another?"

"I'm just askin' if you want me to pull it out, or what?"

Going around about that, shit, it was ruining the mood, the first time they'd had this mood in a long time. LaKelle was more usually concerned about whether Darnell would wipe his shoes before coming in her house. That's the way she would put it, *her* house. Messing with *her* stuff, using *her* electricity. Making ugly pronouncements like that.

Now he couldn't figure why she'd want to have sex, ask out of the blue like that. What was that? That line about another baby, that must be it. Not that he minded, but it was a little soon. This one was barely one.

Lying in bed, looking at each other, LaKelle decided to ask another question. "You ain't got no condoms?"

Always something like that, even as they were moving towards each other. They got close and Darnell's phone started ringing. He moved away to get it and LaKelle said, "Let it ring."

"It might be my momma."

"That's another thing," LaKelle said. "Don't you think your momma wants another grandbaby?"

Oh, man, now she was bringing up his momma and grandbabies in bed. It made Darnell go limp; LaKelle's declarations about Darnell's momma, LaKelle called her Miss Delores; that she might not be so critical of LaKelle if they had another kid.

How Miss Delores wouldn't point out soap scum around the kitchen faucet or tell LaKelle when to plant tomatoes.

Darnell listened to LaKelle, her speech about how much better life would be if LaKeisha had a sibling, until the phone stopped ringing and he heard a chime, that little ding-dong that told him someone left a message.

He rolled over and checked the phone.

It was Max's number.

Johnny was surprised when Raoul told his driver to turn around and take him home. Finally, he told Johnny the guy doing the driving was named Ramon. It didn't ring any bells. Now that he knew his name, Johnny wanted to tell Ramon that he was taking a long fucking time to get back to his house. Took the interstate, sure, but stayed in the right lane the whole time. Didn't get around one person going home, like they did in a hurry to get to Darnell's for nothing.

Ramon stopped the Range Rover a hundred feet or so from Johnny's driveway and Johnny wondered what was going on. Ramon cut the lights and Raoul stared at Johnny like, *What are you waiting for?*

Johnny didn't say a word and got out, stepping over Raoul, who moved his legs out of the way. He got inside the house and it was quiet. He had left a living room light on when he left with Billy and turned it off so the Range Rover couldn't see him watching them. He waited for them to leave, standing there with a crack in the blinds. He hadn't seen the light come on yet. What were they doing? He knew. Waiting for him to leave so they could follow, do something to him away from his residence. Okay, there were the headlights and the Range Rover moved past his house, turning at the next left. They'd be making the block, doubling back to catch him leaving.

What he would do now was wait for them to circle back

around because he knew they would. See his car still parked and think, hey, Johnny's still home, the thought that he would take off on them still in their heads. If he saw Billy walking towards his house—they'd surely send him, Johnny got the idea that Ramon was above that—Johnny would jump the fence in back of the house and hitch a ride to the bus station at the airport or the one on Caribbean Boulevard. See, these guys weren't as smart as they thought they were.

Johnny wondered why he hadn't thought of the bus before. Thinking about his luggage, he'd have to take less, but that wasn't a problem. Be cheaper than driving his car. Max hadn't given him that much, kind of a cheap guy. He had an aunt that lived outside St. Louis, some town that began with a K. He'd have to look her number up when he got there. *Hey, it's been a long time. I'm in town, you mind if I stay with you for a few days?* Johnny had to think about her name. Alice. *Hey, Aunt Alice, how you doing?*

He wondered if she'd let him smoke in the house.

It was the last thing Johnny thought of before he felt the knife in his back.

Max told Darnell to bring a shovel.

Darnell told Max they were going to look suspicious, two men in a dead man's house in the middle of the night. He reminded Max that he said twenty-four hours wasn't going to kill anybody, or something to that effect.

"I changed my mind. The sooner we get our hands on it, the better off we'll be."

Now the man was talking like he *knew* the money would be here. It made Darnell curious and he asked Max how come he was so sure.

"It's just a hunch."

Darnell knew it was more than that.

Max said, "Alondra said she thinks it's here, that they never shut up about it."

Whoa. That made Darnell's eyebrows raise.

They were standing in a dark kitchen, light still off, when Darnell asked, "You been hittin' that?"

Max shrugged, making it look like he was annoyed. "Maybe." Then, "It's none of your damn business, anyway."

Darnell nodded, that self-assured head bob knowing that Max let it slip out, that he'd found out something Max didn't want him to know. Okay, so she was aware of the money. That made Darnell ask, "That pussy ain't going to your head, is it?"

Max had a flashlight out, the beam bouncing around the kitchen, guiding him through closets and an empty pantry. He said, "If you mean, am I looking to give it to her, I'm not."

Max told Darnell to take his shovel outside, start poking around, look for a spot that looked good to dig up. Darnell shook his head. It was about the most preposterous thing he'd ever heard . . . and he'd heard some dumb shit in his time.

Darnell took his shovel and went outside, but was still asking himself, *If he's not giving her the money, what is he gonna do with it?*

The house was empty and deserted, trash laying around. Different from the last time Max was here. It looked like somebody had come in and looted the place.

That thought made Max pull out his gun as he walked through the living area. The place smelled like a sewer, the plumbing had backed up. Something along those lines. Looking around the bedroom, no one there, Max thought back to his conversation with Darnell. He told Darnell he wasn't giving the money to Alondra.

What was he going to do?

Giving it to her didn't feel right. Not like, here, it's yours.

Have a good time. Max meant it when he told her he would have trouble keeping it. He would. He knew Darnell would take it; he'd have to keep watch in the backyard, for all he knew Darnell would hop the fence and take off if he found a gym bag buried out there.

Max kept looking in closets and cabinets. Feeling for loose spots in the floor. The house wasn't on piers, it had a foundation, but still he'd like to think he could tell if there was a dead spot. He looked for a piece of carpet cut out under the bed. Nothing.

Max sat on the edge of the bed, knowing why he was here. It had become personal with Raoul, no doubt about that. The money was something he wanted and Max wanted it first. Still, sitting in the dark, in a dead man's bedroom, the smell of sewage and mildew, had Max questioning himself.

Darnell couldn't figure out where to start. Okay, start poking around. Put the nose of the shovel in the ground, take it out. It's what Max wanted him to do.

Man, this was pointless. How come he had to be outside digging? It must've been something racial. Darnell kept doing what he was supposed to do, wondering if Max was having better luck. He had to be.

Every time he would stab the shovel tip in the ground, Darnell looked in the neighbor's yards to see if someone was looking back at him. Like he said, it looked damned suspicious. What would Max do if somebody called the police and they came cruising up here? Four or five cars, Darnell could see that happening.

He went through the motions, poking and pulling up. He wondered how much good he was really doing. If there was something, it wouldn't be just below the grass. He thought about it and shrugged. Maybe it would, he couldn't be so sure.

He knew LaRon was lazy and was pretty sure Tweety was too, they wouldn't dig deep. He decided to try over by the little tin shed on the other side of the yard, opposite from where he was—because he had tried everywhere else and there was nothing.

So he'd do that section over there to tell Max he did. Shovel in his hand, poking it in the ground, trying harder when he felt like it. Really putting it in there, those tries made his hands hurt. About ready to give up . . .

When he hit something hard.

The Vulture was home now, relaxing in his living room done in a mixture of South Florida pastels and whatever furniture he could find cheap or had given to him. Laying on a couch, stretching out, becoming Armando again; thinking about the people he'd murdered since reuniting with his old friend. He believed "comrade" was the word Raoul used that day, if he wasn't mistaken.

There were three so far: Lester Long, even though that one was an error; arranging for the death of an inmate at the correctional center, a colored one; and, Johnny Stanz. Two, possibly three, more. That depended on Raoul.

Armando sat around. It always looked like he was waiting on Raoul lately. Why was that? His whole life right now disrupted by phone calls, expected to drop everything at a moment's notice.

There was no reason for it, he was the one taking all the risks. What if there was some evidence left behind? He was careful, a professional, but you never knew. How many times had the smartest, most cunning criminals been caught while some dumb one got away? Look at O.J.

If the police came to talk to him, Raoul could have a problem on his hands. Perhaps he could be made to talk. You often hear of long police interrogations, asking questions for hours until you crack. He *was* getting older.

Unless they could work something out. An agreement. He would have to talk to Raoul, tell him about that possibility.

CHAPTER THIRTY-FIVE

It was dark and Raoul still hadn't made a decision; had been thinking about it since Billy told him where they could find Johnny Stanz. Johnny Stanz was over with, Raoul had gotten that phone call. Right now, Raoul was on the patio at the house in Hialeah, Ariel cleaning because they had visitors.

He turned around to look inside and it brought him back to Puerto Rico, his own youth when his mother would clean up, people she didn't know in the house. He could see Ramon, in the kitchen rifling through the refrigerator. Billy was somewhere. In Puerto Rico, Raoul's father would come home at different times of the day, sometimes telling his mother to straighten up, they were having guests. Not like having your boss over to impress him with a fancy dinner, but it was the same gist. His father didn't have a steady job, or not one that Raoul knew of. His mother would clean up and send Raoul to his room with a bowl of *sopon de pescado* if they had fish, black bean soup if they didn't.

All this time passed, nearly forty years, and Raoul saw himself in the same position. A woman cleaning, people unknown to her in the house. Billy playing little Raoul, upstairs tucked away in his room.

Raoul stuck his head inside and told Ramon to call Billy outside. He waited; a long time by his count, Billy stalling to show he still had some control. Raoul had his back turned to see Billy and Ramon stepping outside. Ramon had a plate of ceviche in his hands, Billy looked like he was just waking up.

Raoul said something in Spanish to Ramon and then asked Billy, "What have you been doing?"

"Watching TV . . . the news, whatever was on."

"I hope the news was informative. Maybe you found a funny program? Something too entertaining for you to come down and spend time with us?"

"I had to clear my mind."

"Of what?"

"What I'm gonna do. I'm out, man. This shit is too crazy for me. Y'all do what you want to, but I wanted to tell you man to man so there's no misunderstanding."

"This is what you were thinking about when you were watching television?"

Billy nodded. "Been thinking about it since I was dumb enough to come over here. Just that sitting up there by myself gave me some time to come to my senses."

"Why don't we talk about it tomorrow? Have a nice dinner with Ramon and I." Raoul looked over Billy's shoulder. "I see there's ceviche, that's a start. The way Ariel cooks, I'm guessing it's store-bought, but it's better than a hamburger, no?"

"I like tacos."

"Even better," Raoul said and started to put his arm around Billy. "At dinner, we can discuss one last thing I need you to do for me."

Billy could see it coming.

He said, "What about all that 'Lester deserves justice' talk?" Billy looked over at Ramon, then straight ahead, feeling Raoul's arm across his shoulders. "Far as I can tell, all we've done are things you need."

"Absolutely," Raoul said. "Avenging Lester's death is foremost of my priorities." Raoul touched his heart with his free hand. "It means more to me than anything. But to do that effectively, I have to unburden myself beforehand."

It was Billy's turn to ask, "Of what?"

Raoul said, "I need you to go to the black man's house and bring him to me."

"Darnell? Unh-unh."

Raoul's head snapped back and he faked a surprised look. "This should be no problem for a seasoned professional such as yourself."

"I'm already an accessory on all kinds of fucked-up shit in the last couple days," Billy said. "You want to do that, do it yourself."

"You have skills in breaking and entering that Ramon and I don't have. It would be so much simpler for you."

"You want in, break a window. There, it's that easy. I'm sure there's no alarm, that's why they got bars on the windows. But I didn't see no bars on the windows in back when we rounded the block."

Raoul had his arm off Billy's shoulders by now. "You see, Bill? This is what I mean, you've already got things planned out."

Billy said, "I didn't mean it like that."

"Regardless, we need your expertise."

That was fucking Raoul for you. Always twisting around what you were saying, throwing it back in your face. There was a silence, Raoul standing in front of Billy. His hands on Billy's shoulders, staring Billy in the eye, waiting.

"I told you, I'm out."

Raoul said, "Are you sure?"

Billy nodded.

"Because," Raoul said, "I would hate to make a phone call to a friend, let them know someone I know that attempted to run a federal agent off the road in a high-speed chase. That could be construed as attempted murder."

There was a silence again, Raoul turning it into a pissing contest with that. Billy said, "I could say the same thing about you," prepared for whatever came next. He wasn't sure if Ramon was gonna draw a gun or what.

Instead, in a quiet tone of voice, Raoul said, "You can certainly try. We'll see who walks."

"Why are you doing this?"

"Because I can. And you belong to me. I thought we understood each other about the value of loyalty by now."

Raoul was having his fun toying with Billy, messing with a big, dumb brute. Staring back with that stupid look on his face. Raoul wondered if he actually thought they were going to hunt for Lester's killer. For all Raoul knew, Billy thought he was serious.

"Billy, I'll tell you what," Raoul said. "If it will make you feel better, we'll all go. How's that?"

Darnell said, "What is it?"

Max had to be honest, he wasn't sure. At first glance, it looked like a cardboard box, no bigger than two-by-three. It was hard to tell with some kind of hard shell on the outside. A glaze or glue or something. Max hadn't been looking at it long enough to figure it out.

The feeling he had right now was like when they find buried treasure in the movies. Indiana Jones, Indy busting ass to find some kind of artifact. Making it with the leading lady at the end. *King Solomon's Mines.* The old one, a winner Max had seen a few times. Stewart Granger and Deborah Kerr falling in love in the middle of Africa. *Romancing the Stone,* another good one. That funny scene where they're falling down the mud slide and Michael Douglas's face ends up between Kathleen Turner's legs. Buried treasure movies—it always looked like the guy and girl would fall in love.

Max wondered, *Did they end up living happily ever after when it was over?*

Before they left, Billy wanted to know how they were going to do this. What were they going to do? Would be nice if they had told him that much. Okay, they knew where Darnell lived at, what were they gonna do with it?

He said, "I ain't killin' nobody, if that's what you're expecting."

Raoul was sitting in the living room, a nine-millimeter and hollow point rounds on the coffee table in front of him. Opening the slide, looking around in there, he said, "What good is Darnell to me if he's dead?"

Good, they understood each other. But you know, all this time, that's one thing Raoul never explained. What good Darnell was to him. In the beginning, Billy was getting paid and that was good enough. It was different now.

He said, "I'm glad we got that out of the way." Billy sat across from Raoul. Ramon was in back of him, back there somewhere, stupid enough to be checking out Raoul's woman, on her hands and knees cleaning the spaces between kitchen floor tiles. "You think I could get one of those, for protection's sake?"

Raoul was still looking down the slide, examining it, when he said, "No, I don't." No further explanation, it wasn't up for discussion.

Ramon told Billy, "It's a test."

That made Billy turn, the first time he heard Ramon speak English since they met. "I thought you only knew your language."

"I was in your place once," Ramon said. "Scared . . . Confused." Talking to Billy like he understood what he was going through. With a smile, Ramon said, "Don't worry, you have every right to be."

★　★　★　★　★

"That's five hundred thousand, huh?"

Darnell said it while he and Max were looking at a cooler full of money stacks wrapped in duct tape. Five stacks—they figured a hundred thousand per stack—wrapped in duct tape, then coated with an epoxy glaze and placed in the cooler. *Then,* the cooler was put inside a small cardboard box filled with more epoxy until just the cooler handle was visible.

Max said, "I don't know who was the brains of the operation, but it's a good way to preserve the money. The salt air and damp ground would've worn it away otherwise, depending on how long it stayed in the ground." By now all it took was Max peeling the epoxy cover off and opening the cooler. He was careful with the duct tape, gentle so as not to rip the money.

Max flipped through the bills, looking at packets of money still wrapped in bank bands. Darnell grabbed one of the stacks Max set down and flipped through like he saw Max doing. He said, "Hundred thousand dollars don't look like that much."

Max was still looking at the money, rubbing bills between his fingers, saying, "That's my guess, but it makes sense based on what's here." Max ran his hand through the rest of the cooler, feeling around in case he missed anything. He said, "You didn't find anything else, right?"

Darnell shook his head and looked down. Hundred thousand dollars in his hand. He asked Max, "You tempted to take one of these?"

"It's drug money, right? No one knows it ever existed."

Darnell smiled, saying, "Yeah, me and you's the only ones know it's here."

"You're kidding, right?"

Darnell searched around for words to play it off, then just finally told Max he was. Before Max could get a word out, Darnell said, "Unless you not."

285

"I wasn't the one joking about it in the first place."

"Course not."

There was a quiet while Darnell watched Max looked over the money again; watched him feel around inside the cooler a second time. The man was jumpy about missing something.

Darnell's phone rang in the silence.

Max looked and said, "Why'd you have to bring that?"

Darnell could've given him a couple of reasons. He had a kid, for one. But he didn't say anything, just went into the next room.

On Darnell's way out, Max told him, "Don't be long, we're leaving."

Max decided he was taking everything, no sense in leaving it here. He started replacing the cooler back in the cardboard box, the cash back in the cooler and so on. Bank bands and duct tape in there, too. Everything back in the way they found it. Shit, what was keeping Darnell?

He walked into the next room, the living room, to see Darnell sitting on the couch. Max saw Darnell's shoulders slumped, head hanging down, and wondered what Darnell was doing, it was time to go.

So he asked Darnell what he was doing and Darnell said, "Max, they got my little girl."

Armando knocked on the door and waited until a woman, young and attractive but looking frightened at the moment, came to the door. She asked who he was and Armando told her, "I'm a friend of Raoul's. Is he home?"

Before she could answer—Armando believed she was going to lie, say he wasn't home even though he saw Raoul's SUV out front—Armando heard a male voice from inside that sounded like Raoul. He moved past the girl, closed the door, and moved into a foyer, waiting again. He heard the voice and saw Raoul now—in the living area, talking to someone out of view. Raoul standing up, hands on his hips, saying, "Now we wait," then listening; nodding as the other person said something. "No, I've already called him, he's aware." Nodding again. He said, "Just keep it quiet. She's no good to us in some piss-poor condition." Armando saw Raoul turn to him and walked towards the living area.

Raoul walked fast enough to meet Armando in the foyer, not letting him get far enough to see what was going on.

Raoul said, "My friend, what are you doing here?"

Armando could tell his visit caught his friend off guard.

Before Armando could answer, Raoul asked, "How did you know to come here?"

"I've been here a few times," Armando said, "at your invitation. I went by your other place."

Raoul waited, expecting to hear something more.

Armando said, "I believe it's being watched."

Raoul let out a sigh, breathed out again for a moment, and gave Armando a smile. Put a hand on Armando's shoulder to let him know it was okay, maybe that he knew that information already. He said, "What can I do for you?" and looked back towards the living area.

"I was wondering if we could talk."

Raoul disappeared into the living room for a second and returned, saying, "It's really not a good time."

Armando didn't like hearing that. What if he were to tell Raoul that when he called? *I'm sorry, it's not a good time for me to kill somebody that pissed you off.* He was getting paid to make the time, that was true, but it was the principle.

"It's important."

Raoul let out another sigh, this one to show that this was an annoyance, and said, "Why don't we step outside?"

"Why not right here?" Armando said. "It's hot outside."

"Here?" Raoul said. There were baby noises in the background, crying; two men arguing about what to do about it. "There's too many distractions in here."

Armando looked past Raoul, but didn't see anything from where he was. "I wasn't aware you had a child."

Raoul was walking away when Armando said it, ignoring the remark and holding a hand up while he said something to someone in the other room. Making sure the coast was clear.

After a few moments, Raoul came back. The noise was gone, bodies shuffling that told Armando the baby had been moved. Raoul said, "How about the back patio?"

Armando shrugged and followed Raoul outside. He closed the double doors behind him and sat down, something that Raoul wasn't expecting—a conversation long enough to where he would have to sit down.

So Raoul sat and said, "What is it?"

Getting to it right away. Armando said, "What if the police want to talk to me? What should I say?" Armando knew what to do in that situation—nothing—but was looking for a way to break it to Raoul.

Raoul's face was deadpan. "What are you talking about?"

"I've exposed myself in the last several days," Armando said. "I'm as careful as I always have been . . ."

"What are you saying?"

"I'm taking a lot of risks."

It didn't take Raoul long to figure out what this was about. He said, "And you want more compensation?"

If he wanted to bring it up, okay. Armando nodded, saying, "I think I've earned it."

Raoul didn't understand and hoped the scowl on his face showed it; wondering how Armando could come to him, tell him he's exposed himself, ask what to do if the police came looking for him and he wants—no, deserves—more money?

Something must've happened to him, a realization. An older man now, not The Vulture he grew up with. Too much time had passed, Armando staring at the television, police shows scaring him into thinking he would be found out.

He said, "You have any reason to believe the police suspect you?"

Armando shook his head and Raoul said, "But you're scared anyway?"

Armando wouldn't say if he was or not, but did say, "I'm just being more cautious. It comes with the wisdom that age brings."

Wisdom that age brings, huh? Look here, a cold-blooded killer sitting on the patio giving his philosophy on life. Raoul leaned back in his chair, the first time he gave a hint of relaxation since they were out here, and looked off, thinking to himself. He said, "And more money helps you be more wise, too?"

Armando didn't hesitate to answer, saying, "It doesn't hurt."

Armando wasn't out of the driveway before Raoul found Ramon and gave him instructions.

Raoul had told Armando that he would need time to get some cash, he didn't have the kind of money on him that Armando was talking about.

It made Raoul sad, Armando coming to him and making demands. Threats in there too, the part about the police asking him questions. So much as telling Raoul that he could be persuaded to tattle to save his own ass . . . if he didn't get more money. Raoul shook his head to himself. He thought they were on this journey together.

CHAPTER THIRTY-SIX

Max raced back to LaKelle's, where Darnell said they needed to go. On the way, Max asked if Darnell could tell him what LaKelle said.

Max asked that one question and let it go when Darnell didn't answer. He decided they'd get to LaKelle's and see what happened. They could hear noises from the car as they drove up, then hearing it from outside, LaKelle inside shouting at no one in particular.

Darnell took a second, a serious look on his face that Max hadn't seen before, and said, "Stay out here for a minute, okay?"

Max did that and heard the screams and crying get louder when Darnell walked in. He could imagine what was going on. LaKelle was blaming Darnell for this. Probably Max, too. She'd be wanting to kick Darnell out, maybe come outside to chew Max's ass. That would be her rage talking and Max could understand it. He couldn't pretend to be in their position and wouldn't make the mistake of saying that if he was let in.

Max waited and was surprised when the screams calmed down. Peaceful by comparison now. Man, Darnell had a job in there. Max's head turned when the door opened, Darnell in the doorway telling him to come in.

The first thing Max heard was, "You better get my baby back."

LaKelle disappeared after that.

They heard the bedroom door slam and Max said, "What happened?"

"Two guys. One was a Latino, she couldn't be certain what country. The other was a white guy." Darnell said, "They were after me."

Max took a chair at the kitchen table and said, "You have what he wants." Darnell turned to look at him and Max said, "Or at least he thinks you do. This is his way of finding out."

"What're we gonna do?"

We. That told Max Darnell wasn't sitting this out, letting Max handle it alone. Max couldn't blame him.

"Did LaKelle say if they gave her any instructions?"

Darnell shook his head. "Just took my girl and left." He said, "I 'magine they left LaKelle 'cause she was yelling so much, they didn't wanna put up with that," and was serious.

"No," Max said. "She was able to describe them. When you weren't here, they went to the next best thing. They wanted you to know who it was." He waited and said, "She didn't call anybody else, huh? The police, anybody?"

"She didn't say anything about that."

And that was something she would've said, even in her hysteria. Max said, "Good. We can do this our way, then." Before Darnell could ask what that was, Max told him, "Darnell, this could get messy."

He didn't seem to mind. "Long as they the ones getting messed up."

Okay, that was it. Max said, "We can either wait for them to contact you or we can take the offensive."

"How long we got to wait?"

"Could be anytime." Max shrugged. "My guess, they know you're climbing the walls right now. The longer they make you wait, the more desperate you'll get."

Darnell asked him again. "How long they gonna make me wait?"

"Could be a couple of hours, could be more."

291

Darnell was shaking his head. "Man, I can't sit here that long."

Max was thinking. "Give me a pen and paper."

Darnell went off somewhere and it was quiet for several moments. Max spent the time thinking some more, thinking about the risk he was about to take. If he was right, it would confirm something that had been bothering Max for a long time.

Darnell came back, extending both hands with pen and paper in them, and Max took it.

He wrote a number down and handed the paper back to Darnell.

"Call that number. Tell the person who answers that you have Raoul's money, you want to meet for a trade. Don't say I'm with you."

Max watched him thinking about it, staring at the paper before asking, "Who is this?"

"Just call it."

Ramon had a hard time finding the gray Altima, getting a late start out of the house after Raoul's instructions. It looked like every other car on the road. There, he found it on Southwest 122nd Avenue going south, the license plate number Raoul told him to look for. Traffic was light at this time, the sun almost out of view to Ramon's right.

They passed intersections with green lights that they rolled through. Ramon moved his car slightly and craned his neck, traffic lights for the next few blocks. Storefronts shuttered except for a McDonald's, darkness spreading soon.

Ramon hoped the timing would be good, he tried to time it where they would be the only two at a stoplight. He had to wait two intersections for that, one at 122nd and Miller Drive— where it made a T-junction and dead ended—and a Ford ran the light, making a right onto Miller and heading towards a golf course.

Ramon waited for a car to pass before stepping out and then did, holding a .22 against his leg, away from two more cars making rights onto 122nd and going past them, all the traffic he could see. He didn't think the man in the gray Altima noticed him; didn't see a glance in the side mirror or hear the engine tearing away.

It wasn't until he was at the driver's side door that Ramon could see the man look up. Ramon fired once through the glass, but wasn't sure what that one did. Reached in and pressed the barrel against the man's chest, fired again, and the old man's body jumped, then slumped forward.

Ramon shook his right hand, working the sting out. He looked around, it was quiet, no cars. He walked back to his car, threw the .22 in the glove box and drove off, wondering who that man was.

Chapter Thirty-Seven

Darnell didn't see the guy, one in a plaid flannel shirt untucked over his jeans, until they were right in front of each other. He was hoping he would see the guy coming and be able to ready himself, but it was too late. Standing out here in the dark, an alley in back of a grocery store on North Dixie Highway; it was fucking creepy back here, man. Details that Darnell knew he'd never forget: The way the lights were, nothing but fluorescent lighting from lampposts making it hard to see, steam coming off vents from the back of the store, that guy's shadow out of nowhere telling Darnell to stop where he was.

Darnell wasn't sure about this guy, what to expect from him. Max never said who he was. Walking up to Darnell, he said, "Your call surprised the hell out of me. How'd you get my number?"

Darnell didn't answer the question. He said, "Fuck all that, I want my baby. I got his money. I called you to set up a trade."

"That's what I want to know. How'd you know to call me?"

Darnell didn't have time to make conversation.

"Look," he said and opened a knapsack with a half-million dollars in it, "you wanna do this or not?"

The flannel shirt guy had a gun out now. Darnell could tell it was a .45, even in this light. The guy blew out of his mouth and motioned with his head for Darnell to come closer. When Darnell got close enough, the guy leaned over to look in.

"So that's it, huh? What's all that junk on it?"

"That's something so it kept all this time it was buried. I dunno what it is. I don't care."

The guy hesitated like he was going to make more conversation, but he didn't. He said, "I'm gonna have to ask you for that money."

"What you mean?"

"You're a dumb one, huh?" The guy raised his .45 to Darnell, at his chest, and cocked the hammer. "I said you're going to give me that money that's in your hand."

"What you expect me to use to get my baby back?"

As soon as the guy said, "I don't give a shit," he felt a sharpness at the back of his head. He tried to turn his head enough but felt the sharpness dig in some more. It felt like the end of a gun barrel. That wasn't working, so he tried to move his eyes as far as possible to see what was behind him.

Max's voice was calm when he said, "Stop."

"Max?"

It was the guy in the flannel shirt that said it.

Max kept his gun on the guy, moving around to his left and grabbing the .45 pointed at Darnell. He saw Darnell staring at him, a look on his face like he was trying to figure out what was happening.

Max said, "Tom, I can't tell you how disappointed I am."

"Max . . ." Tom Mako searched for something to say. "Three years ago, we were gonna bust this piece of shit," he said, motioning to Darnell.

Max reacted as if he wasn't even listening. "Why'd you do it? Was it just the money?"

"What else would it be? I got an ex-wife and two kids. Life's expensive."

"That's a bullshit answer," Max said. "Everybody's life is expensive."

Tom said, "You see these jerks with their fancy cars that cost more than a year's salary for us and we get, what, a shitty paycheck every two weeks. You telling me you've never been tempted?"

Max shook his head, tired of this. "We need Raoul's number."

Tom frowned at him.

Maybe he needed some prodding. "Tom," Max said, "he's got Darnell's child as ransom. That's way out of bounds." He waited. "We need that number."

Tom saw Max was serious. The guy had no qualm about pulling out a Beretta and putting it on him. Just like that after all this time. He said, "My phone's in my pocket."

"Which one?"

"In my jeans, right front pocket."

Max told Darnell to get it.

While Darnell's hand went inside Tom's pocket, Max said, "You make a move, Tom, I will shoot."

"You'd do that?"

"I'll make sure it's to wound."

Darnell's hand came out with a small flip phone and he held it, looking through the numbers. "Which one is it?"

Tom told them it was the first one on the list, the last number he called. Raoul hadn't answered.

Max said, "What were you gonna do, set Darnell up? That your idea of busting him?"

"I thought better of it and hung up."

"More money in it for you if you don't let Raoul in on it, huh? You know they damn near killed me in that little stunt when I picked Darnell up?"

"I told them to leave you." Tom started motioning, asking if he could put his hands down. Max told him no. "Was that what tipped you off, the accident?"

"It was everything." Max was moving towards his car saying it and popped the trunk. "Tweety's murder, somebody at the hotel where Johnny Stanz was staying at, the storage unit. I called Miami Metro about that, they said I was the second ATF guy to call about it."

"Damn cops." Tom said it with a slight smile, resigned. "Government guy calls, they can't keep their mouth shut." Max asked who the guy at the hotel was and Tom said, "I don't know. I just made the call."

Max told Tom, "Get in," and watched Tom bend his head and hunch over to climb in the trunk of Max's car.

"This is total bullshit, Max. I can't believe you're doing this."

Max said, "It's better than a cell," and slammed the lid closed.

Max turned to hear Darnell say, "I have your money," into the phone and watched Darnell waiting, listening.

"No, not tomorrow. I want my baby back tonight. You want your money . . . It's got to be tonight." Darnell listened again and said, "No, I ain't going nowhere I don't know . . . We gonna go where I want . . . There's a hunting camp outside Clewiston, way out in bumfuck nowhere. Meet me there in two hours."

Darnell waited for his turn and said, "You got Billy with you, right? Ask him, he knows where it is."

Raoul lost it hearing about the meeting place. A hunting camp. "He knows where it is." Like the black one was ordering him around. Billy thought he was going to kill Darnell's child right there, fuck the whole thing up. Raoul asked, "How the fuck do you know about this place anyway?" Billy said he just did, something about going out there with his dad when he wasn't in the slammer, but didn't elaborate. Ramon was driving an Escalade through Palm Beach County, a vehicle different from the Range Rover they had been driving around in. Raoul said he wanted something else in case someone got the license plate off the Range Rover and decided to be a good citizen. So Ramon disappeared and came back with this. Billy couldn't see why

Raoul would miss his Camaro, the man had a different car every day.

Now Ramon was asking Billy how come Darnell said he would know where they were going. Even if Billy went there as a kid, it didn't make sense. How would Darnell know that? Billy said, "I don't know," getting sick of the questions. Did it matter? What if he led them in the wrong direction, see how they liked that.

Billy said, "You know, we should've gotten a car seat. We can't be driving this baby like this." Billy had the baby in his arms. "This asshole keeps driving like this, we're gonna get in a wreck."

Raoul turned around, looked at the baby, then at Billy and said, "What are you, a fucking wet nurse? Take out your fucking fat nipple, let her suck on it."

Billy heard them laughing, making jokes to themselves in Spanish, having a good time. But it brought up a point and Billy thought they should have fed her, too. That's all babies do—eat, sleep, use the bathroom in their diapers. *She starts crying, they won't be laughing.*

Billy was going to say something about it, but heard Raoul yelling at Ramon first, saying, "What's wrong with you? You're driving like a fucking madman, slow down." That's all that was said until they were on Highway 27, going north towards Okeelanta; Raoul started asking directions before they went too far and ended up in South Bay or near Lake Okeechobee beyond that.

"You sure you know where we're going?" Ramon said. Ramon was starting to speak English all the time now and it was getting on Billy's nerves. He said, "Can you imagine, getting pulled over out here, we have a black baby in the back seat?" sounding as if that would be funny.

Billy would glance over his shoulder at the darkness behind

them. A red tint from taillights was all that was back there. He was pretty sure they wouldn't get pulled over, by themselves out here, but said, "You don't drive so crazy, we wouldn't have to worry about that." He stared down at the baby whose name he didn't know, her head bobbing with the Escalade's motion.

Raoul said, "I haven't seen another car in fifteen minutes."

They drove for a few minutes. Billy would catch glimpses of Ramon in the rearview mirror. Sometimes looking at him, sometimes not, Ramon slowing down to look at crossroads, highway signs, like he knew which one they were looking for.

Ramon said to Raoul, "Are you going to let the black man walk out of there alive?"

"There's not a chance of that happening. As soon as I get my money, he's dead."

"What if we have to go somewhere else to get it?"

A good one that had Raoul thinking, like he was thinking it up as they went. He said, "I'll shoot him in the leg or some other body part that won't kill him. It'll hurt like hell and he'll want to be dead, but I'll still find out where my money is." Raoul let a moment go before he said, "Then I'll kill him."

Man, these guys were full of laughs. Ramon's crack about being pulled over and now this. Billy decided to ask, "What about her?" holding up the baby and nodding.

Raoul turned around to look; what he saw was Billy serious back there in the dark. He said, "What about her?"

"You ain't gonna kill a baby, huh?"

Raoul made a face, trying to show Billy how stupid he thought he was. "No, I don't want that on my conscience. Her daddy is different, he's disrespected me. Disrespected all of us, am I right?" Looking to Ramon for confirmation. "I imagine we'll drop her off somewhere."

" 'Drop her off somewhere'? What the hell does that mean?"

"It means we're not dropping her off at a hospital or a police station." There they were, laughing again. Raoul doing stand-up.

Billy interrupted. "So, you mean like a fucking dumpster, don't you?"

"If that's what it is, it is."

"You do that, you'll never see me again."

Raoul had to fight himself not to say anything, but that was going to happen too.

They drove separate vehicles. Max said he would park his in a turnout area he noticed beyond the camp, a quarter-mile up, right off the road. Darnell could take Tom's truck.

Before they left, Darnell asked Max, "How we going to do this?"

"It's you he wants," Max said. "We'll be there before he is. You need to look like you're alone."

"Am I going to take the money out with me?"

"Leave it in the truck. Don't take it down with you. You'll need to play a game with him for a few minutes, make sure LaKeisha is okay."

Darnell stopped. He stared out ahead of the pickup's front window, the overhead interior light shining down on him. "You think she's not?"

That would be the lowest of the low, but you could never be sure. Max said, "I think she is, but you need to make certain. She's their guarantee that you'll turn over the money. Until they have it, she's safe."

"Do I get a gun?"

Max shook his head. "They'll search you." He backed away from the truck as Darnell closed the driver's side door. Then the whirring noise of the window going down and Max leaned in, saying, "I'll be close, don't worry."

"Are you gonna shoot him?"

Max said, "I'd like him alive," then thought about it. "But sometimes you don't have a choice."

Raoul was still thinking about Billy's threat, that they would never see him again, when he said, "Where do you want us to drop you off at?"

It was all a joke to them. Billy shook his head, leaning forward to see where they were. Coming up on Obern Road, thick brush and swampland canals all around them, he said, "We're getting close now."

CHAPTER THIRTY-EIGHT

They saw Darnell right when they turned in. A white t-shirt in the flash of headlights standing next to a navy Chevy pickup truck.

Raoul got out of his vehicle and said, "You're alone?"

Darnell nodded his head. "I didn't want to take a chance. This is between us. All I want is my little girl." It was just Raoul and another Puerto Rican in front of him, no sight of LaKeisha.

"And you have something I want." Raoul looked over to the truck. "You haven't spent some of it already, have you?"

Darnell shook his head. "That's for a friend." He said, "Where's my daughter?"

Raoul said, "She's in my vehicle," and told Ramon to pat Darnell down. Darnell watched the young Puerto Rican, the one taking orders, stuff a pistol in his waistband and come towards him. He put Darnell against the wall, the outside of the camp, and gave him a going-over while Raoul asked him where the money was.

"It's in the truck."

The young guy backed off Darnell and put his gun on him, a Desert Eagle Mark I, while Raoul walked over, assuming he could reach inside and grab the money.

Darnell said, "It's locked. You pull on the handle, the alarm's liable to go off. You never know about those new vehicles, the alarm is touchy. Could be a car passing, they might wonder what's going on."

The young Puerto Rican used his free hand to land a punch in Darnell's mid-section. A solid one that doubled him over. Darnell was on his knees when the guy pulled his head back and gave him another one in the stomach.

Face down, Darnell heard Raoul say, "You want to unlock it now?"

Darnell took a second to catch his breath, concentrating on breathing through his mouth and letting it out slow. When he was done, he said, "I have to see my daughter first."

"I guess we're at a stalemate then."

Darnell started thinking and liked the idea of LaKeisha staying in the vehicle. He asked Raoul if he could just roll the window down.

Raoul walked over and knocked on the window, raising his voice to let Billy know what to do through the glass. The window came down and Darnell could see her in the darkness, a white and yellow glow from the dashboard lights helping him. Billy held her up by her underarms for a second and the window went up again.

Darnell didn't say another word, just got out the truck remote and hit the lock button twice. It made that little honking noise and Darnell saw Raoul's face change.

He said, "You still being a smartass?" Raoul's face changed again, eyes open wide with a look of surprise when he saw Max come out from around the corner of the building with a weapon on him, pointed right at Raoul.

There was a moment when everybody froze, a mixture of surprise and panic, and Darnell hit the young Puerto Rican next to him as hard as he could right under the ribcage, put whatever weight he had into it.

Max saw it out of the corner of his eye but kept his eyes straight ahead, on Raoul bringing his pistol up. Max beat him to it and shot Raoul in the chest. He turned and saw the young guy getting up, time to get his pistol in his hand before Max put two rounds in his torso. Three shots and it was over.

It was quiet after.

Max stooped to check Raoul's pulse. There was none. He heard a clicking noise and knew it was Darnell opening the Escalade door. He got LaKeisha out quickly, so Billy must have been agreeable. Max stood up and turned to look at Darnell, taking his girl back to the Chevy. He leaned in through the open door and asked Billy, "Did anybody hurt her?"

Billy shook his head. "These guys are crazy enough, but that's where I would have drawn the line. I can't do that."

"You helped them kidnap her, though."

"I didn't have no choice. Those guys are nuts. I didn't like it, but I had to do it."

"So you were under duress?"

Billy wasn't sure what that meant, but by Max's tone of voice it sounded like it made sense.

Max knocked on the door and waited. When it opened he said, "Finally getting a chance to clean up your room?"

Alondra said, "Since I got your message."

Max closed the door behind him and stood there, waiting.

"Max, I haven't seen you for three days. You left a message on my phone and that was it."

He said, "I was hoping you understood my message. It's still not safe here. We never caught the guy who was hanging around."

Alondra nodded, yeah, she got it. She felt a disconnect and wanted to sit down with Max, all of a sudden, and talk about things. She wanted to ask him some questions about where he'd been for three days and why he left in the middle of the night without an explanation.

She would work up to it.

Alondra said, "Yeah, today's my last day here. I have to check out in about an hour. After all these years, I can't leave it looking like this."

Max managed a smile. "I'm sure they'll find something to charge you for." She kept straightening up. He thought it was funny, maybe she didn't hear him.

He said, "Where're you going to set up now?"

Alondra was fluffing pillows now. "Anything but this. Maybe rent some office space . . . a client's hotel. This is too dangerous."

He was starting to feel awkward, standing here watching Alondra do her cleaning routine. He thought the less he said, the better off he'd be. But she didn't look like she was in an understanding mood, that she would realize what he was feeling—the uncertainty about whether she was sleeping with him to get close to the money or not.

She said, "Why didn't you let me know what was going on?" and Max shrugged.

"I had to take off for work."

"I can appreciate that. You could've let me know something later. A call would've been nice."

"I'm sorry."

"Max, is there something you're not telling me?"

He could answer that, but hesitated. In that time, she said, "You think I'm after that money, don't you? You think I'm using you, Max?" She watched him appearing to be thinking about it.

Max didn't feel he was ready to answer all these questions right this minute. She didn't know he had the money, had it three days ago, and she hadn't asked him about it since he'd been here. Still, he hesitated and she used the time to say, "Just talk to me, Max."

So he relaxed and told her, "I had to go to work. It's not the kind of job where I can always let you know what I'm doing or call you and tell you everything's okay. You think this is bad, try having a relationship with someone who goes undercover."

"And you're afraid I'm, what, going to hold you back? That I'm going to stop you from catching bad guys?"

He said, "That's not it. It's just difficult for me to worry about a home life or a real relationship when I'll have to do things like leave in the middle of the night or not contact you for a few days."

Alondra was nodding, like she was taking it all in. She said, "Well, then you'll never be close to anybody, Max."

He didn't say anything or show emotion, but she was right. It was something that had crossed his mind before. Max felt he could go into it, explain to Alondra that that was why he wasn't married anymore, but didn't.

He said, "Maybe I just need some time." Thinking of Tom Mako, he said, "The past few days have been hard for me."

Alondra asked him, "And it's not something you want to talk about?"

Max shook his head, saying, "Not right now."

She started straightening again and didn't seem to mind Max standing there, helping by picking up little things here and there. She made small talk, passed the time with conversation about the weather and what Max's next job was until he grabbed her arm and stopped her.

He said, "I wanted to give this to you," and extended a white envelope, thick with something stuffed inside.

Alondra stared at Max while it passed from his hand to hers. She looked inside and asked, "Max, what is this?"

"It should be enough to cover what I owe for letting me use the room plus some extra."

Alondra stared at it some more, flipping hundred dollar bills through her fingers. She had an idea where it came from, but kept that to herself. "There's a lot more than that."

It was a hundred thousand dollars, but Max didn't give her a figure. He wasn't sure about what he was going to say, but she beat him to it anyway, telling Max, "I don't want all this."

"I'd feel bad if you didn't take it," Max said. He told her, "Like you said, nobody knows it exists," and that confirmed it for her. "Take it and make a future for yourself."

Alondra hesitated this time.

"Max," she said, and he liked the way she was looking at him, a gleam in her eyes. "I'd like you to be part of that future if you want."

Darnell had already finished Colors's two-drink minimum by the time Max got there. Before Max could sit down, Darnell asked him if he could spot him, get these drinks and Darnell would get him back later.

Max said sure, what the hell, and Darnell told the bartender one drink for his friend and another for him.

Darnell was happy to see him, Max could see it in his face, a genuine happiness. Darnell said, "Where you been?" and Max told him he was taking care of business, tying up loose ends.

Darnell knew what he was talking about. He said, "I'm sorry about your friend, man. I know that's hard."

The bartender came, so Max didn't answer. Darnell would understand how it was. Max said, "I don't know how the rest of it's gonna shake out. I'm responsible for two dead bodies, not to mention what Raoul's accountable for."

Darnell set his drink down. He glanced towards the stage and back. "You gonna be in trouble?"

Max shrugged. "Probably not. It's going to take a shitload of paperwork and explanation, though. I've already started. Billy Poe's going to stay out of jail for being a corroborating witness. He's going to say that he was coerced into kidnapping LaKeisha."

307

Darnell could see Max had been thinking about it. He asked, "What about me?" but wanted to ask about the money. He knew it would be a letdown if he did, Max was a straight-arrow guy. At least as straight as he'd ever met. Darnell had prepared himself and was ready, that little optimism fading away over the course of a few days.

Max said, "You're officially off the hook now. You ID'd Raoul. That's good enough for me. You'll be part of my report, though. You have to be, that's how this started. Whether there's a hearing," Max shrugged again, "that I couldn't tell you."

Darnell felt the need to tell Max that he was sorry about his friend a second time and Max nodded, that thank-you nod without saying it.

There was a silence between them while they finished their drinks, shot of whiskey, straight. Then Max said, "If you can tear yourself away from the titties, why don't we go outside? I can't hear myself in here."

Darnell said, "You had your two drinks, it's your call."

They were walking along the outside of the building when Max asked, "Did you tell anybody about the money?"

That surprised Darnell. He shook his head and Max asked him, "Are you sure?"

"Yeah, I never said anything, not even to LaKelle. I open my mouth, I'm gonna have niggas crawling out the woodwork. I don't need that."

That made sense to Max. They rounded the corner and came to the lot where Max's car was parked. Max popped the trunk. "I'm gonna ask you one more time."

Darnell raised his voice and told him he hadn't, not raised enough like he was annoyed but like he was joking around.

Max showed Darnell a bag full of money, cash in a red canvas bag with the Nike swoosh on it, the kind of bag that Darnell didn't think Nike made anymore.

"What you doing with that?"

"I want your girl to have it," Max said. "I want you to raise her with it . . . Put her in good schools . . . Pay for her college with it." He watched Darnell's eyes. "As a father, can you do that for me?"

"I can."

Max handed the bag to Darnell and saw him take a quick look inside. "Don't look like that's the whole thing. You must've kept some."

Max smiled and shook his head to himself. It wasn't said in a tone that was ungrateful, it was just Darnell being himself.

"No," Max said. "The rest is confiscated as part of my investigation."

Darnell closed the bag. That could mean Max was keeping the rest, that's just what he was saying—part of an investigation—but something in Darnell told him Max was being honest. He looked up from the bag at Max, the government agent looking back at him, a couple hundred thousand dollars in drug money in his hand. He knew Max wasn't expecting a thank you, but gave him one anyway and started to walk away when he heard Max say, "I want you to do one more thing for me."

"What's that?"

Max looked across the roof of his car at Darnell. "Try and stay out of trouble, okay?"

ABOUT THE AUTHOR

Brandon Hebert lives in a sleepy South Louisiana town with his wife, Carmen, and two high-maintenance dogs, Lucy and Lily. In his spare time, he enjoys being at home, fishing with his dad, relaxing with family and friends, and dissecting fake Cajun accents in movies.

Odd Man Out is his second novel. His first, *My Own Worst Enemy,* was named to *Kirkus Reviews*'s Best Debut Fiction of 2010 list.

Please visit him at www.brandonhebert.com.